North Coast

A Contemporary Love Story

Oct. 2015

*To Carol —
Many thanks for your
friendship and encouragement!
Alice McCracken
(AKA Dorothy Rice Bennett)*

Dorothy Rice Bennett

outskirts press
DENVER, COLORADO

This is a work of fiction. The events and characters described herein are imaginary and are not intended to refer to specific places or living persons. The opinions expressed in this manuscript are solely the opinions of the author and do not represent the opinions or thoughts of the publisher. The author has represented and warranted full ownership and/or legal right to publish all the materials in this book.

North Coast
A Contemporary Love Story
All Rights Reserved.
Copyright © 2015 Dorothy Rice Bennett
v4.0

Cover Photo © 2015 Dorothy Rice Bennett. All rights reserved - used with permission.

This book may not be reproduced, transmitted, or stored in whole or in part by any means, including graphic, electronic, or mechanical without the express written consent of the publisher except in the case of brief quotations embodied in critical articles and reviews.

Outskirts Press, Inc.
http://www.outskirtspress.com

ISBN: 978-1-4787-5488-6

Outskirts Press and the "OP" logo are trademarks belonging to Outskirts Press, Inc.

PRINTED IN THE UNITED STATES OF AMERICA

In Memory of Vera

Prologue

Gina pushed the battered green Beetle to the limit as she sped up the 101 to Eureka. She had left San Francisco just after dawn, and she wanted to be on the North Coast by mid-afternoon.

With each mile marker she passed, her heart seemed to pound more wildly and she fought a giant lump in her throat.

One thought, one question spurred her on. Would Valerie want her—would Val even speak to her—after all these months?

She didn't know the answer. She didn't know if she could handle a rejection, but she was going anyway...

Chapter One

As soon as Valerie shifted in the bed—her right arm now hanging over the edge—Sam's big red nose pushed its way into her open right palm. Even with her eyes closed, she could sense the golden retriever's tail wagging ferociously. Val had awakened late to one of those perfect Chamber of Commerce mornings, as winter sunlight crept through her bedroom windows to the east. Her western windows were open slightly, and she took a deep breath of the crisp air and imagined gentle surf caressing the shores of Humboldt Bay. This was going to be a beautiful day, she considered with satisfaction, and the perfect time for a romp along the waterfront.

Val changed her position to allow the big dog several sloppy chin licks and then grimaced.

"Okay, Samantha, that's enough. You're drowning me!"

She playfully pushed the dog's big head away and climbed out of bed. Pulling on her sweats and Reeboks and corralling her shoulder-length honey blonde hair with a sweatband, she bounded down two flights of stairs alongside the retriever, grabbed Sam's leash and the house keys from a table near the front door, and stepped outside to face the day.

After a mile trot down into Old Town, the pair ran another mile along the Boardwalk and a pedestrian walkway near the famed Carson House, a well-preserved Victorian mansion dating from 1885. Although it was early winter, on this sunny morning—rare for rainy Eureka—no one would know it. Both Valerie and Sam sniffed the sea air with contentment. Val found a Frisbee that someone had left behind. She picked up the abandoned toy and looked it over. The blue plastic disc seemed clean enough, so she tossed it for Sam. The female dog happily chased the Frisbee and quickly, tail in rapid motion, brought it back to Val as a present.

The two alternately walked and loped for more than an hour, at one point skirting two pre-teen girls who careened precariously on inline skates and one small boy on a skateboard. They, too, were enjoying the unusually fine morning. Exhausted at the end of their outing, Val and Sam worked their way at a much slower pace back uphill to the house. The older, two-story frame job with a two-car garage was a weather-beaten shade of brown with off-white trim. Beds of now dormant wildflowers lined the front walk, which was formed of rough-hewn stone slabs. Valerie noted that the front yard needed a touch up—even in winter weeds managed to grow—but she knew that she needn't worry about it. Her lawn gal, Josie Turner, would be around sometime later to give the yard a good going over.

Val waved to Mrs. Schowalter, the stooped, gray-haired lady who lived next door. The elderly woman was out sweeping her front steps. Her miniature dachshund, Molly, watched her efforts from a safe perch on a porch loveseat. Valerie sometimes walked with Mrs. Schowalter and Molly, but when they did, it was out of friendship and had no real exercise goals. Molly and her mistress walked rather slowly compared to Val and Sam.

On days like this one, Valerie mused, she felt reasonably content. Perhaps she had made the right decision to move to Eureka, trading San Francisco's crowded conditions, traffic, and polluted air for this quieter, if somewhat colder and wetter, northern California town. Eureka thought of itself as a small coastal city, but to Val it was a town, nothing more. However on this day that was enough. She was so glad the holidays were over—her first Christmas season since Doreen had died. Her first alone. She was relieved she had survived the profound sense of loneliness and loss during that highly-touted family time and could now look forward to the coming year.

While on the front walk Valerie leaned down to pick up the morning's *Times-Standard*—a puny roll of newsprint compared to *The San Francisco Chronicle* and filled with announcements of local, not-so-thrilling events. She sometimes had to laugh at the flower shows, tea parties, bake sales, and other similar social activities, but the Eureka paper still had her favorite cartoon and the daily crossword puzzle. She would survive.

"Come, Sam," she said, "How about some breakfast?"

Followed by the still-panting retriever, Valerie entered the spacious house. She passed through the wood-paneled dining room and into the kitchen, checked for messages on the answering machine atop the counter, then started the coffee maker and refilled Sam's water bowl. She threw two slices of bread into the toaster, took strawberry jam out of the refrigerator, and filled Sam's food bowl with a scoop of senior-formula kibble from a large bag in the pantry.

"We won't worry about calories today, Sam," Val mused, her hazel eyes dancing. She considered Sam as the dog slurped water noisily. She was pretty trim for a large, aging dog, but as for herself, at 51 she had begun to put on the inevitable middle-age spread. "I'm just pleasingly plump," she suggested aloud to the retriever. Never overly athletic, Val still felt she had held her own pretty well over the years. And she wasn't about to put herself through some wild dieting scheme or surgical procedure, like stapling her stomach, to lose a few pounds.

While Sam crunched away on her kibble until her bowl was spotless, Valerie slathered jam on her toast and spread the newspaper on the dining room table. Then she grabbed her cordless phone from the counter to return a call from her friend Lanie Olson. The two had planned dinner and a movie later that day.

Valerie dialed. "Lanie, are you up yet?" she asked, when she heard nothing but silence even though the receiver had been picked up. "It's too beautiful to stay in bed all morning! Come on, gal, get going!" She laughed. "Are we still on for dinner and the movie?"

With an audible yawn, Lanie's voice sleepily agreed. "Sure thing, girlfriend. Sorry. I was up late last night." Still yawning she inquired huskily, "Did you find a roomer yet?"

Valerie frowned. "Not yet, but this is a Saturday. Maybe someone will call today. I hope so." She paused to take a bite of her toast. "I'd sure like to get it rented in time to help make my mortgage payment." She sighed. "Oh, well, something will happen."

The two set a time to meet. Lanie would come to the house at 4 p.m. They'd walk on the beach, then grab a bite to eat, and hit a 7 p.m. movie at the local multiplex—one of two local film emporiums, the fancy one with stadium seating. Valerie smiled to herself. No funky art movie houses here. If they wanted art films, they had to get them from cable or Netflix.

Thinking of Lanie Olson always brought a smile to Valerie's lips. They had first met several months earlier in a local real estate office, where Val had gone to sign paperwork for the purchase of her house. She had just put down her pen after signing several pages of legal documents. Her realtor had moved to a nearby copy machine when Valerie suddenly sensed someone looking at her. Feeling a tingling sensation in her back, she turned and looked into the flashing dark brown eyes of a petite, stocky-built woman wearing a western-style pants outfit. Their eyes locked for a moment, and the woman gave Valerie a grin. Val felt a bit embarrassed and turned away. She was relieved when the realtor brought her another pile of papers to look over. As she did, the petite stranger brushed by her and whispered, "Nice house you picked. I wish it had been my listing." Valerie nearly jumped in surprise. The woman placed a business card beside her and said, "Give me a call sometime. We'll have coffee and talk."

Valerie had kept the card but knew she would never make the call. A few days later Lanie Olson showed up on her doorstep. Nonplussed at first, Val found the little gal, in her late 40s with short brown curly hair to match her chocolate eyes, hard to resist. "I can see why you are selling real estate," she quipped. Lanie actually had been a new agent just beginning work with the broker. "Midlife change," she admitted with a grin. Almost instantly, they recognized a shared kinship and became good friends, although Lanie was quite invested—meaning seven days a week invested—in making a success of the real estate game. The two kept contact by phone and enjoyed each other's company when possible.

At this point, there had been nothing romantic between them. Valerie was still grieving for Doreen and wasn't ready for sexual intimacy with another woman. When her mind could get around such subjects, she admitted that Lanie sparkled and was intriguing but questioned whether she would make a good partner. She felt sure that Lanie was attracted to her—in fact Lanie had kidded about it on several occasions—but Val was not about to encourage her. Thankfully, for the most part, Lanie had shown respect for Val's devastating loss and resulting major life adjustment.

After she finished breakfast Valerie went out to the garage, which she had turned into a studio. She worked primarily in oils and sometimes in watercolor, and the large garage was a perfect place to work. Well not quite perfect. Her Volvo station wagon would probably rust, since it was parked in the driveway and often exposed to rain, wind, and ocean salt. The available natural light in the garage was not exactly a painter's dream either, but she had made it work.

Sam sniffed around the concrete floor and then, as was her habit, curled up on an oval rag rug by Valerie's stool as Val put some finishing touches on a painting she had started the previous week. The canvas depicted a coastal scene and featured a majestic lighthouse. She had sketched the natural setting by the ocean—the number of days at this time of the year when she could work outside was limited, so she made it a habit to start a work out of doors when weather permitted and then move indoors to flesh out the details. There was no lighthouse near Eureka that matched what she had in mind, so she used a photograph of another lighthouse along the California coast and sketched from that photograph, placing the lighthouse within her own landscape. Only the purists would know the difference, she thought to herself, and anyway as a painter she was far more impressionist than realist.

Valerie was so totally involved in her work that she was startled when the front doorbell rang. Sam jumped to her feet and began barking, and Val looked at her watch. 11:30 a.m. Hmmm. Could it be Josie, with a question? She had heard sounds outside a few minutes earlier that might have been Josie at work. Val put down her paintbrush, wiped her hands on a rag, and with Sam at her heels returned to the house. She walked into the entryway and opened the paneled front door.

A tall, slender young woman stood on the porch. Her face was pale and ringed with stringy, long brown hair pulled into a haphazard ponytail. She wore glasses with clip-on sunshades and sported a sweatshirt with "Arizona" written across the front in bold letters. Faded jeans and rundown once-white Nikes completed the fashion statement. Behind her, Valerie noticed an unfamiliar green, rather battered VW Beetle parked across the street. She decided it probably belonged to her visitor, who stood holding a map in one hand.

"Yes?" A slight frown marked Val's surprise at having an unexpected stranger on her doorstep.

"You have, uh, a room for rent?" the young woman asked. Her voice was low-pitched and hesitant.

"Yes, I do," Val acknowledged. Perplexed, she still managed to remember her manners and motioned toward the inside of the house. "Would you like to come in?"

"Thank you." With a quick nod the woman stepped into the tile-floored entryway, pulled off the plastic shades, and stole a quick glance around the areas of the house that were immediately visible to her. Sam had stopped barking when Val opened the door. She now sniffed around the unexpected guest.

Valerie closed the door and waved Sam away. "Enough, Sam." When Sam backed off, Val turned to the woman. "How did you hear about my room?" she asked as she appraised the visitor. Although seeming hardly more than a girl—at least from Valerie's perspective—the young woman had a surprisingly appealing quality, despite her rather sloppy outward appearance. A subtle energy radiated from her, and Val now noticed that the shades had covered intense blue eyes.

"At the women's center, at Humboldt State."

"But I gave only a phone number. How did you get the address?" Valerie tried not to be too sharp, but the edge in her voice was apparent anyway.

The young woman blushed with obvious embarrassment, her cheeks, ears, and neck turning bright crimson. "I'm *so* sorry. I suppose I should have called." She swallowed nervously. "But I'm terrible with telephones. I need to see faces. So I asked the clerk where the house was located, and she was nice enough to tell me." The words tumbled out. She was clearly very uncomfortable and shifted back and forth on her feet. "I guess she shouldn't have, right?"

Valerie shrugged. "No, but I suppose it's okay." She suddenly chuckled. "You don't look like a serial killer—or anything dangerous."

The tension broke, and the young woman visibly relaxed. Her fidgeting ceased. "No, I don't think so." She risked a smile and extended a slender, yet muscular-looking hand. "I'm Gina. Gina Fortenham. I just got to Eureka, and I'm looking for a place to stay. Your ad made this house sound really nice," she acknowledged.

"Oh, yes, thank you. Well, I'm Valerie Stephans." Val put out her own hand.

As they shook hands briefly, Valerie noted the younger woman's damp palm and tentative grasp. Their eyes met, and Val's breath caught as she stared directly for the first time into the deepest blue pools she had ever seen. An image of the deep blue hues of Oregon's famed Crater Lake crossed her mind. She gave a little cough and quickly looked away. Still unnerved by the unexpected intrusion and now those intense blue eyes, Valerie took a deep breath, trying to calm down before she spoke. "Well," she finally said, with a sweep of her hand, "this is a three-bedroom house. There are two bedrooms on the second floor, with a shared bath, that I rent out. At the moment, both rooms are empty. Down here is a living room, a dining room, with the kitchen behind, and another small bath and the laundry room along the hallway. My room is on the top floor, in what you might call the attic."

Valerie now noticed, as she waved her hand around, that her arm was covered with specks of paint. She flushed, realizing that she hadn't taken time to thoroughly clean up before answering the door. She pointed to her smock. "I'm a painter," she explained, "as you might guess by my somewhat colorful look. Hope I didn't get you——." She pointed to the paint spots on her arms and hands.

Gina shook her head. After a slight pause, Val swallowed and continued, "My studio is in the garage. Unfortunately, that means all the parking is on the street.

"There isn't usually a problem," she quickly added.

"That's fine." Gina offered a slight smile. "My Beetle is little. I can always squeeze it in somewhere."

Valerie moved toward the stairs. "Here, I'll show you the room that's for rent."

The two women mounted the first flight of stairs, Sam following on their heels. Gina's hand trailed along the polished wood railing.

"I hope you like dogs," Valerie said. "No allergies or anything?"

"I love dogs," Gina replied, "as long as they're friendly. And no, no allergies." Sam sniffed at her again, and she briefly offered the dog her open palm and then stroked the top of Sam's head.

"The house is carpeted downstairs and on the stairways, but the rooms upstairs have hardwood floors. They can be chilly, especially at night. I hope you don't mind that," Valerie said.

"I like hardwood floors. They have a lot of character."

Val noticed that Gina appeared pleased with the bedroom. It was the bigger of the two rooms available and was light and airy, with windows on the east and south. The bay was just visible in the distance over another rooftop. Furniture in the room was old and a bit dark but very serviceable. Across the hall the small bathroom featured a classic, clubfooted tub. Gina acknowledged that the tub was "very charming."

Beginning to relax, Valerie warmed to telling about her home. "This is not a true Victorian, as several houses are in Eureka, but it *is* an older house, with lots of angles and steep roof lines and plenty of oak and redwood in the moldings and trim. The original builder put a lot of love into this house. It had two floors and a large unfinished attic at the top. But an owner at some point decided to convert the attic into a master suite with bath. That set of stairs at the back goes to the top."

Gina gazed at the rear stairs with obvious curiosity, and Valerie surprised herself by offering to show her the room. "Come on up. It's unusual, but I love it."

The two mounted the second, less ornate flight of stairs to Valerie's room, and Gina was clearly impressed. "Wow, you can get the sun from both the east and west and you can hear something. Is that the bay or the ocean?"

Valerie grinned with amusement. "Most likely traffic on the 101. But, I'll admit sometimes early in the morning, when Old Town is still deserted or when the wind is just right, I feel like I'm hearing tide sound. Can't prove it, but I love imagining it."

The room had no regular corners because the roof line ran down almost to the floor on two sides. The area was spacious, however, and Valerie had decorated it attractively with white furniture and a bright blue comforter on her king-sized bed.

When they had returned to the main hallway below, Val asked carefully, "You said you are new in town. Do you have a job?"

"Yes," Gina volunteered, her eyes now sparkling. "I start working tomorrow at Ritchie's Grill on the 101 highway. I have a lot of experience waiting tables, so I'll do fine there." She patted her jeans pocket, pulling herself to her full height. "I have cash for a deposit, or whatever you require."

"Where do you come from?" Valerie was almost sold but was still not certain how trusting she felt toward this person who seemed a tad unkempt and rather transient. And who couldn't, or wouldn't, she reminded herself, talk on telephones.

"I've been in Arizona for several years going to school, but I'm from the Midwest, originally," Gina replied without defensiveness. "I've always wanted to be in California so here I am." Apparently sensing Valerie's uncertainty, she quickly added, "If you need references, I can get them. I have some phone numbers in the car for people I've rented from before. They'll tell you I paid my bills and wasn't any trouble."

Valerie considered this option for a moment and then shook her head. She instinctively felt that if references were offered voluntarily, they would be good ones. "I don't think that's necessary," she said.

There was one possible stumbling block left to cover. Val needed to get it over with. "Now my ad said that I'm renting a room. I'm not sharing the house. That means there will be no kitchen privileges, nor watching TV in the living room. I know that may seem harsh, but I do have a life of my own and I don't want it totally disrupted," she said, her jaw tightening. "And there's no Internet here. I don't even own a computer."

Gina's blue eyes widened just a bit but otherwise her face revealed no concern about these restrictions. "No problem," she said quickly. "I'll be able to eat dinner at Ritchie's and I don't spend much time watching TV. And if I need to use the Internet, I can take my laptop to a Starbucks. The room and use of a bath are fine. That's all I really need."

Still unsure of herself as a landlady—having had just one tenant before this—Valerie could not think of anything else to qualify Gina. When, after a second's hesitation, nothing came to mind, Val capitulated. "Okay, then," she said, "if you want the room, it's yours."

"Thanks." Gina smiled with obvious relief. She quickly pulled out a roll of currency and peeled off several bills. "Here's the first month—$300, right?—last month, and an extra $100 for a deposit. That's $700, total." She carefully handed the bills to Valerie. "I'll be getting a local checking account right away, but I thought you might want cash at the beginning since you don't know me yet."

Val took the money, thumbed through the bills, and then nodded. It was a done deal. She shook Gina's hand again, this time with relief. Then she remembered, "Oh, the keys." Valerie went into the kitchen, cozy with its redwood cabinets and latticed glass doors. She took two keys from a drawer under the counter, returning with them to the hallway. "This one opens the front door," she explained, "and this smaller one is for your room, for your privacy."

"Thanks," Gina said, looking carefully at the keys. "I'll just get my things from the car."

"Do you need help?"

"No, thanks. I don't have a lot of stuff. I can handle it."

A few minutes later, Gina came back into the house with a duffle bag over her shoulder, a box of books under one arm, and a laptop computer bag in her other hand.

Valerie stopped her at bottom of the stairs, offering her a receipt for her rent and deposit. "Oh, I forgot—that door over there," she said, pointing, "goes to my studio. If you need anything or have a question and you can't find me around, I'm probably out there. Please knock first, but don't hesitate to come and get me."

Gina nodded. "Just stick the receipt in this pocket," she said, shoving one hip forward. Valerie flushed at the unexpected intimacy but pushed the receipt down into Gina's rear jeans pocket. Gina smiled disarmingly. "Thanks," she said and took her small number of belongings up the stairs to her new room. Val stood for a second watching her, noting her long legs, her nicely rounded butt, her bouncing pony tail. Valerie's breath caught, and then she shook her head. "Not for you," she murmured to herself as she refocused her attention on the painting project that awaited her. Sam, too, had watched Gina from the hallway but now wagged her tail and followed Val out into the studio.

Gina shut the door and leaned against it, eyes closed. "Thank you, God," she whispered to herself. A place to stay, no more hunting, or worrying about where she would sleep tonight. She knew she had been very lucky.

She found her new abode roomy compared to the last tacky studio apartment she had rented in Tucson. She grinned as she dropped her box of books on the floor and tossed the duffle bag onto the queen-sized bed. This would do fine. Her new landlady, this Valerie Stephans, was an attractive older woman, yet she seemed a little uptight. Gina considered that briefly. Well, maybe there were reasons. Whatever they were, Gina figured she could handle the situation. She'd certainly known worse.

When she surveyed the room more closely, she felt satisfied that the oak dresser was large enough, the one bookcase would certainly hold her small treasury of paperbacks, and the little wood desk would work well for her laptop. There were even some hangers in the closet. She was thankful that, for the moment at least, the bathroom across the hall would be hers alone.

The large bed looked so good to her that Gina was tempted to just drop onto it and go to sleep. She was exhausted from a long drive before dawn, an interview at Ritchie's Grill at 9 a.m., then the hunt for the women's center at Humboldt State, where she had obtained a list of possible rentals. Then the tense initial encounter with Valerie.

Gina actually rolled the duffle bag off onto the floor and stretched out on the bed, luxuriating in the clean fragrance of lavender and comfortable support. It was a good bed, topped by a soft quilt with a brightly colored nautical design. She felt wonderful just lying there. What a relief to have a job and a place to stay, all in one day! Last night there had been so much freeway noise at the funky little motel where she had stopped somewhere north of San Francisco that she had slept little and was now bone tired.

After a moment or two she stirred reluctantly, uttering a deep sigh. She wouldn't be able to sleep just yet.

No, she had to make this place hers. She had to become truly at home here, as quickly as possible. Winter darkness would come early. Tomorrow she would start the job at Ritchie's, and she still had to go find something to eat before she went to bed. Another challenge, when she didn't know Eureka at all.

Reluctantly letting go of the pleasure of lying across the bed, she sighed as she got up and opened the duffle bag, pulling out items and placing them in piles on the comforter. Underwear and T-shirts would fit in the drawers. Two pairs of jeans would go on hangers in the closet. One nice pair of pants and a jacket for dress, also to be hung up. A raincoat, a winter parka, and a fleece jacket to go on hangers. Two pairs of shoes on the closet floor. A couple of baseball caps to be put on the top shelf of the closet.

Then books in the bookcase. She had such a painfully small collection, not much to show for nine years of college and three degrees. She sighed. Oh, well. As she slipped them onto the shelves, she lovingly touched each volume—poetry by Sylvia Plath and Emily Dickinson, novels by Virginia Woolf, a slim tome on dreams by Sigmund Freud. Finally, a bound volume of her doctoral dissertation. All that work, only to end up a part-time waitress? In her exhaustion, she could hardly remember a line of Sylvia Plath's beautiful poetry. Gina shook her head. *Don't go there.* All this would end eventually and she'd find a way to use what she had learned.

The laptop went onto the desk. She looked inside the desk drawers and found that someone had left a notepad and pen. She grabbed both gratefully and made a list of personal items she would need to buy as soon as she got paid. First on the list would be toothpaste.

She put her ditty bag on top of the chest of drawers, leaving the bag open for the moment, so that her toothbrush could air out. She'd deal with the bathroom after dinner.

Gina finally stepped back and surveyed the room. Well, as much as she could be, she was here. In California, at long last. It wasn't her life's dream, San Francisco, but it *was* California. With a job and a place to stay. Her heart raced for a moment and she stopped and took several deep breaths. *Calm down*, she told herself.

As soon as she felt in control again, she grabbed her fanny pack from the rocking chair by the bed—it was nice that Valerie Stephans had put in the rocker and a floor lamp for reading. Gina quickly counted her money. She had placed some single bills at the center of her roll of cash before coming to this house. That way, when she peeled off the twenties to pay her rent, it would seem that she had plenty of money. Actually, after paying first month, last, and deposit, she only had a couple of twenties and a few singles. She wasn't broke, but this cash would have to do until she got paid on her new job. So dinner this evening would have to be filling but cheap. Thinking of that, she'd better get going before she became even more famished and exhausted.

She picked up her blue fleece jacket as she exited the room and locked the door. Gina went quietly down the stairs, paying attention for the first time to the blue-green shag carpeting. It was brighter than most carpeting she had seen—which was usually tan, or beige, or even white. This shag was reminiscent of what, the late 1960s or early 70s? Definitely not current. But, so what? She decided that she liked it.

Valerie was in the kitchen talking on the phone. Not wanting to disturb her, Gina quietly let herself out the front door. She went across the street to the Beetle and retrieved an apple from the passenger seat. It wasn't a lot and it was getting late, but this would have to be her lunch.

The pale winter sun had moved over to the west, and a crisp breeze had come up. Gina could smell the bay, even if she couldn't see it from here. As someone who had always lived inland she had a real sensitivity to the unique smell of ocean air. She zipped up her jacket against the wind, pulled on a knit cap she kept in the pocket, and breathed deeply. Although it was radically different from Tucson's dry air and perpetual sunshine, she felt she was going to like Eureka.

Which way and how to go? She was low on gas, so she left the Beetle. She wanted to see Old Town and explore the waterfront, so she headed on foot along the sidewalk, a gradual descent toward the 101 and the center of Eureka. Aside from her money issues, she needed to stretch her legs and get some fresh air. And, she thought, there would surely be shops along the waterfront where she could find a sandwich or pizza or something. She clipped off the blocks of pavement, her legs moving in a long, artless stride. As was her habit after extended periods alone, she talked silently to herself. "I've never lived on the coast, but I've always thought of myself as a coastal person. And here I am, *finally*, on the coast," she said. Then she laughed.

Gosh, she thought, if anyone heard her they'd think she was nuts. She smiled to herself at the thought.

As Gina had expected, she found Old Town intriguing as she gazed at the nineteenth-century architecture. She wished she had remembered her camera. Oh, well, another day. Then, several blocks down one street, she found a small eatery called Harborside Pizza. Inside she purchased one small thin-crust pizza, fully loaded with toppings. She needed to get as much nutritional value as possible, so olives, artichoke hearts, mushrooms, and hamburger. Her stomach would complain later but, as she pulled apart the slices covered with gooey melted cheese, she chomped down on the first wedge and loved it. She bought a Diet Coke and a bottle of water for later and took the pizza box down by the waterfront. There she found a bench and finished her meal, while watching small waves lapping at the Boardwalk pier. She knew nothing about ocean tides and currents, but the varying intervals between the waves fascinated her. She realized she could watch for hours. She'd have to ask someone or read a book so she could understand better how it all worked. She did know that Eureka was on Humboldt Bay and that the wave action here would be subtle compared to the ocean itself, but still the tide was evident as she observed the water move against the shore.

Having satisfied her hunger and beginning to feel chilled as the winter sun gradually dropped toward the horizon, she allowed her mind to shift to the next morning. She would have to get something for breakfast. She had in her duffle bag a mug, a spoon, and a small electric rod with cord that could be used to heat water for tea. Since her student days she had always turned to it in a pinch. So she needed to find a little market somewhere. Looking up and down the street, she spied one. Perfect. At Sunset Market, she got a package of muffins, a bunch of bananas, a box of tea bags, and a jar of honey. That would do her for a few days. She was set.

As the shadows lengthened, Gina worked her way back up uphill toward Valerie's house, which was now her house as well. Or sort of. A room, anyway.

When Valerie had first moved to Eureka, she had enough funds to put down a large chunk toward the purchase of her home, but she had little extra cash available for living expenses. Eureka, once a busy logging town, had fallen on less fortunate times and was re-inventing itself as a travel destination. Hence the galleries and shops in Old Town and the numerous Victorian mansions scattered throughout the city were central to the area's financial health. But jobs weren't terribly easy to come by, and Val had felt very fortunate to find part-time work in a local photography studio. She needed some predictable income to keep her afloat while she waited hopefully for the sales of her paintings. And, in the beginning, income from renters had also been only a potential.

She had felt especially lucky to find a job that fit into her life so well. Marlynda Cramer, who owned the studio, Portraits by Lyn, was good to her, allowing her flexible hours and tasks that weren't too odious. Although their lifestyles were radically different—Lyn, as she told Val to call her, was married with three children—Valerie respected her creativity, liked her as a person, and felt that, in working for Lyn, she was helping another entrepreneur do her "life's work." In return Lyn had been sensitive to Val's situation and her deep feelings of loss over the death of her life partner, Doreen Hawkins.

Val had spent this particular morning in the photo lab and was just now coming home for lunch, with the hope of having quality time in her studio during the afternoon. The Beetle wasn't parked anywhere along the street, so she assumed that her new roomer had gone to work.

Once inside the house, she greeted Sam and then found several phone messages. She sat down at the dining room table to tackle her calls. The first one was, almost predictably, from Lanie. Valerie quickly autodialed Lanie's number. "Hey, what's up?"

"Nothing much on this end. I'm still sorry about Saturday," Lanie said. The planned evening out had been cancelled at the last moment, when Lanie was asked by her boss to help prepare the contract on a house—tons of paperwork and a deadline.

"I didn't get home until almost 9 p.m.," Lanie explained, very apologetically.

"That's okay," Valerie said. "I've told you before that I understand about your work. You're just getting started, and that has to be the most important thing for you right now. And by the way, the movie was very funny. I stopped for a pizza and, really, it's fine. We'll do it another time." It was true that Valerie had been disappointed on Saturday when she found the message from Lanie, but after all they were friends, not lovers, and such things had to be understood.

Shifting focus for a moment, Lanie commented, "I called to see how you've come along with finding a roomer." No matter the time of day, her voice sounded husky, as if she had just climbed out of bed.

"Oh," Valerie replied, with sudden excitement. "Since we didn't get together on Saturday, I couldn't tell you that I rented one of the rooms. Would you believe some woman just showed up on my doorstep?"

Lanie quickly interrupted. "Is she, like, okay? I mean, how did she get the address? You were pretty careful about your listing." Lanie clearly felt protective of Val.

Valerie grinned to herself. "I think it's going to be fine," she assured her friend. "She seems alright. Maybe a bit nervous and shy, but she has a car and a job lined up. She paid me first, last, and security, all in cash, so I don't have to worry about having a check bounce." She laughed out loud. "Just in time for the mortgage payment. Whew!"

Lanie groaned. "I know you need the money, but I hope this is a good thing. Does she seem independent, or like a kid needing to be adopted? You're still vulnerable. The last thing you need is someone who's needy, like that Debra."

"Whoa!" Valerie exclaimed. "I know you're watching out for me, and I know the last roomer didn't go so well. But I set some firm boundaries this time—the room and bath and nothing else. It'll be okay." She didn't really need to be reminded about her disappointing first tenant.

"Is she a lesbian?"

"Gees, Lanie, how would I know? I just met her."

"Nice boobs? Nice buns? Surely you had time to notice that."

"Beautiful blue eyes, athletic looking but skinny as a rail. Give it up, Lanie."

"Okay. To be continued later. Gotta go. 'Bye!"

Valerie hung up, shaking her head, and strolled into the kitchen, returning the phone to the cradle. *Lanie must have been a bulldog in some other life.*

After dealing with Lanie, Val decided the others would have to wait. She needed something to eat first. In the refrigerator she found the makings for a sandwich and some fresh fruit. She was always relieved these days to look in the refrigerator and see her own things, ordered the way she liked them, and not all of Debra's stuff stuck in everywhere, overflowing the shelves. That silly woman had been a disaster—well, a disaster for Valerie, anyway.

She selected bread and leftover roasted chicken, along with cheese and pickles, and put them on the counter. A fresh orange would make a good dessert. She started the kettle for a hot cup of tea. Never having had a roomer before the "infamous" Debra six months ago, never having had to resort to such means to make ends meet, she hadn't known what to do. Normally assertive but depressed after Doreen's death, she'd been a pushover in this new role and Debra had taken advantage at every turn. Val had been lucky, so her friends had told her, to be able to get her out of the house after three months. Thankfully, the woman had found a boyfriend to move in with. Now here she was faced with a roomer again—and she probably still didn't know what to do, but at least she wouldn't make the same mistakes this time, that's for sure.

Samantha had padded into the kitchen, toenails clicking on the floor, ever hopeful for a treat or tidbit to fall her way. Valerie ruffled the big dog's silky ears and slipped her a piece of chicken. Sam gobbled it down, wagging her tail happily.

After her sandwich was made, Val considered returning the rest of her calls and then decided to wait until later in the afternoon. Although a gray day, the light was fair right now and it was a good time to work.

She took her food on a tray out to the garage, with Sam at her heels, and settled herself before her unfinished painting. Maybe she could get the shadings completed on the lighthouse this afternoon. She had a coat of off-white on the tower, and now she needed to add the shadows and imperfections to give it texture.

As she alternately worked and nibbled at her food, her mind drifted back to her conversation with Lanie, then to Debra, and then to this new roomer Gina. Why, she wondered to herself, would a woman in her 30s be wandering around the country, renting a room, with barely more belongings than she could carry in her hands? This way of operating was so different from Val's experience—by her 30s she had had stable employment, a home, and a committed relationship. And was Gina a lesbian? Who knew? She didn't wear a sign, for God's sake. But those eyes were intense, such a deep shade of blue and so large! She probably had a nice body, sort of tomboyish with small breasts, but how would one know since Gina had so hidden herself behind those glasses, stringy hair, a shapeless oversized sweatshirt, and sloppy jeans?

Valerie stopped in mid-thought. This was leading nowhere. *Thanks, Lanie!* As long as this woman paid her rent and didn't cause any problems, her life, whatever it was, was none of Val's business. This kind of curiosity would only get her into trouble.

Pushing all thoughts of Gina aside, Valerie tuned the radio to a classic music station and went back to work.

Chapter Two

Valerie and her friends—Lanie Olson, Josie Turner, and Judith Marston, or Judee as everyone called her—had gathered around the television set in Val's comfortable living room. They planned on sharing dinner somewhere in town, followed by an evening of poker back at Val's house.

The women had arrived late in the afternoon of a typically chilly and wet winter day. Val first showed them the progress on her latest painting, and they all responded with appropriate appreciation. Then the group moved to the living room—furnished with sturdy oak tables and rich, chocolate-tone leather furniture—to watch a television talk show and share their own happy hour.

"I want a beer," Judee called out. "Me, too," echoed Josie.

Valerie and Lanie both chose a glass of Napa Valley merlot; they brought their wine glasses and two beers out from the kitchen. Conversation in the living room was getting a bit loud, as it often did when the four women were having fun.

Valerie brought out chips and a bowl of nuts and smiled to herself as she listened to the banter. She really enjoyed these times with her "gang." It reminded her of the large number of interesting friends she and Doreen had cultivated in San Francisco.

As Val put napkins, paper plates, and the snacks down on the coffee table, she looked affectionately around the living room at her friends. These women in Eureka weren't as sophisticated as her "City" friends had been, but they were fun to be around. Judee, the newest member of the group, was a student at Humboldt State in nearby Arcata. Granted, the label "student" could be a bit misleading, since Judee was a mother and at least 40, but she was seriously into school, catching up for opportunities lost earlier in her life. She also laughed a lot.

Josie was also a student—part time, anyway. A tall dishwater blonde with muscular build, she really preferred outdoor work. Caring for people's lawns was leading her in the direction of a landscaping career.

Lanie, with her gruff voice, came across as one of those tough women with a heart of gold. A bit shorter than Valerie, she had dark brown eyes and short, dark wavy hair with a single strand of gray. Her figure was solid and trim for her nearly 50 years.

Val sat down on the sofa, joining the group. The women were deeply engrossed in the TV talk show—which focused this day on homosexual relationships—when Gina came down the stairs in her work uniform, comprised of a long-sleeve white blouse, red vest, black Bermuda-length shorts, knee socks, and black walking shoes. She nodded in their direction as she passed the open doorway but didn't speak. They waved in reply and then went back to their TV and their conversation. As soon as Gina had thrown on her parka and was out of the door—and earshot—Lanie turned to Valerie and observed, "So that's the new roomer. Hmmm, kind of puny, washed-out looking."

"And tall!" Judee added. "What, five feet eight or so? Maybe five nine?"

Lanie glanced between Josie, who was nearly six feet tall, and Valerie at five six, "Yeah, I'd say taller than Val but not as tall as Josie. Athlete, maybe? And what's that uniform she's wearing?"

Valerie shrugged. "Ritchie's Grill, I think she said. It's that new place on the 101 North toward Arcata."

Judee jumped up from the sofa and, ever up to fun, enthusiastically proposed, "I vote we have dinner there and give her the once over." Her brown eyes flashed. "Is she one of us?" With a suggestive grin, she focused on Valerie. Judee, the group clown, had dark eyebrows that would shoot up and wiggle at the slightest provocation. Valerie was often reminded of old movies with Groucho Marx.

Val shrugged at Judee's question. "Don't know. I certainly didn't ask. She got my name and address from the women's center at Humboldt State, but that could mean anything. She didn't say, and I didn't think it was any of my business."

Josie chimed in. "Yeah, right. But we can *make* it our business. This town could use some new lesbian blood. I vote that we turn on our 'gaydar' and go check her out." Josie stood out in the group as the most casual dresser, usually opting for some kind of overalls and a flannel shirt. This evening she was wearing jeans and an emerald-green turtleneck sweater, which accented her warm hazel eyes. Although a large gal, she was, Valerie noted, attractive in her own outdoorsy way.

Among the women, Lanie alone was resistive to the plan. "I think the less Valerie gets involved with this girl the better. Remember Debra? Let's leave sleeping dogs lie," she commented. "No offense, Sam," she added, with a warm laugh, as she looked toward the retriever stretched out on a nearby rug. Sam's head had come to full attention at the word "dog."

Val waved them into silence. "Look, I don't want to go to Ritchie's just to check on Gina. However, Ritchie's is a rather new restaurant, and I haven't been there. I've heard that it's reasonably priced, and I'd be willing to have dinner there. I don't want curiosity about Gina to run my life, but I don't want to avoid things because of her either."

Lanie raised an eyebrow. "You're about as subtle as Samantha."

They all laughed and Valerie blushed, but in the end they decided to have dinner at Ritchie's Grill. They finished watching the talk show, downed their beverages, and then, bundled up against the cold, soaking rain, climbed into Val's silver Volvo for the short trip across town to the restaurant.

Ritchie's sported "retro" red, white, and black décor. The four women found a booth to their liking, stripped off their outdoor gear, and turned their attention to the plastic-coated menu that the young, smiling hostess had provided. They soon agreed that if they liked the food, they'd be eating here often because the choices were varied and the prices moderate.

"Look," Josie pointed out, "they have chocolate mud pie for dessert. Wow!"

Judee feigned a pained look. "Do you have to mention that when I am trying to watch my calories?"

They all laughed. Judee, after giving birth to her two sons, had continuously struggled with her weight. Her battle, however, had never prevented her from enjoying herself.

Valerie looked around and noted that the restaurant's 50s theme was uninspired but adequate. She had initially been amused at eateries in Eureka and how they generally lacked ambience, compared to the trendy restaurants she had enjoyed in San Francisco. She hated to sound snobbish, but living in a smaller community was certainly an eye-opening experience. After trying almost every restaurant in town, she had decided that if the food was decent in Eureka she had to be satisfied. And, she reminded herself, it wasn't Eureka's problem. *She* had decided to move here.

A young woman server took their order. A trim blonde of college age and obviously heterosexual, she was not particularly interested in dealing with these four women. She handled their orders efficiently but without displaying any warmth toward them.

While Valerie waited for the meal to be served she glanced around the seating area, hoping to spot Gina. At first she didn't see her, but eventually Gina emerged from the kitchen carrying a tray loaded with several plates of food. She headed for a corner table. Val noted that Gina appeared friendly toward the customers she was serving and that they seemed to be responsive. As Gina went back toward the kitchen she caught a glimpse of Valerie and her friends out of the corner of her eye. Her face registered some surprise. She quickly nodded to Val, who was caught gazing right at her. Their eyes met briefly, then Gina looked away.

Once Gina had disappeared into the kitchen, Josie leaned over and whispered, "So what do you think? Is she a lesbo?"

"You better believe it," Judee said loudly, with a raucous laugh. The bushy eyebrows danced.

Valerie pleaded with them to be less obvious. "Come on. We're all out, but let's keep it down," she said very quietly. "Especially you, Judee." As they all did, Val stressed the "ee" and called her "Judeeeee."

"Okay," Judee shrugged, "I'll change the subject. Who do you think is going to win the Humboldt State basketball game next Friday?" Her voice was still loud enough to be heard by everyone in the dining room.

A few heads turned their way, and Val, Lanie, and Josie all squirmed. Valerie frowned at Judee, who just wiggled her eyebrows in return. What could one do with such an irrepressible gal?

In the kitchen, Gina shoved her glasses up on her nose and waited for her next order to be hefted onto the counter by Carlos, the portly, middle-aged Mexican cook. She looked at her watch. Valerie and her friends made her nervous because they were obviously here checking her out. She could handle the job fine, but those four women, who as a group looked so overtly lesbian, were something else. They were loud, if not obnoxious.

When she'd gone to the women's center looking for housing she had definitely wanted to share space with a woman, and she knew there was at least a possibility that the woman would be a lesbian. Valerie had been reserved, hadn't made any comments about her personal life, which was fine, and Gina wanted to keep it that way. Now she found the whole bunch of them unnerving. Valerie was feminine in appearance and could fit in any crowd, but the other three were very butch. Gina hoped they didn't try to talk to her.

With a sigh, she reached up to the counter, took the plates that had just come up with her order, and headed back to the dining room. "Well, gal," she grumbled to herself, "this is part of the game. You can't avoid it, so you might as well learn how to live with it."

Gina waved her pay envelope at Ritchie's manager. "Thanks, Tino," she called out as she left the restaurant. Climbing into her Beetle, she clutched the envelope tightly. Now on to the bank.

Her personal survival tools included a cell phone—which she detested but kept for emergencies—the simplest of checking and savings accounts, and one credit card, also used only for emergencies. Now that she had her first paycheck, the bulk of it, beyond what she needed immediately for gas and food, went into Bank of America at F and the 101 downtown. Next Gina walked along the 101 to the nearest post office. She needed to open a post office box and pick up her general delivery mail, which consisted of a few advertisements and one envelope that appeared to contain a bill. The ads she tossed into a nearby trash barrel. Then she tore open the envelope, pulled out a sheet of paper, and quickly read what it said. She resisted a sudden impulse to wad up the paper and toss it in the trash, knowing that destroying it would feel great but wouldn't in the long run help anything.

Uttering a deep sigh, she looked around the room and spied a counter with free space for writing. She went over to the counter, pulled her checkbook from her backpack along with a plain envelope, and quickly wrote a check. She addressed the envelope, enclosed the check, and went up to the window to buy some stamps. She then paused just a second to study the envelope thoughtfully before dropping it into the outgoing mail slot.

Outside the building, she bought a local newspaper from a sidewalk rack and pulled her parka tighter against a brisk wind. It was a cloudy winter day, but no rain was forecast until later in the afternoon.

To sit and study the paper, she could go to the library—which was several blocks away—or go down to the waterfront, perhaps almost as far. Despite the cold and wind, she chose the waterfront. She needed to walk, to think, and to make some decisions. The Boardwalk was a good place for that because, on a day like this one, she could count on solitude there.

Gina hiked for several blocks and finally came to the Boardwalk, where there were benches at water's edge—just across from typical Old Town businesses, including a restaurant, an antiques store, and a couple of art galleries. She sat with her newspaper, thoughtfully, frowning now and then when the gusty wind threatened to whip the pages out of her hands. She carefully went over the want ads, then folded the paper, found a pen in her backpack, and circled two ads in the Help Wanted column. She jotted some figures in the margin, totaled them up, and nodded. Next she pulled a map of Eureka from her backpack.

After checking the map, which she held tightly against the wind, she pulled her belongings together and walked briskly back down the sidewalk along the same direction she had come earlier. She looked at building numbers on the other side of the street until one caught her eye. That was it, The Music Recycler. Pausing for a moment to let a car pass, she crossed the street and approached the faded brick building. A small "Help Wanted" sign had been placed in a window next to the front door.

Crossing her fingers for good luck, she entered the store. A few moments later the "Help Wanted" sign disappeared from behind the glass. Gina came out shortly thereafter, a broad smile on her face. She pumped a fist into the air. *Perfect*, she thought to herself. *Just what she needed. A job in the mornings opening the store for the owner, a job that would fit into her schedule at Ritchie's Grill.* Gina couldn't believe her good fortune. Jobs were scarce in Eureka—she knew that even though she hadn't been in town very long. Maybe the fact that the store owner was pretty clearly gay had helped her get the job. Whatever, she was just grateful to have it.

A Saturday morning dawned much warmer than in recent days. A light fog started breaking up early, and the afternoon promised to be sunny. Valerie was thrilled. It was going to be a rare, late winter day during which she could go to the ocean and paint. She'd do that after lunch, but first she would take Sam for a much-needed walk. They had been cooped up the past few miserable days during a storm that had blown in from the Pacific Northwest, and Sam was getting a bit testy—as all big dogs tended to do when they didn't get enough exercise. Tossing Sam balls inside the house was no real substitute for an outdoor romp.

After a light breakfast for herself and the retriever, Valerie pulled on her sweats. Then she said to the dog, "Leash, Sam." Immediately, Sam turned in circles, barking and wagging her tail. The retriever ran to the front hallway and brought back her harness and leash, which Val always kept within easy reach. With an "atta girl," Val put the harness on the dog, grabbed her keys, and took the big animal out the front door and down to the bay.

It was such a good morning that the two of them ran for what seemed miles along the water's edge and through the streets of Old Town. Valerie stopped now and then to throw a stick for Sam to fetch so she could catch her breath. She grinned to herself—middle age was catching up with her. Or maybe she was just winded by the cold air.

During one of these stops, she noticed The Music Recycler across the street. She liked that store but hadn't been there for a while. Jim

Rannish, the owner, always took time to chat with her and could always find music that she really enjoyed. She assumed that he was gay, although they had not said anything to each other. He took in used CDs and cassettes and even LPs, mostly for trade, and had an excellent collection—for a smaller community, anyway. She grinned to herself. *Stop Eureka-sizing everything.*

As Valerie looked toward the store she noticed a figure putting the "Open" sign in the window. It wasn't Jim, but someone who looked rather familiar. Then she saw a green Beetle parked near the building, a Beetle that looked very much like Gina's.

It occurred to her that she hadn't seen much of Gina in the past few days. Now curiosity got the better of her. She crossed the street and went into the store. A bell tinkled when Val entered. Sam followed, tail wagging.

Sure enough there was Gina behind the counter, making notations in a ledger.

"Hello." Surprise was evident in Val's voice.

Gina looked up briefly and nodded, her mind obviously still on her task.

"What a surprise to see you here. You're working for Jim now?" Val asked.

Gina seemed embarrassed. "Yes, for about a week now," she said.

"What happened to Ritchie's Grill?" The words just tumbled out before Valerie could think.

"Oh, I'm still working there." Gina studied Val for a second, and then a smile crossed her face. "You're worried about getting your rent, aren't you?"

Val blushed. "Umm, not really, I just—."

"Well," Gina interrupted, "you needn't worry. This is a second job. I can't get enough hours at Ritchie's to get ahead. So I found this job to help out, and the hours are perfect. I'm here in the morning, opening for Jim, and then later in the day I go to Ritchie's."

Their eyes met for a moment, Gina's deep blue ones boring into Val's hazel eyes, until the older woman nearly gasped. An unexpected shiver went down her spine. A bit embarrassed at her own emotional reaction, Valerie glanced around the store, with its many racks of CDs, posters on the wall, and at the moment, music—Abba, she thought—playing in the background. "I've been in here before, and I really like this place. Jim is very friendly and he has a good collection."

"Yes," Gina agreed.

"He lets me bring Sam in here, and I appreciate that because the weather outside is sometimes not so nice for her." Valerie patted Sam's head.

Gina grinned, leaning over the counter and looking down at the reddish-gold dog sitting patiently beside Val and panting slightly. "Oh, Sam. I wouldn't want to ignore you—you're welcome in here, too, whenever I'm on duty." Gina came around the counter, stroked Sam's muzzle, and gave the dog's back a brisk rub.

Gina glanced up at Valerie. "Is there something I can find for you this morning?"

Val shook her head. "No, not today. I just saw your Beetle outside and was curious. I'll come back another day and pick out something, a CD probably." Valerie heard that nagging voice in the back of her head, telling her not to get too involved with her roomer. "Well," she added, "I'd better be going. I was taking Sam out for a good run along the Boardwalk, and we should get back to that."

Gina winked at Sam and returned to her ledger. "Yeah, I've got work to do, too, while it's quiet this morning. When the customers start coming, they can keep me hopping. I'll see you later. Bye, Sam," she called as the two went out the door.

Despite her determination not to get mixed up in Gina's life, Valerie found herself thinking about her. Gina was actually an attractive young woman beneath the loose, casual clothing she usually wore, the straggly hairdo, and those terrible black-rimmed glasses. But what kind of expenses did she have that required more than one job? What did "getting ahead" mean for her?

Val grimaced. "Don't go there," she muttered, quickly squelching thoughts of Gina and resuming her run with Sam.

Spring announced itself with flowers blossoming everywhere along the North Coast. Daffodils came first. Then buds appeared ready to pop on rhododendron bushes. Even though the nights were very chilly, the afternoons became milder and the rains less frequent. And warm sunshine was beginning to appear more often, breaking through patches of persistent fog.

Gina's routine had settled down, and she was handling her two jobs quite easily. People in this town, she had learned, were pretty friendly and she didn't have any trouble getting along.

Money, however, continued to be a troublesome issue. On one Saturday Gina put her paychecks from both jobs in the bank and then went to the post office to pick up her mail. Again, that single letter that ominously resembled a bill. When she opened the envelope and read the sheet of paper, she frowned. "Will this never end?" she grumbled to herself. Then she wrote out a check, addressed and stamped a small envelope, and posted the sealed missive. With a disgusted look, she bought the day's newspaper, scanned it quickly, circled yet another want ad, and then marched off down the street to get her Beetle. This time she was headed to a local cinema complex to the south on Highway 101.

Gina's—incredible, she knew—luck in finding employment held yet again. The manager, a tall gray-haired woman, was available and gave her an immediate interview. Having worked in a multiplex in Tucson, Gina was able to sell herself easily. Within an hour she had lined up a third job, one which was mostly on weekends, the only time slot she still had available and the time when the movie theater most needed help. Ritchie's didn't use her often on weekends because their more senior servers wanted those times, with bigger crowds and larger tips. She was assigned to the evenings during the week when business was slower.

So Gina came out of the theater building with yet another uniform to be added to her small collection hanging in the closet at Valerie's house. *You're young and strong,* she reassured herself, *so you can do three jobs. When you're older, you won't need to.*

The new routine would not be fun, but she would be too busy to worry about anything and the money would help bring an end to those dreaded monthly envelopes. The sooner the better, she thought.

The next Saturday evening Valerie and her now ever-present friends decided to go to the movies. The group vote went to a comedy, a popular romance that was playing at one of two mall theater complexes along South 101. By pure coincidence they selected a film showing at the same complex where Gina had just started working, and they chose a night when she was on duty behind the snack bar. "I'll get the popcorn," Val had called out after an usher had torn their tickets. When she went to the concession stand, Valerie found herself face to face with Gina. Val felt her hazel eyes pop wide open.

Gina merely smiled at the foursome, served up the popcorn, and took their money. The gang walked off to see their film, each looking at the others with questioning glances.

As they settled into their seats, Josie whispered to Valerie, "Don't you think she's cute?"

"I guess so." Val shrugged. She didn't want to admit how the intensity in Gina's blue eyes seemed to take her breath away. Covering her own confusion by grabbing a handful of popcorn and passing the container to Josie, she asked herself silently what in the world could be going on in that young woman's life that she needed all these jobs.

The warming sun, so welcomed and needed by North Coast residents, went into hiding shortly thereafter, and the weather reverted briefly to winter as rain and wind pelted Eureka almost continuously for the next several days. Valerie forced herself to rise above a minor wave of depression, since the weather controlled what she could and could not do. Late on the following Saturday morning she sat in the dining room, newspaper in hand, cup of tea on the table. She had decided to work a crossword puzzle since it was another dark day—no sun, tons of clouds and rain threatened, yet again, later in the afternoon. Definitely not a good day for painting, so she planned to do some laundry and other chores.

Teacup in hand and pen poised to fill in a needed word, Val found her mind wandering for the millionth time to the young woman upstairs. Gina had barely been in the house during the last week—with all those jobs, the girl was in and out several times a day and only around long enough to sleep. Val had to admit Gina was quiet when she came and went, never disturbing anyone. Sam would barely raise her head. A deep sigh was the only signal that the dog even knew of Gina's movements in the house. Valerie greeted Gina whenever they passed on the stairs, but beyond those simple courtesies there was little conversation between them. Thus her thoughts about Gina always met a dead end, because she had nothing to go on. She knew absolutely nothing about her. So, as she always did, she let the subject drop. She could imagine all kinds of backstory scenarios—a bad marriage, an abusive boyfriend, a business failure—but, having no information, she found it pointless to even think about the possibilities.

While Valerie worked her puzzle, Sam lay at her feet, head on paws. Then the dog abruptly looked up. Gina was coming down the stairway, dressed in a wine-colored turtleneck knit top and jeans, covered by a gray parka. Sam rose and went to greet her, tail wagging. Gina reached down to pat the dog. Sam in return licked her hand and Gina laughed.

Val put her *Times-Standard* down and studied the bundled-up young woman. "Hi, Gina," she greeted automatically, and then surprised herself by adding, "It's cold and dreary out there. Before you brave it, would you like a cup of tea to fortify you?"

Gina hesitated for just a second, looked at her watch, and then nodded. "Sure," she said, clearly warming to the idea. "That would be nice."

Valerie indicated a chair. "Come and join me."

Gina slipped out of her parka, hung it over the chair back, and then slid onto the upholstered seat.

"I made a pot of Earl Grey, so there's plenty to share. I'll just go get another cup. Do you like sugar, honey, lemon, or milk with your tea?"

"Honey would be wonderful." Gina continued to stroke Sam's head. The dog stayed by her feet, basking in the attention.

Valerie came back with the teacup and saucer. She poured a cup of tea from the pot and set it in front of Gina. "There," she said, with a smile.

"Thanks," Gina acknowledged, as Val went back into the kitchen for the jar of honey.

Sam put her nose against Gina's thigh. Gina chuckled and petted the dog.

When Val returned to the table she noted that, while Gina barely said boo to her, she gave a tremendous amount of attention to the dog.

"Sam seems very fond of you," Valerie observed.

"Yes, and I like her, too." Gina rubbed Sam behind an ear. "Even if Sam is a funny name for a girl dog."

Valerie laughed. "Well, it's short for Samantha. She already had that handle when I got her, so I didn't bother changing it." She looked at the dog with open adoration, then studied Gina. "Did you ever have a dog of your own?"

Gina nodded, while taking a sip of tea. "When I was growing up," she said a moment later. "We had a big outdoor dog, kind of a collie-shepherd mix. He was a sweet dog. We named him Jaxx, and he was a little like Sam. Maybe that's why I feel so at ease with her."

The two women were quiet for a moment, enjoying the warmth of the tea.

"I never see you anymore," Valerie finally risked. "That is, I never see you here, always at work. You are terribly industrious. What, three jobs now?"

"Yes." Gina made no further comment.

Trying to find an entry, Valerie observed with concern, "I hope your arrangements here aren't the cause of your needing to work so much." She smiled at Gina, her hazel eyes crinkling kindly.

Gina gazed at Val questioningly for a second and then shook her head. "Oh, no, I just had to piece some part-time jobs together until I find one full-time job. Ritchie's gives me weeknights, the record shop gives me mornings during the week, and the movie theater gives me a big chunk of the weekends."

"That's a lot of hours," Val observed. "When do you have time for yourself?"

Gina smiled over her teacup. "I do get breaks here and there, sometimes in the afternoons during the week and then usually Saturday mornings, like today. But my free time right now is less important than making money."

"Investing for your retirement?" Valerie probed. She tried to keep her voice light.

Gina studied Val for a second before answering. "No, I just have some bills to pay off. I wish I could say that I was saving for the future—but that will come, in time." She put the cup down in the saucer and abruptly stood up. "Thanks for the tea. I have some errands to run, got to get to the post office, so I'll see you later." She patted Sam again, grabbed her parka, and was almost instantly out the door.

Valerie looked after her, thoughtfully. Maybe money was the root of Gina's problems. A student loan, perhaps. Val shrugged. Such a strange young woman, very distant and untrusting. Debra had been all over the place, taking advantage, feet up in the living room, watching television to all hours, leaving beer cans around the house, and just generally being a pain. Val had been glad to see her go. Now she had a bird that scarcely lit on the branch, but, she mused to herself, she had to admit that she had set some very firm limits. Maybe Gina didn't feel she had a right to ask for anything.

She caught herself wondering to herself, *Who are you, Gina Fortenham? You little bird with intense blue eyes? Are you one of us, as Lanie, Josie, and Judee think? You give me no signs, even though I would like to know you. Why do you hide?*

Valerie caught herself and sighed. What difference did it make, really? The crossword puzzle beckoned, and she turned her attention to it. Easy entertainment without problems.

Chapter Three

Valerie sometimes felt as trapped as a prisoner in a cell. She recognized that she had done the trapping herself, but that didn't make the feeling any easier to tolerate or make it go away. She followed Sam along the Boardwalk and then through Old Town on a Saturday morning when the fog had burned off early and the sky was filled with puffy white clouds—the sun coyly peeping out among them.

Sam's tail wagged furiously and the dog was, as usual, quite happy. But on this particular day small town life seemed suffocating to Valerie. She missed afternoons in Golden Gate Park, walks along the ocean, cable car rides to Fisherman's Wharf, evenings at the opera, movies, theater, and visits to favorite bars or private clubs with lesbian friends. In Eureka her daily routine had become terribly predictable. She went to the photo studio in the morning, worked on her paintings in the afternoon, fixed dinner, watched television or read in the evenings, went to bed. She made phone calls to her friends, walked the dog, and once a week had dinner and played cards or went to the movies with the gang. Once in a while, there was an outing with Lanie, but that friendship had distinct limitations. There was definitely a lack of drama and excitement in her life.

Well, she admitted to herself as she jogged along at the end of Sam's leash, if she was totally honest she suspected the biggest hole in her world was not *really* life in Eureka but the lack of Doreen—or now, the lack of a lover with whom to share everything. Although Valerie had always had a lot of interests, being within a dedicated and loving partnership had been the real key to her happiness. It was probably no accident that she had been born under the sign of Cancer.

Hearth and home, she mused wryly.

Her personal reverie of discontent ended abruptly. She and Sam were passing The Music Recycler, just as Gina emerged from the shop. Sam wagged her tail and strained against the leash to get to the young woman.

Valerie smiled. "Hi, Gina, what a nice surprise to see you this morning." She allowed Sam to go to Gina and Gina leaned down to give the big dog a hug, accepting some ear licks in exchange. "Are you working here on Saturdays now?" Val asked.

"Oh, no." Gina shook her head and laughed. "Just stopped in to get my paycheck from Jim." Glancing up at the promising sky, she added, "It's a nice day for your walk."

"That it is. We've been all over Old Town and now we're on our way home. Sam never gets worn out but, me, I get exhausted before we get back," Valerie admitted. "Just feeling my age." The last words were barely above a whisper, almost to herself.

Gina seemed to ignore the last comment. "If you're going this way, I'm on my way to the bank and I can join you. I could use the exercise, too."

They fell into step together and walked along in silence, Sam looking back and forth between the two of them, tail pumping away.

"The weather really is improving," Valerie finally said. "The rain lets up, so they tell me, about now and we begin to have some nice days. I'm really looking forward to that. I've been feeling so cooped up. There's more rain up here than in San Francisco, and I thought it rained a lot there! If this everlovin' downpour really lets up for awhile, Sam and I will be able to get out more regularly."

Gina nodded but remained quiet.

"In the spring, here, they have a rhododendron parade." Val tried to work up some enthusiasm. She didn't particularly want Gina to know how down and alone she was feeling this morning. "And then there is some unusual race where entrants build people-powered sculptures that have to go on land and sea—they start up in Arcata and have to cross Humboldt Bay to end up down to the south in Ferndale. That sounds like fun, if a little unusual."

"Yeah, different for sure. I'd like to see that one," Gina affirmed.

Valerie sighed deeply. "I was thinking," she admitted, despite herself, "how nice it is to walk with Sam but that I enjoy having human company at the same time. Maybe sometime you can join us."

Gina looked directly at her, her blue eyes seeming to search Val's face. "Maybe I can," she said, "once in awhile." Then she suddenly stopped in her tracks. "Well, here's my bank. See you later." She waved goodbye as she entered the front door of the bank building.

Val and Sam walked on. *What a puzzle*, Valerie thought to herself, not for the first time. Gina, she considered, was looking cute this morning in a casual way, tall and slender in her sweat pants, fleece jacket, and watch cap. She was always friendly at first, but seemed so reluctant to engage in any real contact. Val sighed. Well, maybe that was better. At least there wouldn't be a repeat of her last roomer. On the other hand she couldn't help but feel curious as to what was keeping Gina so isolated.

After depositing her paycheck at the bank Gina made her weekly trip to the post office to collect her mail. Today there were a few advertisements, a letter from her mom that had been forwarded from Tuscon, and the monthly envelope containing a bill. She stuck the letter in her pocket for later and then went through the now routine motions of writing a check, addressing an envelope, putting on a stamp, and posting the letter.

Outside, she walked to a nearby lunchroom and ordered a grilled ham and cheese sandwich, a Diet Coke, and a bag of chips. She sat alone at a small table with her drink and read the letter from home. Her mom sounded good, but her dad was on medication for high cholesterol. *Farm diet*, she mused. She had been remiss in not writing home sooner to tell them where she was. She wouldn't give them a lot of detail—just let them know where she was living and that she expected to be moving to San Francisco soon to look for a teaching position. No point in worrying them about her problems when there was nothing they could do about them. She slipped her mom's letter into her backpack and studied the bill she had received. She made a few math notations on the sheet of paper, shook her head, and sighed.

"Gina, your ham and cheese is ready," the counter clerk called out.

She picked up her sandwich and ate at her table, occasionally glancing out the window at people walking along the sidewalk and traffic moving through the street.

She nibbled on her chips. This arrangement she had made with Valerie was becoming difficult. Val was pleasant enough but renting a room from her, while reasonable by itself, was costing a lot. Gina couldn't fix food at the house but must eat all of her meals out. At first she hadn't minded, but as time wore on and she had tried every little restaurant in the area, she was tiring of the fare. She wanted salads that would be healthy and she didn't want to waste gas driving for miles to find just the right place to eat. If she treated herself to a nice meal out, she wanted to be able to take the leftovers home and enjoy them the next day.

Gina had hesitated, not wanting to say anything about her problem. Valerie had rented her a room when she first arrived in Eureka—when some people would not have—and had not demanded references. But Val's strict house rules were becoming a nuisance. Gina wanted this confounded bill paid off as soon as possible and she needed every penny to do that.

"Man," she whispered aloud, "I wish I could afford an apartment with a refrigerator and a little stove." Visualizing herself in a little place of her own, she mused, "And maybe a TV set. A little television would be good, now and then, to forget about work." She was beginning to chafe, feeling a lack of personal accomplishment. "Time is just passing me by. I'm getting older, and I'm not doing anything but working. Not the writing I want to do. No friendships. Nothing."

Oh, well, she sighed, she'd figure something out eventually. Right now the issue was just getting through the day and through each job without any problems. She certainly couldn't afford any difficulties.

Valerie's lower back was complaining. She was stooped over in the storage closet off the garage sorting through a pile of boxes, hunting a waffle iron she was sure she had brought with her when she moved to Eureka. Unexpectedly, she came across an old hotplate and a porcelain teakettle that she hadn't used in years. She grabbed the two and stood up, surprised that she had dragged them along with her from San Francisco instead of giving the items away to charity.

But here they were, kind of jumping out at her—mementos from her past with Doreen from a small walk-up apartment they had shared in the Marina District before they bought a condo. Looking at the blue teakettle and remembering when they had selected it together in a little shop near Union Square, she sighed wistfully. Then she suddenly thought of Gina. That girl had absolutely nothing to make her really comfortable in this house. Maybe, Val considered, she should let Gina use these things.

Just as she was weighing this idea, she heard the front door open. It was Gina, she knew, because Sam went bounding back into the house in search of her.

Valerie followed, carrying the hotplate and teakettle. "Oh, Gina," she called out.

Gina stopped at the foot of the stairs. "Yes?"

"Hi," Valerie said, feeling a bit embarrassed. "I just found this old hotplate and teakettle in the storage closet. I think the hotplate still works. If it does, would you like to have it in your room? It might be nice for you to be able to make yourself a cup of tea now and then."

Gina pushed her glasses up on her nose, a curious little habit she had, and looked at the two objects. A small smile crossed her face. "Yes," she said, the smile growing into a lopsided and enthusiastic grin. "Yes, that would be very nice. It would really help to be able to make some tea in the mornings, and sometimes at night before I go to bed."

As she accepted the items Valerie held out for her, Gina added, "Thank you. I appreciate this." She turned to go up the stairs, while promising, "And I'll take good care of them."

Warmed by Gina's positive acceptance of her little treasures, Val suddenly wanted to do more. Ideas rushed to her mind. "I could maybe get a little refrigerator that you could use up there, too," she suggested, before Gina could get away.

"That would be great, but it would be expensive for you. You don't need to do that," Gina called down as she climbed the steps. "You didn't offer that and I certainly don't expect it."

Abruptly, Valerie had an insight. *Her house rules must be very hard for Gina.* Maybe a compromise was in order.

"Well, I can't do it right away, but if I can I will," she said. Then, surprising herself, she added, "Meanwhile, I have a big refrigerator in the kitchen. It's not overly crowded. I could make some room on a shelf for you, so if you want to bring something home, like leftovers, or keep a soft drink or something, you could use it."

From the top of the stairs, Gina appeared taken aback. For a second Val thought she saw a tear form in the corner of her eye. "You don't need to do that, but it would be very nice. Thank you very much. I won't have a lot. And I won't overdo it, believe me."

Valerie heaved a nervous sigh. "Well, I'll clear a place. You can put things in there. You'll recognize the spot."

"Well, thank you again," Gina said as she turned toward her room.

"I've got to rest for a little while before I go to Ritchie's."

"Okay," Valerie acknowledged. "See you later."

Val walked out to her studio and sat down before her painting project. *Be careful*, she told herself, *keep your boundaries intact*. Although she could feel her stomach churn, she did believe she had done the right thing. "Gina isn't like Debra," she said aloud to herself. And truly Gina had not taken advantage in any way since moving into Val's house.

Gina held the hotplate and teakettle carefully, pushing open the door to her room with her foot. Entering, she placed the little appliance on top of the bookcase. There was a wall plug in just the right location to hook up the hotplate. She prayed that it would work. It wasn't the teakettle that was most important. She had other ways of heating water. But if the hotplate worked, she could warm up other things. She could get a little saucepan and heat soup or make hot chocolate.

She plugged it in and punched the "on" button. The hotplate immediately began to heat.

Gina heaved a sigh of relief. This would be very good. It would make her life easier and also save her much needed money.

And if Valerie did allow her to use the refrigerator, that would be even better.

She closed the door and stretched out on the bed. Maybe she wouldn't have to move to another place after all. She didn't really want to go. Generally, this place was fine. She was chilly sometimes and the hardwood floors could be cold on her stocking feet in the mornings, but that wasn't important enough to cause her to move someplace with carpeting. Unlike Arizona, Eureka was almost never hot—or so she had been told—and just about anyplace she would live around here would probably feel chilly by comparison to Tucson.

Overall it was pretty good here. She was lonely, but she would be lonely anywhere. And she would stay lonely until that damnable debt was paid off. No way was she going to pursue a close relationship while dragging around that kind of baggage.

Meanwhile she had her computer, her books, and her music—and they would have to be enough.

Her mind wandered back to Valerie. Gina was relieved that Val seemed to be relaxing a bit. Maybe she had a good reason from the past to protect herself. Whatever it was, something had made her rather inflexible. Yet sometimes she could be very nice. And attractive, too, Gina considered, realizing that she hadn't thought much about it before. A smile crossed her lips. Yes, attractive—medium tall, with that honey blonde, shoulder-length hair and a full figure. Beautiful hazel eyes that sparkled with intelligence. Gina grinned to herself thinking of Valerie. Then she frowned. Val was older by maybe 15 to 20 years and much more stable with a house and a nice car. There was just too much separating them to allow for any feelings of attraction. And Gina wasn't going to pursue *any* relationship right now, least of all with someone at such a different place in life.

With a resigned sigh she reached for her CD player and headphones on the floor beside the bed and put on some music. Anne Murray, soothing. She listened to Anne's crooning and was soon asleep.

The next few days zipped by for Valerie because her latest painting project kept her occupied beyond the demands of her job and the hours she devoted to Sam.

Another gray, rain-filled week—an emotional downer that reduced Sam to pacing the floor and whining, which she seldom did—somehow seemed to pass in the blink of an eye. Val had been true to her word and had left some space in the refrigerator. Gina had cautiously placed a few items there on the clearly designated shelf but was careful not to overload the space. Valerie had noticed some jelly, butter, and a six-pack of English muffins in the refrigerator and had gotten used to seeing them there. They didn't multiply and she began to relax. Gina was obviously not taking advantage, and Val began to wonder if she had been overreacting to her experience with Debra. Maybe there was no real reason to hold Gina at arm's length, other than the fact that Gina was also holding her at a distance as well.

So on the next Saturday morning, an unusually fine day with tiny wisps of white clouds and warm sunshine, Valerie took Samantha for a long stroll along the waterfront. "Hey, Sam," she said to the retriever as they walked, "isn't it good to be outside again?" Sam merely wagged her tail. Wondering about Gina, Val steered Sam past the music store. As luck would have it, their timing was perfect. Gina again came out with her week's paycheck. Seeing Valerie and Sam, she waved, crossed the street, and joined them.

"We're out for a long walk this morning, because it's so nice today," Valerie said. "Sam has been too cooped up this winter so we've got to stretch out our walks, for both of our sakes. Do you have time to join us?"

Gina looked thoughtful for a moment, glanced at her watch, and then said, "Sure, I've got a little while."

"Good," Valerie said. Sam wagged her tail as if she understood the conversation and the three of them strolled on together. Old Town early in the morning was usually quiet, before all the art galleries, antique stores, and other shops opened. The cars and the pedestrians would arrive a bit later in the day.

"I like this time of year," Gina said as they walked up one street and down another. "The spring is always so hopeful, filled with new beginnings and the promise of nicer weather."

"Yes," Valerie agreed. "If it were this beautiful all the time, Eureka would be a metropolis. Maybe it's better that it is so chilly and wet here so much of the time. We get clean air and we're not overrun, like in the big cities."

Gina nodded. "I didn't always feel that way about spring in Arizona, because the summer came after and it was always so terribly hot. Winters are great there, but it's unbearable from mid-May to nearly October."

"You told me, right, that you are not originally from Arizona?" Valerie questioned.

"Oh, no, I'm from a small farm town in Illinois," Gina explained. "I'd probably still be there, in my overalls in the corn fields, if my mother hadn't been a school teacher who pushed me to get an education and move beyond the limits of our rural life."

Val smiled to herself. Well, there was a good reason that Gina, with her wisps of hair dangling from a ponytail and her big glasses, looked a little like a Midwestern hayseed.

"So you were a good student, I gather," Valerie suggested.

"Yes, especially in English. I wasn't so hot in math or science, but I really loved literature. I read several books a week from our little town library. And thanks to Mom I got a scholarship to the University of Illinois. Then I went to the University of Arizona for graduate school."

"You were planning to teach?"

"Yes, English lit. I got my doctorate in it."

Valerie was taken aback. "My, that's impressive," she exclaimed. Then she paused for a moment. "But you aren't teaching now."

Gina's face clouded. "Well, some things happened that got me off track. I may teach someday, but I had to let it go for a while." She frowned and visibly withdrew into herself, crossing her arms and staring down at the sidewalk.

Valerie sensed that she should change the subject. "I've always lived in California," she admitted. "I grew up in the Bay Area, went to school there, had my jobs, and started painting, as a hobby at first, in the city. I'd never known anywhere else until I moved here."

Gina looked at her in surprise. "San Francisco is so beautiful. How could you leave?"

"Well, something got *my* life off track, too." Val paused a moment, considering how much she wanted to risk sharing. "My life partner," she finally said, "Doreen Hawkins, died of cancer a year ago. We were together for nearly 20 years, and it tore me apart to watch her go through all the chemo and radiation treatment. Her hair fell out and she lost weight until she was skin and bones. Then she was gone." She swallowed a lump in her throat and looked toward Humboldt Bay, trying to mask the tears that instantly filled her eyes when she thought of Doreen.

Gina was quiet for a long moment. "That's really sad," she offered finally.

"Yes, it was," Valerie agreed, wiping away a tear and pulling herself together. "Everything in San Francisco somehow related to Doreen, every place we had enjoyed together. After a while I couldn't stand it. It was like having my heart cut out of me, whether I stayed home with all the memories there or went out anyplace. After six months of agony I sold the condo and moved here—still along a coast, still in California, but in a very different environment. I felt I needed to start a new life, with nothing here to remind me."

"Wow," Gina said. They were both silent for a moment.

Finally Valerie asked, "I hope it isn't uncomfortable for you, my being a lesbian?"

Gina shook her head. "Oh, no, I'm——." She stopped and looked away. Then she continued, "No, it's not a problem. I'm just sorry you lost your partner. A loving relationship of 20 years is rare, straight or gay, and to lose it that way is very unfortunate."

They walked along without speaking. Sam padded along between the two women, looking from one to the other and seemingly checking them out. They had arrived at the Boardwalk overlooking the bay and the marina. The two stood by the railing, staring out at the water as it lapped against the shoreline in a light breeze.

Valerie suddenly chuckled. "A Ph.D. in English lit. I can't get over that. You must have been really young when you got your doctorate," she noted.

Gina nodded and smiled ruefully. "26. I was just about the youngest person on the platform when I graduated," she said. For a second her face lit up with obvious pride in her accomplishment.

"Too bad," Valerie observed, "that you can't be using all that education instead of slaving away at all these menial jobs."

Gina frowned again and swallowed. "Yeah." She hesitated, took a deep breath, and glanced up and down the Boardwalk cautiously, as if checking to see if anyone could be listening. Then she grabbed the railing tightly for a long moment, her fingers pressing against the wood until her knuckles turned almost white. She glanced at Valerie briefly and then looked away. Finally she shrugged, as if forcing herself to relax, and spoke. "I don't talk about this often, but after I got out of grad school and was putting in applications for teaching positions I had an upsetting experience, which led to, sort of, well—" she paused and then blurted out, "kind of a nervous breakdown. In all honesty, I had probably been headed in that direction for a long time, but school sometimes holds you together—the structure and definite goals."

Her face twisted for a second in obvious pain. Valerie waited, not knowing exactly what she should do or say.

Gina then swallowed and began to speak again. "Anyway, after I fell apart and was in the hospital for a short time I had to go into heavy therapy. I didn't feel strong enough to teach. It's too demanding, getting up in front of a class, having all those students focused on you. I was jittery and scared. I felt very much exposed somehow, like everything about me was written all over me for everyone to see. So I had to work jobs that didn't demand so much until I got things straightened out in my head." Her hands gripped the railing again.

Valerie was touched, and she realized that Gina had taken a huge risk in sharing this much of herself. She resisted an urge to encircle Gina in her arms and give her a comforting hug. Instead she gently put a hand on Gina's arm. "I appreciate your trusting me to share that piece of personal history. I know that isn't an easy thing. I'm no expert on such things, but I can guess as much."

Gina gave her a tentative smile. "It has been hard to talk about it with anyone," she admitted. "I try not to dwell on it, because I want to get on with my life—or maybe get started with my life, at last." The tension gradually left her body and she let go of the railing. The two turned to continue their walk.

Valerie sighed. "Well, you are obviously very intelligent and you went through a lot of schooling. Whatever happened must have been something major to rock you so completely."

"Yes," Gina agreed with a nod, her eyes on the ground as she walked along a stretch of uneven pavement. "I grew up an only child, in a family where marriage and children were expected. I always assumed that I would complete my education, get a teaching job, meet someone and get married, have kids, you know?"

"Sure," Valerie said, smiling gently. "That is what most people expect, and the majority do just that."

Gina took a ragged breath, then continued. "Well, when I went to work this woman approached me for a relationship—I mean a sexual relationship. I was totally thrown. Somehow I had blinded myself to this whole side of life, even through all those years of college. I saw others living alternative lifestyles but I never thought of it applying to me. When it hit me, it came like an explosion."

Valerie nodded but kept silent. Anything she could say would probably seem trivial.

"When I got into therapy," Gina continued, "the therapist explained that my breakdown had to do with repressed sexual feelings that I had hidden from all my life." Her voice had an edge of bitterness.

"I didn't want to hear that," she admitted, "and I told the woman that I wanted to be normal, to be heterosexual. She told me she could help me do that. So I stayed in Tucson and had a lot of therapy. I worked dumb jobs and had hundreds of sessions—and I ran up a big bill. And it didn't work out. I just couldn't change what nature had intended for me."

Gina's shoulders drooped. She looked totally beaten down for a moment, but then she took a deep breath and pulled herself up. "Finally, I had to walk out. Just leave. I had gotten angry over all the digging we had done in my mind, and all it had cost me, and all to no end. Now when I get that bill paid off I'll be free of it at last and can put Tucson behind me. Then I will be able to do things for myself—hopefully even teach someday."

They had reached the end of the Boardwalk and stood silently for a few moments, looking across the bay toward the giant saw mill that belched steam and smoke into the sky through its tall stack. When Valerie looked at the mill, she was always reminded that it was possibly the last vestige of the huge logging industry that had once been the heart of Eureka.

Val came back to their conversation. "Did you ever come to any peace with yourself? Are you okay with the way you are?" She asked this very carefully.

Gina sighed before answering. "I've had some relationships along the way," she said. "They didn't last long, because I was too fragile and too distressed, but they lasted long enough and there were enough of them to convince me that I am a lesbian. But I don't want that fact to run my life. I'm a person, first, and I have to be comfortable with my life as a whole."

Valerie nodded, trying to imagine what it must feel like to be in Gina's shoes. "I'm sorry it has been such a trial for you. I always knew that I was gay, and living in San Francisco I had many models around me of the gay lifestyle. It wasn't hard to adapt to it. My pain was losing a really loving partner too soon. I saw us going into old age together, and now here I am alone with probably 30 to 40 years yet to live. That's what makes me feel fragile sometimes."

She reached down and stroked Sam's head. "Sam understands," she said. "I got her at a dog pound. She had been abandoned and found wandering, thin and hungry. I thought that we might be able to keep each other company. She's been a good dog." Samantha licked her hand. "Yes, you're a good girl, aren't you, Sam?"

Gina watched them for a moment. "I don't know you really well, but you seem genuine and I'm glad we talked. I haven't had many people to tell. And you don't seem shocked."

Valerie chuckled. "I've lived too long to be shocked by much. And what you've told me isn't going to make me think you are weird or anything." She gave Gina a warm smile.

Gina appeared relieved. "I always worry that if I open up about myself I'll turn people off."

Valerie nodded. "Sometimes we do have to be careful in choosing our confidants," she admitted, "but your story is safe with me—and Sam won't tell."

Finally, Val felt comfortable enough to give Gina a warm hug. Gina accepted her gesture with a hesitant smile. The two stood in an embrace for a moment. Then, subject closed, they chattered about lighter things and resumed their walk.

Chapter Four

"How's school going?" Lanie asked Josie while Judee shuffled a deck of cards.

Josie stretched her long legs and took a big sip of beer before replying. "Pretty good. If I can just get through this semester I'll be ready for the landscaping course they offer in the fall." She watched a moment as Judee began to deal a hand of poker. "I can't wait. That's what I really love, the hands-on stuff. All this biology and botany gets my goat. I'm not really a student, you know." Josie's warm chuckle turned into a sigh as she looked at the cards Judee had dealt her. "Great hand, Jude!"

Lanie, Josie, Judee, and Valerie were gathered at Val's dining room table, poker chips mixed in with beer bottles and glasses of wine. Lanie, the clever poker player, was cleaning up as usual. No matter who dealt the hand, she always seemed to get the best cards.

Betting among them was limited to nickels and dimes. Two of the four women were students and the other two didn't have a lot to lose, either. But it was a fun way to get together on Saturday evenings, and none of them was involved romantically at the moment. "Small town demographics," Judee had once quipped. "Getting a date with a woman here is about as hard as finding a penguin in the Panama Canal."

Over the past few months Valerie's spacious and comfortable home had become their poker palace. No other place was particularly convenient. Josie had a roommate, Judee had two kids at home, and Lanie lived in a small apartment over a garage with little space for entertaining.

On this particular Saturday evening they were playing Texas Hold 'Em. And Lanie had just drawn two Aces. Possessing a great poker face, she gave no clue that she was about to win yet another hand.

Just as Josie was about to fold—not having drawn anything she could consider useful, a five of hearts and a three of clubs—Gina came down the stairs dressed in a wine-colored polo shirt and tan slacks. Rain gear over her arm, she was headed out the front door, presumably for her work shift at the movie theater, Val thought. Sam got up from her spot under the table and ran to Gina for a farewell lick and a pat.

"Hi, Gina," Val called out, looking up from her cards and quickly introducing the women to her renter. This formal introduction was long overdue, Val knew, but Gina was so rarely home.

The others nodded and murmured hello as Gina smiled and patted Sam.

With a sideward glance at Valerie, Judee called out, "You should join us for poker sometime."

"I have to work at the movie house," Gina said, pointing to her work outfit.

"Yeah, I can see that, but you don't work all the time, do you?" Judee quipped, her dark eyebrows wiggling.

"Most of the time," Gina affirmed.

"Well, there must be SOME time you don't work!" Judee refused to give up.

Gina gave her a thoughtful look and her face relaxed into the hint of a smile. "Try me on a Friday, with a little warning," she said. "Maybe if you ever play on a Friday, I could join you then."

"Well," said Judee, "we'll just have to find a Friday for you. Soon."

"Okay, let me know. See you later." With a final rub behind Sam's ears, Gina pulled on her rain slicker and let herself out the door.

Sam padded back to her spot near Valerie's feet and the poker game resumed.

Judee faced Valerie with a hint of apology in her piercing brown eyes. "I hope I wasn't overstepping my ground. She's your roomer. I hope it's alright with you that I asked."

Valerie shrugged. "Sure. I don't mind," she said.

Josie was counting her poker chips. "Judee still wants to check her out, I think," she observed, with a knowing grin in Judee's direction.

Judee stared down at her cards. "Well, she looks like a lesbian to me, but we're never gonna find out if we can't get a word with her. Poker's as good a way as any to break the ice, especially since this young thing works all the time. What didja say, Val, three jobs?"

"Yep," Valerie acknowledged, carefully avoiding any details. "By the way, Judee," she added, "she *is* a nice young woman. Don't pick on her."

"Oh, being protective, huh?" Lanie asked, kiddingly. "Maybe you like her a bit?"

Valerie grinned. "No, not at all—not in that way, anyway," She picked up her cards and quickly changed the subject. "Let's play, before Judee has to go home."

"I'm good," Judee said. "The boys are with their dad this weekend, so I'm free as a bird. Except for studying for that big fat exam on Tuesday."

Lanie saw a chance to give Judee a ribbing. "Just like a lesbian, to get married and have a couple of boys to raise before you get your head screwed on right."

"I'm not falling for that one," Judee quipped, wiggling her heavy brows and flipping her shoulder-length dark brown ponytail. "They're good kids, and I love 'em. But let's play cards." Despite the teasing Judee's brown eyes were twinkling.

The banter went on throughout the evening, at the end of which Lanie doubled her money, Judee broke even, and Valerie and Josie each took a loss.

The house was dark and silent when Gina arrived home from work shortly after midnight. Saturdays were always busy at the movie multiplex. She was kept running behind the snack bar, filling popcorn bags, pouring sodas, serving hot dogs, and ringing up orders. Being a newer employee, she landed all the less-desirable jobs at closing—washing dishes, cleaning the popcorn popper, or hauling supplies from the storeroom. On Saturday evenings the crew was usually there late because, thanks to the bigger crowds, there was so much more trash to pick up and cleaning to do. She had recently been given ushering duties, which meant collecting sweaty drink containers, tossed popcorn bags and candy wrappers, sweeping up in individual theaters, and checking the restrooms for needed toilet paper, towels, and other supplies. But at least this task got her away from the intensity of the snack bar—where packed-in bodies bumped into each other as they literally ran to fill orders—and she didn't mind.

On this evening Gina felt bone weary and, after climbing the stairs to her room, she shrugged off her clothes, pulled on a nightshirt, made a quick trip to the bathroom to brush her teeth and splash water on her face, and gratefully fell into bed. She could not get there too quickly.

Despite her tiredness it still took time for her to get to sleep. She had to slip on her earphones and listen to music for a while. Working all the time kept her mind from worrying anxiously about money or her future, but late at night when she stopped running, her mind caught up with her and sleep was sometimes difficult to achieve and even harder to maintain.

This night she drifted off finally, only to awaken at 3 a.m. to her heart pounding and her body bathed in sweat. She had been dreaming and, as she lay panicking in the dark, the covers thrown off in a heap, the dream came back to her.

She was sitting in a big leather chair in a small, airless room. Across from her, in another leather chair, was an older woman. She had dark hair with streaks of white around the temples. Wearing heavy horn-rimmed glasses and dressed in a business pantsuit, the woman held a notepad and a pen. Gina's chair seemed huge and she felt tiny within it, almost enclosed, trapped in the giant seat.

The bespectacled woman had a gleam in her eye. She stood up, towering over Gina—who could only look up at her with wide eyes, terrified. "You have a homosexual transference on me," *the woman said, putting one hand on her hip and posing like a movie star. Gina heard her words, as if they were exaggerated, stretched out, intimidating.* "You will feel strange for a time, but it will go away eventually. You must allow this to happen, allow these feelings, to find yourself."

Gina's heart, here in the night, pounded rapidly. She quickly flipped on the light beside the bed, bringing the present into focus. Gazing around the room, she breathed a deep sigh of relief. She was here in Eureka and not back in Tucson. She would be okay. But would the woman in her dream, Dr. Reitman, ever fade from her memory, ever truly be part of the past?

Forcing herself to think of other things, she finally began to calm down. Eventually Gina was able to turn out the light and drift back to sleep.

Judee was on the phone. "Hi, Val, how are you?"

"Fair to middlin," Valerie quipped. Covered from head to toe with flecks of blue paint, she was in the garage touching up a nearly finished painting.

"Well, guess what! I got an A on that paper for Humanities class, and the boys are going with their dad again this weekend. He's actually picking them up on Thursday. I'm so looking forward to some free time with no class paper hanging over my head." Judee's enthusiasm was obvious, even over the phone. Valerie could imagine her brows wiggling and her eyes sparkling.

"So what are you going to do?" Val was filling in a section of blue sky, trying to hold the phone and paint at the same time. She was going to have to get some kind of hands free phone one of these days.

"Well on Saturday I'm going to Trinidad to the beach. They say it's going to be sunny this weekend. But I was thinking. We were talking about a Friday night poker game so we could invite your roomer, Gina. And this is one of the few Fridays I'll ever be able to get away. What do you think?"

Valerie considered the idea. "I can't think of any problem, for me anyway. You want to call the rest of the gals? I'll check with Gina to see if she can come. I can't promise, you know. I don't know if this is something she really wants to do."

"Yeah, oh, well, it's just a thought, but I will check with the others if you'll talk to her." With a quick goodbye, Judee hung up.

Valerie considered the idea. This was a Tuesday, and Gina hadn't been in the house all day. Probably wouldn't be until late this evening. Maybe the best thing to do was put a note on her door. She'd have to be careful in wording it. Her friends wanted to meet Gina, and they would undoubtedly pester her with insinuating questions. Val realized that she was feeling a bit protective after Gina's recent revelations. The young woman was really sensitive and didn't need to be given the third degree.

Of course, the structure of the poker party might help. The game could take them away from conversation if the questions got too touchy. Valerie would have to pay attention and take some responsibility on Gina's behalf, if she felt it necessary. She didn't want Gina frightened off or made uncomfortable in this house. After all, she was a roomer and Valerie needed the money, if nothing else. She considered that for a moment. It sounded crass, even petty, and she suddenly recognized that needing money wasn't the only or even the most important reason. She had begun to like Gina, and she didn't want to see her hurt. And she knew that her friends, all in the name of fun, would take no prisoners.

The poker party was on. Gina, after a few moments of hesitation, had decided to accept the invitation. She worried about it periodically between Tuesday evening and Friday but she didn't have any real friends in Eureka—other than maybe Valerie and her acquaintances at work—and she needed some kind of social outlet. She wasn't a bad poker player, after all. She had learned to play during graduate school when there wasn't much money for entertainment. Poker provided a good release from the ongoing tension of classes and research papers. Maybe this would be a good thing, she considered.

So just after 7 p.m. on Friday evening, the women gathered in the dining room. The wine and beer came out, along with chips, dip, and pretzels, Valerie's personal favorite. Judee arrived first, still enthusiastically looking forward to her free weekend. Then Josie, who seemed sullen at first but loosened up after admitting she had just had a little tiff with her roommate, Sarah Green. Lanie came armed with a six-pack of her favorite beer and a bottle of wine.

Dressed in jeans and a red and white University of Arizona sweatshirt, Gina came down the stairs when she heard all the buzz of conversation below. She was followed by Sam. The retriever had trotted upstairs to find her. Samantha always seemed to know what was going on in the house, without being told. And the dog showed partiality toward Gina, who would get down on the carpet and tussle with her. Gina could play the way a child would and Sam had started wagging her tail and following her throughout the house.

Valerie gave Gina a more complete introduction to the gang, one by one.

"You remember Judee. She made this evening possible by dumping her kids on her ex for the weekend. She's a student at Humboldt State, and you can usually find her buried in a textbook when she isn't chasing the kids," Val announced.

"Hi, again, Gina," Judee nodded with a wide grin. "And I didn't DUMP my kids! I LOVE my kids, by the way." Judee's laugh, which followed, was loud and infectious.

"Be prepared, Gina. We do a lot of teasing around here," Valerie interjected. "And next we have Josie—another student, but a reluctant one—a landscape gardener at heart. You may have seen her around the house. She does my lawn for me and keeps the flowers alive. And she'll turn a bright rosy pink if you ask her anything about her love life."

"Not fair!" Josie complained, as her cheeks immediately turned bright red. Josie could kid, but basically she was an introvert who listened rather than spoke. Valerie had noticed, however, that sometimes when she did speak up, she seemed wise beyond her 28 years.

"Moving on," Val quipped, "we have last but not least, Lanie, my best friend and a budding real estate lady. Another one who tried marriage and then thought better of it. She has no pretensions and lots of street smarts."

"Wow, Val, you get down and dirty," Lanie grumbled. But she smiled anyway. Valerie didn't add that she had always assumed that Lanie had had lots of lovers and would probably have many more in her lifetime. Although her friend never discussed such exploits, Val had her own suspicions.

Gina looked around at them, clearly nervous. "Great. Um. Good to meet you," she said, her smile tentative. "You know I'm, uh, Gina. And you know I work at all kinds of jobs around here. So you are likely to run into me anywhere in town."

"We have already." Lanie offered a mischievous grin.

"That's right," Gina said, with sudden recognition, "you all came to the movies one night."

"And we had dinner at Ritchie's one night." Josie put in.

"So you have The Music Recycler yet to go," Gina said, allowing a smile.

"Oh, really?" Josie looked thoughtful. "You work there, too?" She studied Gina seriously.

"We're playing Texas Hold 'Em," Valerie interrupted, trying to take the pressure off Gina. "And we're all having something or other to drink. Do you like wine, beer? Lanie brought some good white Zinfandel, if you are into white. Beer is in the refrigerator. There are some cups there on the counter. And help yourself to the snacks."

Gina poured herself a glass of white wine, grabbed a few pretzels and a napkin, and sat down at the table. Valerie had pulled up a chair next to her own.

Val then explained how they played. "Truly for small change."

Gina took a couple of dollars from her jeans pocket and purchased her chips. They dealt a hand and Gina played tentatively, folding early even though she had a couple of high cards.

"Most of us here are Californians, born or adopted," Lanie mentioned to Gina. "You sound different, maybe a slight twang in your speech. You from the South?"

Gina shook her head. "No. Illinois, but farm country. Rural people in the Midwest often have a twang that sounds kind of Southern. I've just moved here after several years in Arizona and that might really give me an accent. Lots of Arizonans hail from the Midwest and the South. Local speech, at least in Tucson, is pretty casual and laid back, I've noticed." She smiled at Lanie.

"You sound real smart to me," observed Josie. "You been to college, I bet."

"Yes, I went to the University of Illinois," Gina acknowledged.

"What did you study?"

"English lit."

Judee came to attention. "What writers do you like?" she asked. "Now mind you, my level is Rita Mae Brown." She laughed, her eyebrows doing a dance, and the others joined her.

"I gravitated toward American and British women writers, including poets like Sylvia Plath. And I did thesis research on Virginia Woolf," Gina said.

"Thesis? Then you've been to grad school, too?" asked Judee with amazement.

This time Gina's cheeks turned pink. "Yes, I did graduate work in Arizona," she admitted, looking uncomfortable. She recovered in time to point to her Arizona sweatshirt.

"Wow!" Judee exclaimed. "But why are you working at those piddly jobs? Shouldn't you be teaching in college or something?"

Gina's knuckles turned white as she gripped her poker chips and suddenly looked as if she would bolt from the room. Valerie put a hand gently on her arm. "Okay, gals, that's enough of the inquisition. Let's play poker, huh?"

Judee backed down. "Sorry, I didn't mean to pry or anything."

Gina took a deep breath and nodded to Judee. The subject was dropped.

They returned to the game, and at the start of the next hand Gina drew two Aces. She was delighted, and a small smile played at the corner of her mouth. Valerie saw the smile, as did Judee across the table. They glanced at each other and Val winked. They'd play along. Gina would win this hand, but they'd give her a little tussle over it so that the pot would be a bit bigger. They wanted her to feel more comfortable. She was, after all, the new kid on the block.

Neither Val nor Judee had been dealt a particularly good hand, but they played almost to the end before folding. Gina ended up with several coins as her two Aces ultimately won the hand.

Obviously delighted with her first success, Gina smiled, settled into her chair, and began to take more risks. As the evening wore on, she proved an apt poker player. When she had a good hand, she played it well. When she didn't get high cards, she folded early to hang on to her little pot. The initial tension in her body gradually melted away, and she began to study the other women.

"How many kids do you have?" she asked Judee.

"Two, both boys, 10 and 12. They run me ragged," Judee admitted. "I'm just lucky their dad lives here in town and wants to take 'em regularly on weekends. I don't know how I'd keep up with school and chasin' after 'em if I didn't get a breather now and then."

"What are you studying?"

"Oh, I have this crazy idea I'd make a good counselor—school or family, I'm not sure, but some kind of counselor—so I'm takin' all the psychology and educational prerequisites. I'm about halfway done with my bachelor's right now. Gotta long way to go," she sighed.

"Is Humboldt State a good school?" Gina asked. She had only been on the campus that one time, when she had visited the women's center.

"Yeah, I think it's pretty good. Meets my needs anyway. But then I don't have anything to compare it to," Judee quipped. "It's pretty open-minded, pretty liberal. That's good for those of us living 'alternative lifestyles.'"

Everyone shifted and glanced to see how Gina would take that remark. She didn't react overtly but instead looked studiously at her cards.

Valerie quickly picked up the conversation. "Josie here can give you the real lowdown on Humboldt State, can't you, Josie?"

Josie turned pink again. "Come on, now, you know I'm not really into college. I just hafta take these courses there so I can get on with my work. Don't pick on me now," she admonished.

They played several more hands of poker, keeping the conversation light, and at the end of the evening Gina, citing beginner's luck, claimed the biggest pot. She thanked all of them for inviting her and, excusing herself, went upstairs to her room. Sam trotted after her.

"You're going to lose a dog," quipped Lanie as she helped clean up the table.

"I see that," Valerie observed. "I'm wondering if I should seriously start to worry."

With stretches and sighs the women all stood up and gathered their belongings, ready to leave. They also gave each other warm hugs before pulling on coats and caps.

"I think she's a lesbian," Lanie whispered to Valerie before she walked to the front door.

Val smiled. "Time will tell," she replied wryly.

Gina awoke, bathed in sweat. She looked at the alarm clock. It read 2:06. Another bad dream had disturbed her sleep. Another scene back in Tucson.

Now, trying to cool down, she lay in the dark with covers askew. She wanted to think of something else besides the dream. Her mind drifted back to the poker game.

She had to admit that it had been a fun evening with Valerie and her friends. Since Gina didn't have much time for amusement these days, it was really nice to talk and play cards and just be with other women.

Well, not just any other women. Lesbians, obviously.

She liked Judee, right off. Her good sense of humor and openness was winning. But Gina couldn't imagine trying to live as a lesbian and at the same time deal with an ex-husband and two sons. It couldn't be easy. She assumed that Judee had started out straight, or trying to be straight, and it hadn't worked for her. Maybe someday Gina would ask her about that.

Josie was cute but seemed younger than her physical age, and she was still trying to get an education so she could get started with her life. Gina didn't feel she had too much in common with her, beyond some degree of athleticism, although she liked the girl. While there actually wasn't too much difference in their ages, Gina had been through so much psychologically that she felt much older—older on the inside and probably much older than she looked to others on the outside.

Lanie, she thought, was very brusque, and her roughness kind of turned Gina off. Yet she had noticed that Lanie paid a lot of attention to Valerie. Maybe there was something going there, at least on Lanie's side. Val had introduced her as her "best friend," and it could be exactly that or maybe something more. Funny, they didn't seem at all alike. Valerie was more of a lady and Lanie—well that tough exterior was a bit too much.

Looking back on the evening, Gina instantly berated herself for becoming overly sensitive when the questions got too personal. She sighed. It was going to be this way until she worked through her personal issues. Until she was teaching and there were no questions, or until she stopped feeling apologetic about *not* teaching after getting all that education. Perhaps she should just learn to say she was going to be, or was, a writer—it was partly true, anyway—and then people wouldn't comment so much or hint about her "wasted" schooling.

She wondered if she would ever become comfortable in social situations, with people in general and with lesbians in particular. Leaving her emotional problems out of it, maybe she just wasn't a social person. She had always been more of a loner than many people she knew.

"Shoot," she said to herself and tossed a pillow across the room. She didn't want to be alone forever. But at the bottom of everything was the same old issue. This damnable debt and the memories of her devastating therapy sessions with Dr. Reitman!

In the dark she heard a padding sound. She looked down at the side of the bed and saw Sam. Her big eyes were shining in reflected moonlight, searching for Gina in the darkness while her tail wagged tentatively.

"Oh, Sam," she said. "You are my friend, aren't you? And you know when I need comforting." She hugged and stroked the big dog. "But I'm okay now, and I'm going back to sleep." She gave Sam a loving pat and then suggested, "You must get back to Valerie. Now go, Sam."

As if understanding her every word, the dog padded out through the doorway and bounded up the stairs to Valerie's attic room.

Gina pulled the covers up around her and gradually drifted back to sleep.

Chapter Five

The next morning dawned clear with the promise of unseasonable warmth. After their late night of poker Valerie had planned to sleep in, but the band of sunshine peeking through her windows awakened her. She found it intriguing, if not surprising, how much weather affected her moods these days. In San Francisco she had seldom cared, but when it rained or was gray and overcast in Eureka, she got moody. But not today! She bounced out of bed and with Samantha at her heels, pulled her white fleece robe about her, hurried downstairs, and went into the kitchen to start breakfast.

Given the wine she'd drunk the evening before, the intensity of the poker game, and her 1 a.m. bedtime, Val felt pretty good. An excellent day, she decided at once, to get work done in the studio.

With determination she quickly glanced at the morning paper, downed a piece of toast topped with her favorite Oregon marionberry jam, and drank a cup of tea. Then she fed Sam, took the dog outside, and decided to work for a little while before showering and getting dressed. "Good girl, Sam." She ruffled the dog's fur after Sam had done her business. "We'll take a long walk later this morning."

Valerie took a mug of steaming tea out into the garage and settled herself on her stool, surveying the nearly finished piece—a rather large painting of a deep foot path through coastal redwoods. Highlights of luminescent green for the leaves and auburn tones in the tree trunks. In the reflected light within the garage the painting was looking good, even if she did say so herself.

Suddenly her mind drifted off to Doreen. Doreen would have loved this painting, with its ferns, tall trees, and play of light and shadow.

Before losing her battle with cancer, Doreen had often stood just behind Valerie while she was working. Very sensitive to Val's feelings, Doreen had never interfered or criticized. She had just stood there watching and had always known when to support, when she could tease, and when she needed to massage Valerie's tense shoulders.

As much as Val loved painting, as much satisfaction as it gave her when she came to the studio and put in several hours of devoted work, it was during those quiet hours that Doreen most often came to mind. Val could almost feel her presence over her shoulder, so much so that once in a while she would turn to look at her. But no one was there and the emptiness was devastating.

The two had had such a unique relationship, which had blossomed and matured despite the harshness of the world around them. Even in diverse San Francisco, judgments and fear were often directed toward homosexuals and their lifestyle.

Thinking back, she would first remember the good times and feel Doreen's presence. That made her happy. But then the positive image would fade into a haunting memory of Doreen in a hospital bed, with sunken eyes and a gaunt look, reduced to skin and bones and waiting to die. Val's breathing would stop for a moment and her stomach would tighten.

It was hard to accept that Doreen was gone forever. Even though many months had passed, the memories and the feelings came back just as intensely as they had when she had first lived them.

"Damn," Valerie cursed and slammed down her paintbrush. She had put a single daub on the canvas. There would be no more. Her buoyant mood had been destroyed.

She would not, after all, be able to work today.

"Spoiled, Sam," she admitted wryly to the dog at her feet. "I spoiled it. There's no one to blame but me. Now I'll have to pick myself up again."

Sam wagged her tail and fussed slightly.

Valerie studied the beautiful and loyal dog. Thank goodness she had Sam.

She had found the retriever at a local dog pound just a few weeks after moving to Eureka. Doreen had said to her that she should get a dog, something to keep her company. "You're going to be very lonely," Doreen had whispered, late in her cancer battle. "Now you're here with me every moment. When I'm gone, there will be a lot of empty hours to fill."

Val had walked along the chain-link cages inspecting dogs, large and small, hoping for a sign. She didn't know exactly what she wanted. She stopped before a few animals and studied them, watching their reactions.

Sam had been curled up on a mat dozing, but the retriever came to attention when Valerie paused before her cage. First the head came up, then the dog sat up, and then it rose and trotted to the fence, its brown eyes gentle. Valerie put her fingers hesitantly against the fence, and the dog sniffed and then pushed its tongue through the links to give Val's palm a lick.

That single gesture was enough to drive her into heaving sobs. A stocky volunteer attendant appeared at her side. "Are you all right?" the young woman asked.

Valerie nodded, taking deep breaths and fishing in her pocket for a Kleenex. "I've recently lost someone close to me and gentleness sets me off," she admitted.

The volunteer agreed, nodding at the retriever. "This dog will get you every time," she said, offering a warm smile.

When Valerie felt a little more in control, she asked the woman what she knew about the animal.

"We found her wandering the streets of downtown Eureka. She was very thin and her coat was matted. She looked lost and neglected, with no collar or tags, but she didn't show any signs of abuse. We brought her in, gave her a thorough cleaning up, and she had no injuries or scars. But she was very hungry and ate everything we could give her," the volunteer explained. "No one has come to claim her, so something must have happened to the owner."

"How old is she?" Valerie didn't want something else dying on her.

"At least five, perhaps six years old. She's had some training, because she responds well to basic commands, and she's young enough to learn more. She's a good dog and she'll adjust." When Val still looked doubtful, the woman added, "She has no big health problems. And if you're worried about her age, she's strong and should have several years ahead of her as a good companion."

Valerie studied the dog thoughtfully, and the retriever looked back at her, tail wagging, eyes beseeching.

The worker noted, "She has such a sweet disposition that we called her Samantha. We just put her up for adoption this morning actually, because she's shown a good weight gain and has been given a security chip and updates on all her shots. She will eat a lot and need a good deal of exercise."

Val nodded. "That would be good for me, too. The exercise, that is."

"Do you have children?"

Valerie shook her head. "Just me."

The worker hesitated. "Retrievers are good family dogs, great with kids, but," she added after a moment's consideration, "this one has been through some kind of trauma and loss. She might do well with a single adult—just understand that she will be with you every minute. Retrievers are very affectionate."

Val's heart was touched by the dog's pleading look. "I think Samantha wants me to take her," she said, a lump forming in her throat.

"Looks that way," the young volunteer agreed.

So Valerie had taken the big dog home, and the two had been inseparable ever since. And as Doreen had predicted, having a dog by her side had helped Val deal with the immense sadness and loneliness that still surrounded her months after her partner's death.

"You want to help me feel better?" she now asked the golden retriever.

As if she understood Valerie's words, Sam stood up. She turned in circles, wagging her tail and barking, and ran to a box in the corner of the garage. She picked up a large red rubber ball, which she carried back and dropped at Val's feet.

"Okay, Sam, I get the picture. We're going for an outing."

Followed by Sam, the ball in her mouth, Valerie went into the kitchen and pulled a cooler from the pantry. She started filling it with drinks, snacks, and peanut butter and jelly sandwiches that she quickly threw together. Plus some snacks for Sam.

"I'll just pull on some sweats, and I'll shower when we get back. Where do you want to go? Up the coast, maybe?"

Sam's tail wagged harder.

As Valerie climbed the stairs to her room, she passed a sleepy Gina on the second floor. The oblivious younger woman was yawning and just emerging from the bathroom, her blue terry robe hanging open. Val couldn't help noticing her nakedness and stared at a delicious, small rounded breast standing at attention and the mound of light brown curls between Gina's legs.

When she suddenly realized that Valerie and Sam were there, Gina gasped, turned beet red, and quickly pulled her robe together. She crossed the hallway and disappeared into her room, closing the door sharply.

Val smiled in spite of herself. Then she considered that it wasn't nice to tease Gina. Crossing to the bedroom door, she tapped gently. "I'm sorry," she said. "I didn't mean to stare." She wanted to add, but didn't, "I'm a lesbian, after all."

There was no answer from behind the door. Valerie felt awkward, but then she suddenly had a brainstorm.

"Sam and I are going on a drive," she called out, "up the coast, north of Arcata to a nice, rustic beach we know, so we can have a good run. It's a beautiful day out, and it's going to be very nice this afternoon. You want to come?"

Gina finally opened the door, one arm clutching at her tightly closed robe. She studied Valerie dubiously. "I don't know."

Val waited hopefully.

Gina stared at her for a moment and considered the idea. "Let's see, I don't go to work until 5 p.m. today and I don't have anything else I absolutely have to do." Gina looked down at Sam and then said a bit hesitantly, "Well if you're sure you'll be back in time for me to get cleaned up for work, I guess I could go. It would be fun, if you really don't mind having me along."

"Oh, please come. I'm just jumping into my sweats. I've got some food and drinks in a cooler, and there's plenty for all of us."

Gina finally agreed. "Okay. Give me five minutes and I'll be ready."

The ride along Highway 101 North began quietly. Gina watched the scenery in silence as they passed by the northern end of Humboldt Bay and the small city of Arcata, home of the Humboldt State campus. Valerie glanced at her out of the corner of her eye and decided not to push conversation. Samantha hunched on the floor behind them in the Volvo wagon and put her big head between the front bucket seats. With tongue hanging out, Sam looked at the scenery and then glanced back and forth between the two women. Once or twice she risked a lick of Valerie's cheek. Val giggled but said, "That's enough, Sam."

For having been so miserable earlier in the morning, Val now felt content and warm inside. It was great fun having Gina and Sam in the wagon with her, like a little family. She and Doreen had had a couple of cats during their time together. The two women had been gone a lot to parties, stage presentations, and films. With their jobs and social activities, they had decided that a dog would be left alone too often. Now Val had time for an animal and, with Gina in the passenger seat, Val felt strangely and unexpectedly complete. The idea of her "little family" produced a nice sensation that she fostered for a moment or two and then pushed aside. Gina was, after all, a renter and nothing more and would likely walk out the door one of these days. *No attachments,* she reminded herself. *Live for the day and expect nothing else.*

Soon they turned off the 101 and drove along a narrow two-lane road through open countryside for what seemed like several miles. Gina pointed out the crops growing on both sides of the roadway. They made a right turn at a "T" intersection and then a left turn near an old steel bridge. After another mile or so, they arrived at Valerie's destination—a driftwood-strewn deserted beach surrounded by sand dunes, called, she explained, Mad River Beach. They unloaded the car and Sam, who didn't need a leash on this beach, trotted ahead of them with her red ball toward a familiar path that led from the parking area down to the water's edge. Val smiled at the dog's rapidly flapping tail, which clearly monitored her degree of happiness at this outing.

Valerie had a beach blanket stowed in the wagon and she brought it along. Gina carried the cooler. They found a spot just at the foot of a large sand dune, laid out the blanket, and put their things on it. The sun was warm but the light breeze was still chilly. The sand dune afforded some protection from the cool air currents. "Everything should be safe here," Valerie commented, "until the wind comes up and starts blowing the sand all around."

Sam circled them teasingly, wanting to run. Valerie tussled with the dog over the ball, took possession of it, and then she and Gina followed Sam along the beach. Gina had brought her little camera and she took some shots of Sam chasing the ball after Val gave it a long toss.

As the two women walked in the soft sand, Valerie risked a question. "Did you enjoy last evening?" Her tone was tentative.

Gina nodded. "Yes, your friends were really nice."

"They can be a bit overwhelming at times," Val admitted.

"Well, yes, for me anyway," Gina acknowledged. "But you're very lucky to have several women friends."

"Yes," Valerie agreed, "I know."

"How did you meet them? I mean everybody knows there are a lot of gay people in San Francisco, but how did you find them up here?" Gina asked.

"Well," Val recalled, "I really expected to be very much alone after the enormous gay community in 'Frisco. But I met Lanie almost immediately in the real estate office when I bought my house. She was just starting out in the business. We discovered that we enjoyed each other's company, and it was so nice for me to have someone with whom I could be open about my lifestyle."

Valerie grinned, remembering. "Then I needed a gardener, and Lanie knew of Josie because she provided yard services to some of the local realtors. Josie had met Judee at Humboldt State and introduced us. Then all of a sudden, I had a group of lesbian friends."

"That's really neat," Gina commented. "I've never been good at meeting people. Kind of introverted, I guess. In Tucson my therapist put me in therapy groups and then pushed me into community activities where I would meet women." She sighed. "Now I've got to learn how to do that on my own."

Valerie was thoughtful for a moment. "Well," she said, "you know me, and now you've met some other women. If you want to become friends with any of them, I'm sure the door is open. They can be kind of raucous, especially Lanie and Judee, but underneath they are all decent women."

"I appreciate that, Valerie." Gina nodded and fell silent.

Val continued throwing the ball, and Sam delightedly raced after it and brought it back to her, kicking up beach sand as she did so.

"What made you pick Eureka?" Valerie eventually asked, continuing the thread of their conversation. She was glad in a way that Gina had mentioned her therapy again. They could explore that history some more. It might give Gina some peace to talk about her experiences in detail.

Gina stopped to examine a piece of driftwood before she answered. "Well, my life so far—in Illinois and Arizona—has all been inland. I've always had this attraction to the ocean. It's so radically different, the way it feels where water meets the land. Before I left Tucson, I did some reading about California. I thought that any place along the coast below San Francisco would be entirely too expensive for me, at least until I get this debt paid off."

She picked up a small rock, examined it, and then tossed it into the surf. "So I drove from Tucson to the Bay Area but turned north and skirted San Francisco. Even though that's where I want to be eventually, I didn't even drive through the city. Too much to deal with right away. Then I stopped in each coastal town and looked at the local newspaper for job listings and apartment or room rentals. When nothing appropriate showed up, I drove on. I was beginning to think I'd end up in Oregon or maybe even Washington, but when I got to Eureka, I got my first nibble on a job that would work for me. Then I located the women's center, with the listings of rooms for rent. That seemed a sign to me that this was the place I should stay."

Valerie's heart skipped a beat at Gina's mention of San Francisco and her plan to go there one day. She had sensed somehow that Gina would only be temporarily part of her life. Val swallowed and forcefully stopped herself from continuing any personal thoughts about that idea. She tossed the ball for Sam. "I guess Eureka makes sense, for your 'coastal launch,' if you will." She smiled at Gina thoughtfully. "You know I ended up here because of the Victorian architecture, the price of houses, the ocean, and a job opportunity I was lucky enough to find that supported my painting. There are a lot of artists here on the North Coast."

Gina nodded. "Have you always been a painter?" she asked.

Valerie stopped to lean down and pick up an unusually colored rock lying in the sand. She studied it for a moment and then slipped it into her pocket. "No, I got a business degree in college and worked as an accountant for several years. I took up painting as a hobby, kind of an outlet to balance my mind from all that 'left-brain' activity during the day. I was actually surprised when I discovered I had some real talent for it."

They had reached the end of the sandy beach and started to turn back. Sam was running through the surf, happily carrying the red ball in her mouth.

"Are you hungry?" asked Valerie. "This cool breeze makes me feel ravenous!" Her ankles and calves were beginning to tire from fighting each step through the deep, soft sand.

"Yes, I'm getting there." Gina admitted. "I only had a muffin for breakfast and this brisk air really does sap your energy. I could use some carbs."

The tide had receded and, in returning along the beach, they walked on the cool but flatter, damp sand, wind to their backs. This made their going much easier.

"I've never been to an ocean beach before," Gina shared as they walked.

"Really?" Val was surprised at first. But as soon as she considered it, that fact made sense.

"When I was in Tucson, some of the students made weekend runs to San Diego or down into Mexico to the Sea of Cortez, but I just didn't have the time or money to do it. I've been dreaming of California beaches for a long, long time." Gina paused as she mused to herself for a moment. "Movies give you an idea of what it's like, but films can't capture the warmth of the sun, the wind rustling in your hair, or the sensation of shifting sand on your skin." She reached down and picked up a couple of shells and studied them in her hand.

Val felt a sense of emotional warmth pass over her. "Well," she said with a smile, "I'm really glad you decided to come and that Sam and I could enjoy this experience with you." She put her arm around Gina's shoulders and gave her a pat. Gina smiled in return.

Minutes later they reached their sand dune, where the blanket and supplies still waited for them. The cooler and its contents were safe, although dusted with sand.

"I hope you like peanut butter and jelly sandwiches," Valerie commented, as she opened packages and simultaneously threw some treats toward Sam to keep her occupied.

"That was my favorite as a child, made with Mom's home baked bread," Gina allowed.

"You said your mother was a teacher?" Valerie asked, trying to put the pieces together.

"Yes," Gina replied with a nod, "she was and still is. My family comes from a long line of farmers, but many farms in that part of Illinois aren't terribly large. By the time my dad inherited the family acreage, it was hard to make a living. He knew Mom from high school and he kind of waited to ask her to marry him until she was out of college. I think he saw the handwriting on the wall—that he would have to have a wife with skills to bring in some outside income."

"That makes it sound a little calculated. Did they love each other?"

Gina paused a moment, considering the question. "Oh, yes, well, I think so anyway. At least they've always gotten along pretty well. But Mother was also from a farming family and she knew the life. She was lucky that there was enough money available for her to get an education and she loves teaching. But after school hours and on the weekends she is truly a farmer's wife. When I was growing up, she trucked home seed and feed and other supplies for the farm, picked up parts for the tractor and other machinery, ran errands for my dad, kept the books—along with the usual tons of laundry, cleaning the house, and baking every Saturday morning. The best breads and rolls and pies you could imagine." Gina looked off into space, as if recalling her childhood. "During the harvest, she cooked for all the field hands as well. That's not all, but it will give you an idea of her many responsibilities. I don't know how she ever graded papers in the evening because she must have been exhausted by then."

Valerie smiled. "I see where you get your energy to work all these jobs. Your mother was a real role model for that!"

Gina nodded and gazed out at the ocean, lost in thought. For a few moments she was back on the farm of her childhood.

Val silently passed her a sandwich. The two women ate quietly.

Soon Valerie found herself watching Gina, her mind playing over the things she had said. Val watched as the wind pushed Gina's ponytail over her shoulder, where it danced. "You're tall and slender," she finally observed. "Are your parents tall, thin?"

Gina laughed, pushing a strand of hair out of her face. "My dad is tall, but he's built like an ox. He's from German and northern Italian stock—blonde, really strong physically. I got my height from him, but my being kind of thin came from my mom. Her family background is English, short, thin: kind of wiry, with brown hair and blue eyes. So I'm a mixture of both of them. My dad named me Gina—if I had been a boy, I'd have been Gino."

Valerie finished her sandwich and offered Gina a cookie. "How did you feel about growing up on a farm?" she asked, still trying to make sense of Gina's very different world.

"When I was a kid, I loved it. We had several chickens and a few milk cows, a couple of goats, and lots of corn. I helped gather the eggs when I was really little and before long I was riding the tractor out to the fields with my dad. I learned to tell when the corn was ready to pick and how to identify pests that could destroy it. I could read the sky and know when the weather was a threat to our crops."

Gina smiled to herself. "I was a tomboy, so I was happy that I could wear overalls, have short hair, and play softball with the boys in our town," she recalled.

"Did you ever feel different from the other girls?" Valerie asked.

"Between school and helping on the farm, I didn't have a lot of free time to think about what made me tick. I was just typical. Farm girls often wear overalls and have short hair. It's either a pony tail, cropped head, or those funky curls from a boxed permanent. When you're getting dirty out in the fields, short hair is the easiest," Gina explained.

"So, "she added, "I didn't look different from anyone else." She stared down at the sand. "I didn't know what I was supposed to feel, about sex and stuff, but I just thought I'd do what everyone else did. Many of the women in town had been tomboys when they were young and were still that way as adults. But they got married and raised kids and that was life. If any of them were different, they didn't know it or they just pushed it down because life was about working hard to survive."

Gina looked out at the ocean. "Maybe if I had stayed there, that's the way life would have turned out for me too. I'd probably be depressed, but I'd go along with what had to be done. If I hadn't gone away to school, I don't know if I'd ever have known any other life."

"Maybe that would have been easier for you, in a way," Valerie observed.

Gina nodded. "Yes, it probably would have been. I know how I am now, and someday maybe I'll be glad about that, but right now it just seems hard." She took a bite out of a chocolate chip cookie.

"Were people in your town prejudiced against gay people?" Valerie asked.

"Nobody said anything one way or the other. The subject just didn't come up, at least not in my hearing. The main occupation of the town and the farming community was getting by. And most people there are conservative and pretty religious. Living a gay lifestyle would be considered kind of selfish, I think. And that's without looking at issues of morality or sin. So if anyone was inclined to follow that path, I suspect they left town. At least I never saw anyone there that I knew was 'gay.' There were, of course, a few people who lived alone. But I never gave their sexuality any thought."

Gina heaved a sigh. "My therapist would say that I've been living in denial—that homosexuality was around me even in that farm town and I just didn't want to see it. Things also might have changed since I left. There is so much discussion on television and the Internet these days." She stared at small waves lapping at the sand for a long moment.

She was ten or eleven and throwing feed for the chickens out in front of the barn. She noticed something unusual, something she had not ever seen before. One of the hens followed another hen around the yard, clucking. The other hen stopped, turned, and the two approached each other, touching their beaks together. The clucking turned to a cooing sound, and they stood like that, ignoring everything, for a long time.

Gina's father came out of the house, heading for the barn. She looked up at him, questioningly. "Dad, why are those two hens acting like that?"

Her dad put his hand on her shoulder. "Yes, that is unusual, isn't it. Normally, those two gals would be keeping their space. Unless the rooster is around." He grinned at her.

"But why are they doing that?"

"Well, honey, sometimes animals are different. They are born that way, apparently, with some interest in others of their kind and the same sex. We don't know why, but it does happen every so often. We just kind of ignore it, because they aren't hurting anyone. It's just nature."

Gina studied the hens. "But what about people? Do people do that, too?"

Her father looked at her thoughtfully. "Humans are different from animals. We have the power of reason. God gave us reason so we can be responsible and make responsible choices. Animals just follow their instinct. We know what's right, and we can choose to do it."

Gina looked at him quizzically. She didn't really understand, but he was her dad and he must be right.

Valerie saw Gina's attention come back to the beach. She had allowed her some space for what was obviously a personal memory but now hauled out potato chips for a treat. The two women finished their soft drinks and then bundled everything back up in the cooler. Sam had settled down beside them with a rawhide bone and seemed very happy with her chewing. The red ball was at her side.

"How have your parents accepted your being a lesbian?" Valerie finally asked very gently.

Gina swallowed a potato chip before answering. "I didn't tell them for a long time. When I did talk to them, Dad was more hurt personally, like it was somehow his fault. I had to do a lot of reassuring. I think my mom thought of my being a lesbian as a choice I was making—that I could be straight if I wanted to. She had a hard time recognizing that her daughter had emotional conflicts and that this gay thing wasn't going away."

Gina sighed and ran her fingers through the sand between her feet. "It's still touch and go, but we're communicating better. I've never told them about the huge debt I have to pay off. They wouldn't have the money to help me out anyway, and since it really is my problem I'm the one that has to deal with it."

Valerie thought for a moment. "Do you think it might help if they understood how much you have sacrificed to try to be the daughter they wanted you to be?"

Gina shrugged. "I don't know. It might. Maybe someday I'll tell them, but not until the debt has been paid." She grinned. "Sometimes I can be one of those stubborn Midwesterners."

They were both quiet, listening to the ocean waves as the new tide began to roll onshore—and to the crunching sound of Sam working on her rawhide stick.

Gina slipped off her shoes and pushed her toes into the sun-warmed sand. After a considerable silence, she turned to Valerie and asked, "How did your parents react to your being a lesbian?"

Valerie smiled. "My mother was a psychologist. My father was an art historian. They knew I was a lesbian before I did. We had this very unusual birds-and-bees discussion, when I was maybe 13—about how some birds and bees did things differently and if I was one of those, it was fine with them."

She sighed, thinking back. Even her younger brother Daniel hadn't cared about her sexuality. When she started dating during college, he was into his own hormone explosion and barely noticed what was happening for her. "I was really lucky," she admitted to Gina, " because I grew up without my sexual identity being a problem. I never had to keep secrets about it. I brought my girlfriends home and my parents welcomed them. It was a little unnerving at times because no one else that I knew had it so easy."

"You *were* very fortunate," Gina observed wistfully.

"Yes," Valerie acknowledged, "and I think that's why I was able to have a healthy relationship with Doreen for two decades. I didn't take that kind of baggage into the relationship. I had the built-in expectation that two women could love each other, just like a man and a woman. There was no shame, no angst, to stand in the way."

Gina looked as if she wanted to say something. Val paused, giving her room to speak.

"If it isn't too touchy a subject, how…how did you meet Doreen?" Gina asked, her voice soft and hesitant.

Val smiled wistfully. "It wasn't at a gay bar, I can assure you." She mused a moment, staring at the waves rolling onto the shore. "I always loved art, even before I realized that someday I would be a painter. So I hung out in art galleries whenever I had free time."

She was twenty-something—in short curls, a turtleneck, bell bottom pants, and pointed-toe shoes—standing in a San Francisco gallery staring at paintings for long moments and sometimes getting all teary-eyed over a work that especially touched her.

That day Valerie had gone to the Palace of Fine Art, where there was an exhibit of paintings and sculpture by new artists. She had stopped before a modern yet classic oil of two nymphs in nearly transparent silky robes, standing in the forest in the light of a full moon, smiling shyly at each other. The oil so captured the essence of young love between women that she couldn't leave it.

She had gotten physically tired from standing there, shifting from one foot to another. Enthralled and unable to take her eyes off the painting, she felt a presence nearby. Her space and mood were being invaded and she turned sharply to see who it was. Just over her shoulder, maybe a foot away, stood a auburn-haired, brown-eyed young woman in a red T-shirt and jeans. She was staring at the same painting.

Valerie gave her such a look of annoyance that the young woman blushed and apologized for gazing practically over Val's shoulder. "I'm sorry," she said, "so sorry. I didn't mean to intrude. The painting just grabbed me." The young woman, in her early 20s, was very pleasant and the two began talking about the work of art.

They went for coffee together and before they knew it they were dating. Soon afterwards they became lovers. Val knew immediately that their pairing was idyllic, compared to the traumas and struggles that many lesbians went through before—and if—they found a loving partner.

"So, I was at a gallery one day," Valerie continued, when her mind returned to the present. "I met Doreen there. She was a graphic artist, a freelancer at the time. She had kind of coasted through life, taking it the easy way. But after she met me and we both realized we were serious about one another, she settled down and developed a real career for herself. And I have to admit that watching her work with artistic elements, even though with a computer instead of paints, intrigued me. My life developed a new dimension beyond the business world. I began to think more creatively, and soon I was seeing in a new way and then drawing what I saw in reality, or visualized in my mind, on a pad. My art grew from there. Doreen really inspired me."

She paused a moment, adjusting her headband to prevent the wind from tousling her hair. "I know this all sounds too good to be true. And for the most part it was. But like all couples, Doreen and I had our issues. We sometimes fought over the dumbest things, like who got to read the Sunday funnies first." She sighed. "The worst, though, was the cancer. It tore our lives into a million pieces. No one should ever have to go through that hell." She passed a rock back and forth between her hands, pressing it tightly with her fingers. Her jaw tensed for a moment. She hadn't mentioned that Doreen's parents had never supported their relationship and at times had been truly mean and cruel to them. Val didn't want to even think about what they had done after Doreen's death.

Gina studied her but didn't speak. They were both quiet, lost in their own thoughts.

Then Gina's eyes focused for a while on a series of waves gently brushing the shore. She took a deep breath of the ocean air and let out a sigh. She smiled and turned to Valerie. "This is a wonderful way to spend the day, isn't it? It's so peaceful here it's almost like being in church."

Valerie returned from her reverie, looked at Gina thoughtfully, and asked, "Are you into church?"

Gina shook her head. "Not any more. When I was growing up,

it was church every Sunday. As regular as clockwork." She smiled to herself.

"What religion?"

"Oh, Methodist. Everyone in town was Methodist or Lutheran or Presbyterian. I think, for me anyway, Methodist was the easiest to swallow." She smiled at Val. "When I went to graduate school in Arizona, church was the first thing I dumped. I started spending my Sundays outdoors in the sunshine and open air. No preaching anymore for me."

Valerie considered that idea for a moment before speaking. "My parents were intellectuals, and neither of them believed in formalized religion. I never saw the inside of a church until I met Doreen. She was a devout Catholic. I sometimes went to Mass with her, but it didn't mean much to me. And years later, I got pretty angry that this God in whom she believed so much would allow her to get cancer." Valerie frowned and became quiet again.

Gina put a hand on Val's arm. "I'm sorry that you had to have that kind of experience," she said gently. She looked out at the ocean thoughtfully. "I used to go to a desert park, up in the hills near Tucson. There was a very old saguaro cactus, a really big one. Saguaros sort of look like people, you know. This one had a bent head and two arms outstretched." She put her head slightly to one side and stretched out her arms at odd angles, helping Val visualize that cactus and forcing her to laugh. "I decided one day that this saguaro was God," Gina continued, "extending love and peace to everyone. I came to the conclusion that God is present in all things—so I don't need to go to a church."

Valerie studied her for a moment. "That seems like a good way to believe."

Almost simultaneously they both stretched out on the blanket and let the sun warm them for awhile. Val watched the breeze play with Gina's hair and then she closed her eyes, feeling good and at peace.

It seemed they both had stared at some personal demons and maybe the breeze would waft them away. Sam, too, seemed at peace as she rested her big head on Valerie's thigh. Val wished this day could go on forever—the sun, the sand, Gina, Sam, and her, all together. It was such a nice fantasy.

Her mood was broken abruptly when Gina looked at her watch. "What time were you planning on going back? Is it time to go soon?"

Val sighed. She glanced at her own watch.

"Yeah," she said, standing up, "We should go. There's actually plenty of time left, but neither of us is tanned and we shouldn't be in this sun too long. I don't want to get burned and I doubt that you do either."

Gina agreed and began helping her collect their things. Then a thought occurred to her. "Oh, wait. I want a picture of you and Sam." Secretly delighted, Valerie knelt next to Sam, while Gina took a couple of shots.

"How about you?" Valerie asked. "How about you and Sam?"

"Oh." Gina seemed surprised. "Sure, if you don't mind. It's an easy camera to work—just point and shoot, as they say."

Valerie took a picture of Gina with her arms wrapped around an accommodating retriever who seemed to be grinning through it all. Momentarily the thought crossed her mind that it would be nice to have a picture of herself with Gina, or the three of them together, but there was no one on the beach to ask. And perhaps that was better anyway. *Gina was planning to move to San Francisco before long. Never forget that.*

They gathered up their things and trooped back to the Volvo wagon. On the way to the freeway, they were surprised by a cow standing in the middle of the road. Next they saw another cow and then another. Gina grinned and Valerie gasped in surprise. A whole herd of cows was being moved from field to field, and their milk-laden udders hung heavily between their rear legs. Valerie had no choice but stop and let them pass. The line of cows seemed endless, and several of the brown and white spotted bovines looked up with curiosity at Valerie and Gina and the Volvo. Sam could hardly contain her excitement.

Finally a young, dark-skinned man on a small tractor closed a gate and followed the herd down the road. He nodded pleasantly as he passed the station wagon.

"Oh, those poor things," Valerie said.

"I'd almost think I was back home." Gina leaned out the window to take a picture with her camera. "Those cows are obviously being well fed."

"What is that slogan about California cows being happy cows?" Valerie asked with amusement.

When the herd had moved along to the next field, hopefully headed in the direction of the milking barn, the women continued their return trip to Eureka.

After each film showing Gina was assigned, along with a skinny red-headed fellow named Rick Hendricks, to clean up the auditoriums. The two worked well together and got a lot done in a short period of time. Gina noticed that every Saturday she and Rick were placed in the same rotation. Not being turned on by men, Gina paid very little attention to him. He would sing while he picked up the trash from the auditorium floor or chatter away about something that didn't mean anything to her. Sometimes he talked continuously and Gina would just nod and move on after her own work was done.

One particular Saturday Rick was more of a chatterbox than usual. Gina tried to ignore him, but this time he was unusually pointed in his comments. "I'm surprised I haven't seen you at the Purple Priscilla," he said to her, abruptly and very directly.

"The what?" she asked, not knowing what he meant.

"You don't know the club?" One eyebrow shot up.

"No, I'm sorry, I don't know what you're talking about," Gina admitted, a bit sharply.

"Maybe I've got you figured wrong," Rick mused, waving a hand in the air.

"What do you mean?" Gina's heart suddenly began pounding very hard.

"I thought you were MOT," he said.

"What's MOT?"

"Member of the Tribe. You know, gay," he said, frustrated at having to spell it out.

Gina froze in her tracks, her broom held in midair. She nearly gasped. So people at the theater—well at least Rick—had figured out that she was a lesbian. Could it be that the two of them were assigned to work together because Rick had requested it or the manager thought they would understand each other and enjoy each other's company?

Gina felt exposed, as if she were standing there naked. Her first impulse was to flee. Then she took a deep breath, let it out, and resumed her sweeping. Maybe being recognized wasn't totally a bad thing. It took a load off. She could relax a bit and not worry about being "outed" any longer. If they knew and hadn't fired her for being a lesbian, then maybe it was okay.

After a moment of working in silence she looked at Rick. "Where is this Purple Priscilla?" she asked. That was the closest she could come to admitting he was right about his supposition.

He picked up some drink cups and a popcorn bag and smothered a private grin. "It's a new place up in Arcata, near the university," he said. "If you haven't been and want to go, maybe you could join some of us after work. It doesn't have to be tonight. The invitation is open, whenever you feel like it."

"Thanks, I may take you up on that sometime."

The gang wasn't getting together this weekend. Judee had the boys because her ex was out of town on business, Josie was studying for a big botany test she had to pass, and Lanie was caught up with some old friends who had arrived unexpectedly from out of town.

So Valerie was at home with Sam, her book, her television set, and her feelings. She tried to read a mystery novel that she had been slogging her way through, but when she started reading the same paragraph for the third time she decided to switch on the TV instead. Surfing the channels, she found a tear jerker movie. She got up, made some herbal tea, and popped some popcorn, sharing the warm kernels with Sam.

No matter what she did, she found herself, thinking, remembering, feeling. She liked the group activities on Saturday night. They occupied her mind and suppressed memories of Doreen for hours.

But with an empty evening and no one there to distract her, she was remembering the good times she and Doreen had enjoyed. Saturdays had been very special for them, usually involving an elegant dinner out or a romantic meal with candlelight at home. Because they had been together for several years, they both knew the importance of keeping romance in their relationship. They worked at it, buying flowers and bringing home balloons, sweets, and wine.

Her body ached for Doreen's gentle touch. Doreen had been physically beautiful and a perfect lover—sensitive, imaginative, and flexible. During their intimate moments Doreen had also massaged her tenderly, helping her to relax from hours spent over an easel. Thinking about it, she could almost feel those hands.

Valerie's hand grasped the paint brush tightly. Hour after hour she struggled to make her brush strokes as broad or as narrow, as deep or as feathery as she wanted them. As a beginner at painting, her goal was discipline and control, just as a pianist might play scales for hours to gain mastery over the instrument. Her hands began to ache, her arms trembled, and the muscles in her shoulders and neck started to scream.

She was sitting in the guest bedroom of the condo she shared with Doreen. She had just turned this room into a makeshift studio. Her easel was positioned to capture the natural afternoon light. A small table held her paints, brushes, and wiping cloths. She wanted so to learn, to put on canvas what she could see and feel in her mind.

Fingers lightly touched her shoulders and, at that touch, her body began to relax instantly. The fingers stroked and the knots gave way.

"That feels so good, Doreen," she whispered.

"I'm glad, my love. You've been at this for hours and you are exhausted."

"I know, but I want so much to do it right!"

Doreen leaned down and kissed Valerie's ear lobe. "You are doing it right. Every time I come by, I can see your increasing skill. I see a Monet or a Seurat in the making, and it will happen. It will come. But you need to rest now and then, sweetheart."

"I know." Valerie sighed and leaned against Doreen.

"I'm so proud of you, but now please come and eat and take a little time for yourself—and for me."

Before they had met in their late 20s, both had had their fair share of sexual encounters and brief affairs. Both knew what they liked and needed in a partner and in sexual play. Their relationship had been balanced from the beginning, which was in part what had made it so special to both of them.

"Oh, Doreen," Valerie sighed. A tear ran down her cheek, and she brushed it away. "Why did you have to get sick?"

Had it been too perfect? Was that why Doreen had been taken from her? She pushed away that thought. It made no sense. Like any couple, they weren't perfect. But their love had just been bigger than all of that.

Val sometimes wondered if she would ever have another lover. She wasn't avoiding that idea. She just felt there would never be another Doreen. That kind of love came once in a lifetime.

The previous year Doreen had told her, "You're too young to live the rest of your life alone. I hope you find someone eventually, someone who will be good for you. I don't want you to spend the rest of your life pining away for me. It's been wonderful, but you have to let me go."

Even in her illness, which had taken a toll on both of them, Doreen had been unselfish. That, too, often made Valerie cry when she remembered.

Suddenly she noticed that Sam's head was resting on her knee. The dog's eyes were beseeching. How long had she been sitting there, Val suddenly wondered, lost in memories, old feelings and losses?

"Okay, Samantha," Valerie said, stroking the dog's head. "I know. I'm not really alone. You've been here for me since I found you. And you're right here now. I guess I should pay more attention, shouldn't I? I've been thinking that you are going to become Gina's dog instead of mine. But I would deserve it, when I get into these moods and forget about you. You need loving, too." She hugged Sam and Sam gave her a big sloppy kiss on the cheek.

Val then noticed a burr in Sam's heavy coat. "You look like you need brushing," she said to the dog. Walking over to a cabinet where she kept Sam's things, she selected a slicker brush and comb. She sat back down, pulling Sam to her. The dog was very patient with the brushing, which had to be done nearly every day. Val carefully ran the brush over Sam's back, legs, and tail, removing loose fur and tangles. Finally the retriever rolled over on the rug so that Val could work on her tummy. "You're such a silly dog," Val said, smiling to herself. "You just love this, don't you?" Sam's tongue hung out of her mouth, and she looked deliriously happy.

When Val finished the brushing, she took the comb and cleaned out the slicker brush, putting the fuzzy pile of fur into the wastebasket. She gave Sam a final pat, and the dog licked her hand and then curled up on a nearby rug.

Val picked up her book again, but her thoughts wandered. This time to Gina. Now Gina, that was another one. She liked her. If she was honest with herself, she *really* liked her. Gina was a good person and Val found her physically attractive. At the same time she was like a little chicklet—and a chicklet with problems. She was so self-protective, cautious around people, and obviously fragile. Those were all red flags, although Val had to give her credit—Gina was paying her bills, being responsible, not causing trouble around the house, and generally being a good roomer. She had goals, and she seemed to be steadily working toward them. She also had a basically positive attitude, despite the problems she had encountered. And she was opening up, sharing her past, her personal pain. Valerie felt good that she had gotten Gina to trust her enough to do that.

Val really wanted to be supportive of Gina. At the same time, she had decided that she would *not* become emotionally—let alone sexually—involved with her. It would be so easy to pursue Gina. Val was lonely and Gina was not in a relationship. She was young and—Valerie had to admit—good looking in a tall, stringy sort of way with those goofy glasses sliding down her nose all the time and the floppy ponytail. Gina did have a kind of casual charm. But how could they ever be equals in a relationship? Surely they'd always be mother-daughter on some level, and that wouldn't be healthy. Too many lesbian relationships were symbiotic, like mother and child, and filled with neurotic—even destructive—elements. No, involvement with Gina was to be avoided at all costs she told herself as she returned to her book.

Chapter Six

After her eye-opening conversation with Rick at the theater Gina's life changed in very positive ways. She learned that the Purple Priscilla, a relatively new business in Arcata, had been named after the popular cult film, *Priscilla, Queen of the Desert*. She had never heard of, let alone seen, this film but was lucky to find a copy at a local video store. Intrigued, she brought the DVD home and slipped the disc into her computer. Within moments of the start of the movie she felt an emotional lift. The picture's enthusiastic attitude about being gay, along with its spirited music, mesmerized her.

Gina had finished watching the movie just in time to go to work at Ritchie's, but that night she watched it again. The film even invaded her sleep, and she watched it three more times before returning the DVD. As the film played on her computer the last time, Gina stood up and danced around the bedroom floor until she began to sweat and felt lightheaded. She had to sit down on the bed for a moment and wondered how she could have missed so much for so long. In Tucson she must have been walking around in a fog. More and more Gina sensed how narrow her life had been from her rural childhood, to school, therapy, and then work. She had obviously been missing a lot in life. *Like a lot of fun.*

The next weekend she went with Rick and two of his friends, Eric Watkins and Paul Kaufman, to this mysterious Purple Priscilla tucked away in an old warehouse near the Humboldt State campus.

The foursome sat together at a small table, and Gina put her hand on Rick's arm. "Thank you so much for telling me about *Priscilla, Queen of the Desert*. I've got all this music in my head now, and when

I go to work I keep replaying it. The time just flies by, and I feel so much energy."

Rick grinned. "Glad I could share." He nodded toward the dance floor, where several couples, men and women, were gyrating to a tune spun by a disc jockey. "Now you'll have to use all that energy here on the dance floor."

Gina grimaced and then forced herself to relax into a hesitant smile. She wasn't sure that she was quite ready yet to—what? Let it all hang out, she guessed.

Rick and his friends were considerate of her inexperience in all things gay. They introduced her to friends—including a couple of women who seemed pleasant, positive, and open about their lifestyles. The young men told her about more music and films that could help her feel less like an outsider. Eric and Paul were a colorful duo, both in dress and behavior, and Gina couldn't quite figure them out. Yet she did enjoy their company.

As they all talked, she could feel some previously unrecognized weight inside her lifting. She certainly hadn't realized just how uptight she had been. The future was beginning to appear more hopeful.

Amid this new enlightenment she found that she could look forward to Saturday evenings at the multiplex—not just for the job, but as a place where she could meet her own kind. Rick would signal her when someone came into the theater that he recognized as gay or lesbian. Her own "gaydar" began to develop.

Rick was tall, what they would have called a "string bean" back home in Illinois, with curly red hair. He could be silly and a tease. And now that she understood him better, he made her laugh. She hadn't known how much she needed to laugh. Everything had always been so serious in her life, especially since her emotional breakdown. Laughing, she now began to realize, helped her heal inside. She recognized that

Rick wasn't threatening to her. They were becoming buddies, and that was all.

When no one was around Rick would call out, "Hey, Doc, coming to the club tonight?" She had admitted to him that she had a Ph.D. and had had emotional problems, but he didn't care. "That's heavy, girlfriend," he had said when she told him about her experiences in Tucson, but he hugged her and gave her a big kiss on the cheek. Being gay, he told her, exposed him to all kinds of stories. Gina's tale wasn't even particularly unusual to him, and he admitted as much. He was still empathetic and encouraging.

Gina liked laughing at his theatricality, which was a big part of his personality. He kept it down in front of straight people, but when the two cleaned auditoriums together, now that they were open with each other, he let himself go. He swished and talked with a lisp, and Gina laughed and truly enjoyed his antics.

On a Sunday morning Valerie awoke to sounds and smells coming up the stairway from the kitchen. She was taken by surprise. The house was usually very quiet at this time of day. She looked over the edge of her bed for Sam, but the dog was gone.

Curious, Val struggled to her feet, grabbed her robe, and virtually sailed down the two flights of stairs.

Gina stood by the kitchen stove, Sam at her feet watching her every move. She had the teakettle simmering. The oven was hot and the aroma of baked goods strong.

"Hi!" Gina greeted Val with a smile. "Did I wake you? I was hoping for a complete surprise, but it's hard to whip up breakfast without making at least a little noise."

"This smells wonderful," Valerie admitted. "I love waking up to breakfast cooking."

"How about scrambled eggs with ham?" Gina asked. "I've got

blueberry muffins in the oven. They're almost ready."

"Perfect." Valerie was amazed. Since she had moved to Eureka, no one had cooked for her. Actually no one had since Doreen became ill. Val waited a moment for some kind of emotional downer to hit after she thought of Doreen, but nothing happened. She remained in the moment, delighted with the promise of a beautiful breakfast.

"I'm fixing hot tea but I'll make you coffee if you'd prefer."

"Tea is fine."

Gina poured her a cup of Earl Gray and motioned her to take it into the dining room. The newspaper was sitting beside Valerie's customary place at the table. Impressed, Val sat down and allowed herself to savor the steaming tea.

In a moment Gina came out of the kitchen, first with her own tea, then with plates of eggs and muffins.

"Wow," Valerie said, "this is stupendous."

As soon as Gina sat down, Valerie took a bite of the eggs and found them delicious. "You are a very good cook," she said, a hint of surprise in her voice. "Did you learn this from your mom?"

Gina laughed, her eyes sparkling with amusement. "I guess so. You can't survive in a farm family without knowing something about cooking. Farmers are big eaters."

After taking a bite of the muffin and stowing away most of her eggs, Valerie asked, "Is this a special occasion?"

"Not really. I just woke up feeling hungry for home cooking. I haven't seen anyone have a really big breakfast since I've been here. I've been kind of living on muffins and bagels and stuff like that. Sundays were always special where I grew up, and I was just hungry for that. I hope you don't mind that I had to use some of your supplies," Gina apologized.

"No problem," Valerie replied, with obvious amusement. "Eggs this good are to die for. I can forgive you anything, for this!"

The two women enjoyed the meal for a little while in silence. Sam waited patiently, hoping.

Finally, after swallowing the last bite of her muffin, Valerie observed, "I'm surprised to see you up so early this morning. You usually sleep in after the theater and the late hours."

"True, but this morning I just couldn't stay in bed. I guess I'm feeling good—things are going better for me."

"That's good. I'm really glad for you."

"I've made these friends at the theater—Rick Hendricks, who's gay, and some of his buddies. They've taken me to the Purple Priscilla a few times. I just feel more relaxed now. I'm so glad to be able to have a good time."

Valerie looked at her thoughtfully. "I've heard of this Purple Priscilla. It's mostly a men's bar, isn't it?" she asked.

"Well, yes, but women do go there. I've met several women. I've even danced with a few and it's been fun," Gina said.

"Anybody special?" Valerie probed.

Gina blushed. "No, I'm not ready for that yet. Just fun, you know, with a group. Like your group—like Josie, Lanie, and Judee.

"You should come sometime," she added.

Valerie considered that idea as she continued eating her eggs. "Maybe. Sometime." She focused on her plate quietly and conversation again came to a halt.

After a moment or two, Gina looked at her watch and abruptly stood up. "Glad you liked the breakfast," she said. "I've got to go to the theater early today for the matinee shift, so I need to shower and get dressed."

"I'll clean up the dishes," Valerie offered. "It's the least I can do after such a wonderful meal."

"Thanks. I appreciate that. Glad you didn't mind my using your kitchen. See you later." Gina disappeared up the stairs. Sam looked after her and then back at Valerie and decided to stay put at her feet. In reward for this show of loyalty, Valerie passed the retriever the small morsel of scrambled egg still on her plate. Val then glanced through the Sunday *Times-Standard*, got up and put out a bowl of food for Sam, gathered up the dishes, and took them into the kitchen.

As she cleaned off the plates and slipped them into hot soapy water she thought about this unexpected treat. She remembered how she and Doreen used to fix breakfast for each other, but her mind quickly returned to Gina and the changes in her lately. Gina was opening up. Becoming less reserved and intense. Even though, in making the breakfast, Gina had crossed one of the boundaries of their landlady-tenant relationship, she had not done so in a negative, dependent way. Debra would have made herself a plate of food, left the dishes all over the kitchen and gone into the living room to turn on the television, loudly of course, to entertain herself. Gina had fixed breakfast to share with, and to surprise, Valerie. Her actions were far more adult and more considerate. Instead of feeling threatened and as if her kitchen were being taken over, Valerie discovered that she felt liked and respected—even nurtured—by Gina. It was a good feeling, and she allowed herself a moment to enjoy it.

Valerie had never wanted to be a parent. That this decision had been a wise one for her was reinforced by an unforeseen visit from her brother Daniel, his wife Susan, and their two bratty—Val's definition—children.

Val had been an only child for eight years when her parents had found out, quite by surprise, that they were expecting another child, a boy. Not surprisingly, this late-life arrival had upset the family dynamics. Daniel was the light of his father's eye and both parents spoiled him to no end. Valerie had resented him from day one, and he had lorded it over her as soon as he could toddle around.

Because of the difference in their ages, they operated in totally separate worlds. Val was in high school while Daniel was still in the elementary grades. She did her best to pretend he didn't exist and managed to succeed, except when she was asked to babysit.

Once Valerie went on to college and began her own adult life, she rarely saw Daniel. But every so often he would show up on her doorstep.

This time he and Susan were taking the kids to Seattle for a family vacation, complete with riding at least one ferry, seeing the aquarium, and visiting the Space Needle. Daniel had asked by phone, since they were driving the coastal route, if they could stop in Eureka for a couple of nights and stay at her house. Biting her tongue, she had agreed.

She put Daniel and Susan up in the second bedroom across from Gina. Val made a camp for the kids, Petey and Mariah, by putting up a tent in the living room, furnished with two sleeping bags.

It was panedemonium from the moment they came in the door. Petey and Mariah started running up and down the stairs, whooping and hollering. Their own house was on one level and having stairs was a big thrill. Soon Samantha was following them up and down as well, barking all the way in each direction.

Daniel must be 43 by now, Valerie surmised, and Susan was probably 37 or 38. They had had their children relatively late in their own lives, and as a consequence, Val felt that they should have been mature adults able to manage their kids, but obviously that was not the case. She had to admit to herself that children today were a lot more boisterous than they had been when she was little, but knowing that sociological fact didn't make the noise any easier to take.

After the household finally settled down for the first night, Val tossed and turned in her bed. Why had she said yes to them? They must have money or they couldn't do this trip. Why did she have to put up with them? She knew she was being uncharitable and not very sisterly, but she did like her quiet. She had liked being an only child and she liked her peaceful life the way it was now, with little or no disruption. She wondered if this was the onset of menopause or if she had always been that way. Or did these feelings of annoyance stem from the depression she still felt over Doreen's death? Susan was a pretty good conversationalist and the kids could be cute, if she'd allow herself to see it.

She was still mulling this over in the kitchen the next morning while fixing breakfast for the brood. The kids were watching TV in the living room and their parents were getting dressed upstairs. It had been planned that they would go sightseeing in the local area for most of the day. Val couldn't wait for them to leave the house.

Gina came into the kitchen, already dressed, to get her muffins and juice from the refrigerator. Val almost jumped as she caught movement out of the corner of her eye.

Recovering, she asked, "Did you get some sleep last night?"

Gina smiled. "I'm fine."

"Wish I could say the same," Val grumbled.

"Guess this isn't a good day to ask to use your toaster for my muffins," Gina commented. Her mouth was turned up in a slightly evil grin.

Val waved a spatula at her. "You are no help!" Then she relented. "Go ahead, use the toaster. And then get out of here."

"Okay, boss." Gina spoke lightly and did as she was told.

Val stared out the window after Gina had disappeared up the stairs. She had to get a grip. She would get through today, and tomorrow they'd be gone. She'd get back to her painting, and her nerves would settle down.

The phone rang. It was Lanie. "What are you up to, girl? I haven't heard from you in days!"

Valerie chuckled. "Not much. I'm just sitting here with the morning paper, feeling very full and satisfied. Guess what? Gina fixed breakfast the other morning and again today. She's a very good cook!"

"Mmmm," noted Lanie. "That sounds intimate. Is something I don't know about going on over there?"

Amused, Valerie shook her head. "No, Lanie. If there were, you'd be the first to know. And there isn't. Gina was just up early and feeling good and she decided to fix breakfast for us. My brother and his family have been here the last few days, and with all the noise and door-banging, my nerves are shot. Gina hasn't seemed to be too bothered by all the pandemonium, and she wanted to do something to make me feel better, now that they've left at last. It was very nice of her and I'm duly grateful."

"Mmmm," Lanie repeated. "I thought you were going to have tight boundaries, no fraternizing with your roomer—no more Debra kind of stuff."

"Quit worrying, Lanie," Val said. "The boundaries are still there. I won't let a Debra happen again. I assure you, it's not the same."

The two friends talked for a few moments and then said goodbye. As she worked the daily crossword, Valerie replayed the conversation with Lanie in her mind. Was Lanie a bit jealous of Gina? That was a funny thought. There had never really been any overtures on her or Lanie's part. Nothing beyond teasing now and then. They were just good friends. Val had already concluded, for herself, anyway, that Lanie would not make a good long-term partner. She was a restless sort, always seeking new challenges, and that would not suit Valerie. She needed a loyal and dedicated lover—if and when the day came when she was ready for a loving relationship again. *Which certainly isn't now*, she said to herself.

Val patted her full stomach and thought about Lanie's protective comments. She found she liked both the food and the attention. This morning she felt a little bit less lonely and that was a good thing.

Rick cornered Gina at the theater while they were cleaning an auditorium. "J.J., a friend of mine in Arcata, is looking for a roommate. I think she wants less than what you are paying now. She's got a nice place, and I think you'd get along," he said.

"Oh." Gina was surprised by the information and her heart skipped a beat. "Well," she managed, "thanks for the tip. I'll think about it."

"Well, think quick because it'll go in a heartbeat," Rick shot back, "and it will help you get that debt of yours paid off sooner." He wheeled his trash cart out the auditorium door.

Gina finished sweeping up and pushed her cart along after him. She'd sure like to save more money. That debt was going down, but not fast enough. Every time she got the bill it seemed longer and longer before it could be repaid. At the same time, she was comfortable at Valerie's and she didn't really want to move. She'd have to give it some deep thought.

Valerie lay in bed that night, wakeful. She couldn't seem to relax, and she couldn't put her finger on the reason why. It had been a good, productive day. She had taken Sam for a long walk and had put several hours in on her painting. The canvas she was working on was nearly complete. She even had an idea about what she wanted to paint next and that was a *very* good sign.

So what made her so restless?

Gina's fixing breakfast, twice? Lanie's expressing a little concern, which might be masking jealousy? Gina's asking her to go dancing at the Purple Priscilla? Any and all of the above?

She tried to relax by stretching out in bed, arms way over her head, legs extended to the fullest under the sheet and blankets. Mmmm. Felt good and she did seem to relax a little.

But there was a body tension that was still there.

She allowed her hands to reach under her nightgown—moving over her skin, massaging here and there, trying to soothe away the tightness. Her fingers passed lightly over her breasts and they responded to the touch. She thought about the fact that she hadn't made nice to herself like this for a *long* time. She didn't even want to acknowledge how long it had been since she had really touched her own body. Probably not since Doreen had died and for months before that while Doreen had been gravely ill.

Her body, she realized with some surprise, was hungry for attention and she stroked and massaged herself with growing intensity. How could she have neglected herself this way? With her sadness over Doreen, the move, the settling, and the adjustment, it all made sense that she just hadn't thought about her physical needs. Everything else got in the way. Maybe she was becoming a little menopausal as well. She was nearing that age, but she hadn't seriously considered it since she was still getting her periods.

Little goosebumps formed on her skin as she touched herself. Even her own touch caused a tickling sensation wherever her fingers fell. She put her hand over her mound of honey-blonde curls and she could feel her muscles pulling. Her fingers gently slipped between her legs, and she discovered she was wet. Surprised and delighted, she could not stop herself. She stroked her clitoris and found it hardening and rising beneath her touch. Almost instantly her back arched and she went into a strong climax, gasping for breath. Ripples of heat and pleasure passed throughout her entire body.

Covered in perspiration, she fell back against the pillows. She was astonished but satisfied by the reality, the strength, of her capacity for sexual response. It had been such a long, long time.

Downstairs from Valerie, Gina lay soaking in the clawfoot bathtub. She hadn't felt sleepy, despite the late hour, and she thought a soak might help her relax. She loved this old bathtub. Initially she hadn't been too sure. Having always been a shower freak, she felt this tub wasn't very conducive to taking enjoyable showers. Because there was a showerhead sticking out of the wall and a metal ring above the tub, with a plastic shower curtain attached, showers were technically possible. But the whole setup was awkward and inconvenient. Over the months, with her exhausting schedule, she had gradually started taking baths more often—especially at night, when she could soak away the soreness of being on her feet for hours at Ritchie's and then again at the theater. So this night, her head abuzz, she took her body to the bath.

She wondered what was making her restless. Was it the full moon or something that had happened that day that would not let her even feel sleepy?

Rick's information about a possible roommate in Arcata was on her mind. He knew that she was working three jobs to pay off a large debt, and he also knew that she had only a room and bath—no real house privileges—where she was living. He might have been concerned about that and wanted to see if he could help her out.

This place in Arcata could save her money, if his information was correct. On the other hand, she had become comfortable here. And her jobs were all in Eureka. It could cost her more in time and gas to drive from Arcata, even though it was only a few miles up the highway.

But she needed to get the debt paid off, and every dollar counted. Maybe she should call Rick, get his friend's name, and at least look at the place.

Yet she would miss Valerie. And why? Val was nice, but there was nothing between them. Just a pleasant friendship. Sure, Valerie was good looking in a mature sort of way, but Gina just couldn't see her as a possible romantic interest. And why would she? It wouldn't make any sense—especially when she was getting ready to go to San Francisco to work and build a life there. So why the big deal about moving out?

But when Gina was honest with herself, some part of her didn't really want to move away from this house or from Valerie or even from Sam.

Gina's cell phone rang. She was working at the record store the following Friday morning and the call took her by surprise. She normally kept her cell on but rarely got a call.

Picking the phone up off the counter, she said "Hello" into it.

"Gina, this is Valerie."

"Yes—what's up?" Gina was startled to get a call from Val.

There was a slight hesitation on the other end. Then, "Did you say that you and your friends are going to the Purple Priscilla tonight?"

"Yes," Gina replied, a bit surprised by the question.

"Well, you had asked me to go sometime and I wondered if I could meet you there. Tonight."

"Sure," Gina said, grinning to herself with amusement.

"What time do you think you'll be going?"

"I'll be done at Ritchie's by 8:30, I'm sure. Rick will pick me up there, so we'll be at the club by 9 anyway. We usually get a booth and the dancing will be in full swing by then. I'll keep an eye out for you if you decide to come."

"Okay, I'll come by about 9:30. What's the dress code?"

Gina chuckled. "California casual. Don't sweat it. See you later."

As she put the phone down, Gina was both shaking her head in disbelief but somewhere inside she was also dancing with glee. And why? She wondered about that with amusement.

The first time Gina visited the Purple Priscilla, she had been so nervous that she barely looked at the décor. Later all she could remember was dark, noise, and purple.

After a few more visits, she was relaxed enough to take notice of this unique alternative bar. It was, not surprisingly, decorated in purple. From the street the bar was almost invisible, in an old warehouse, looking rather run down, with a weed-infested asphalt parking lot next to it. No one would guess what was inside, and there were no obvious signs posted anywhere. If you didn't know it was there, you'd never find it.

Inside the bar was another story. Purple bar, purple booths, purple tables and chairs, purple helium-filled balloons flying from the rafters above, purple dance floor, purple curtains behind the stage, purple neon signs over the bar and inside the front door. Other than these garish purple highlights the bar was very dark and painted black. The floor was covered in sawdust.

On this particular Friday evening Gina, Rick, and his pals, Eric and Paul, had a booth—the same one they usually commandeered. They were all on their second beer. Rick could go swishy, but he was usually pretty ordinary in his attire. His friends, Eric and Paul, were more "flaming," with spiked hair, gold studs in their ears, nose, and belly, and tight silk shirts tied above the waist over low-slung black leather pants. They looked almost like twins, at least in dress. Gina often thought of them as rock stars, and this wasn't too far off because both were members of a punk rock band. On this night they didn't have a gig, so they were hanging out.

A band commanded the stage. This evening it was an all-girl band called "The Amazons." Female performers were a rarity in this male-oriented establishment, Gina had been told. She enjoyed listening to the tall, blond, leather-clad lead singer, who handled her guitar quite well, the dark-haired keyboardist, a devilish looking drummer whose neckline came down to her waist, and a fourth chunky redhead, who switched from flute, to clarinet, and then saxophone. The group seemed to have a large repertoire of music from several genres.

At the moment most of the dancers were male, but two lesbian couples were also gyrating on the floor. The atmosphere, overall, was decidedly loud and sweaty.

Gina sat with Rick. The two were talking about the multiplex and people they worked with there. Eric and Paul seemed to be in a world of their own. They periodically took to the floor with a jaunty "Bye."

Although she was excited and a bit anxious as she waited for Valerie to arrive, Gina still focused on Rick.

"If you don't mind my asking," she said to him unexpectedly, "I always see you with Eric and Paul. Don't you have a main squeeze of your own? Or are you all a threesome?" She blushed.

Rick gave her a big grin, shaking his head. "No, no threesome. It's too much fun playing the field."

"You've never had someone special?" She was sure there was a story there somewhere because she had never seen him with anyone.

Rick shifted in his seat and looked down at his tall mug of beer, running his finger around the rim. He frowned. "There was one, once," he admitted, with a sideward glance at Gina. "A guy I knew from Humboldt State. He was studying acting." Remembering, he smiled, "A real good looker. Like a movie star." He was quiet a moment.

"What happened to him?" Gina persisted.

"Split. Went to New York. Didn't ask me to go, and I've never heard from him since." He took a deep breath and Gina wondered how much he had grieved over that loss.

She started to say something, but Rick quickly recovered and gave her a silly grin. "I just enjoy what's around. No expectations, no regrets."

Gina studied him. "Sounds like a good excuse to me. I'm not sure I buy it." She considered it for a moment and then risked saying, "Maybe you only want what you can't have."

"Oh, a psychologist tonight." Rick had a sarcastic edge in his voice.

Gina decided she'd better back off. "Well, whatever. You're too sweet and too much fun not to have someone special making over you," she observed. She then steered the conversation back onto neutral ground.

Shortly after 9:30 Gina glanced around the bar and saw Valerie standing just inside the front doorway, her eyes searching anxiously across the darkened room.

"Over here," Gina called, standing and waving.

Val saw her, heaved an obvious sigh of relief, and quickly worked her way among the tables to the booth. Gina motioned her to sit and introduced her to Rick.

"You made it." Gina gave Valerie a warm smile.

"Yep," Val responded, her own smile somewhat forced. Her hazel eyes darted and she looked like she might run at any moment.

Gina touched her arm. "Would you like a beer?" she asked loudly, trying to be welcoming and yet make herself heard over the din.

"Beer's okay, although I'd prefer white wine if it's available." Val also had to shout to be heard over the music.

Gina motioned to the server, a slender young man with purple spiked hair who was dressed in a purple vest over a black long-sleeve T-shirt and purple slacks. The server appeared at their side and took Valerie's order.

As he scooted away Val commented wryly, "They must really like purple in here."

Gina laughed. "It just about puts your eyes out, doesn't it?"

Valerie nodded and smiled. She was clearly beginning to relax a little. She allowed herself to look around at the couples dancing and at the women's band on the stage.

Rick, on his third beer, was feeling no pain.

"So this is Valerie," he said. "Gina's landlady, right?"

Val nodded hesitantly, one eyebrow raised, clearly not sure how to take his comment.

Rick grinned. "Gina said you were older so I imagined this little gray-haired lady, but wow, you aren't what I expected," he said.

Valerie looked bemused at what was obviously a backhanded compliment. She looked from Gina to Rick, as if wondering what this was all about.

"Now I know," Rick continued, "why Gina didn't want to move away."

Valerie gave him a puzzled look and then turned to Gina. "What?"

"Would you like to dance?" Gina suddenly interrupted, almost pulling Val out of the booth and toward the dance floor. She gave Rick a stern frown as she did so. Rick shrugged at her, suggesting that he was sorry for having spilled the beans.

Sensing that his comments might be payback for her having questioned his personal life, Gina tried to put that aside as she led Valerie out onto the dance floor. Thankfully this rhythmic number encouraged personal expression but not close dancing. Gina began gyrating and Val soon picked up the rhythm and the movements.

"Hey, you're pretty good," Gina enthused.

"Thanks, but what was that all about?" Valerie questioned.

"Oh, nothing really. Rick knows someone in Arcata who was looking for a roommate. He thought it might be good for me, because I could save some money and get my debt paid off sooner," Gina explained as they shook and turned and twisted on the floor. "But I figured out that the added time and gas to go from Arcata to my jobs would just about equal the savings in rent, so I turned it down,"

"I see." Discomfort and confusion were written on Valerie's face.

"Besides," Gina said with a little smile, "I'd miss you and Sam."

"Oh. I see, I guess." Val seemed a little relieved at Gina's additional explanation.

The number ended and the two women returned to the table. Eric and Paul were now seated there. They greeted Valerie, who appeared to find them charming. "I haven't seen a social scene like this since San Francisco," she whispered to Gina.

When the two men trotted off to dance again, Val quipped, with an amused smile, "I must be living a sedate life."

"Careful," grinned Gina, looking at Rick, "you'll blow your cover."

Rick started to make a crack and Gina kicked him under the table. He considered that for a moment, rubbing his ankle with his hand, and then offered, "Gina says you're an artist. Painter?"

"Yes." Valerie gave him a friendly smile.

"What do you paint?"

"Landscapes, mostly. Outdoor scenes. Kind of impressionistic, sometimes a little whimsical."

"No nudes?"

Val laughed. "No nudes. At least not recently. I've done them in my time, especially when I was studying art," she said.

"Well, if you start doing nudes again, I'm available to model." He posed flamboyantly. "I'm just dying to model for someone."

Valerie smiled and Gina wondered what she was really thinking. If Val wanted to do nudes, Gina suspected she'd most likely be doing women. But then maybe men—especially gay men—saw themselves at the center of everything.

The band had started a new set, and Gina asked Valerie if she wanted to dance. Val nodded with just a hint of hesitation and the two went out to the dance floor. This number was a slow one and Gina took the lead, circling Valerie's waist with one hand and holding her other hand out for Val to take.

As they moved around the floor, Valerie quickly admitted that Gina was a good dancer. "Doreen always led, so I am accustomed to that but, Gina, since you are younger and more slight of build I didn't automatically expect you to lead. But here you are, leading away." Val blushed slightly.

"I'm glad you came," Gina said, covering Val's obvious discomfort. "I wasn't sure you would."

"I almost chickened out," Val admitted. "Then I thought about having to face you tomorrow morning and I decided I'd better make a go of it."

"Well, you're here, and you're a good dancer. I think it's harder to follow than to lead, and I'm happy you do it so well," Gina said.

"Where did you learn to lead?" Valerie asked.

"Farm girl, remember. We had to do just about everything."

Their bodies were beginning to mesh with each other and Gina pulled Valerie closer. As she did so, she felt the quickening heartbeat, the warmth and tingle of excitement between her legs that she had come to recognize when she was with a woman. Being with men had never done that for her, and feelings like this on the dance floor were part of what had convinced her she was a lesbian. Now she had to accept, as her heart skipped a beat, that despite the difference in their ages Valerie was a turn-on for her as well.

Chapter Seven

"Val, this is Lanie." Her voice over the phone sounded tense. "Josie's in the hospital. She fell and mangled her leg. I'm here at St. Joseph in the ER waiting room."

"I'll be right there." Valerie dumped the phone in the cradle. She had been working in the studio, but now she tore off her painter's smock, grabbed her purse, scribbled a note for Gina and left it on the hall table, patted Sam, and quickly left the house. "You wanted drama in your life," she mumbled to herself as she ran to the Volvo wagon.

Fifteen minutes later, Val met a strained-looking Lanie in the hospital waiting room. "What's happening? What do you know?" she asked breathlessly.

"As best as I can understand, Josie was on a ladder trimming a tree," Lanie told her. "The ladder buckled beneath her. She fell at an odd angle, twisting her left leg. It's not good. It's a complicated break and will undoubtedly require surgery."

"How did you find out?" Valerie asked.

"I guess she was out cold for a few moments," Lanie explained, "but when she came to she was able to reach her cell in her shirt pocket and dial 911. Then she hit a speed dial number and got me. I was here at the hospital just as the ambulance pulled up."

Still shaken from Lanie's call, Valerie held onto her best friend's arm. "I'm so glad she had the presence of mind to call one of us. But how terrible for Josie," she said. "I wonder if she has any insurance."

Lanie shrugged. "Student policy, I suspect. It will cover some of this but not enough, I'm sure."

"What about her family?"

Lanie shook her head. "No support there. Josie is pretty much on her own."

Valerie stood silently for a moment, thinking and worrying about Josie. *That poor girl.* She couldn't imagine what it must be like to be totally alone without family in a time of trial. Her own parents had always been there for her as long as they were living. Val knew instantly that there must be something she and her friends could do to help.

Moments later Judee rushed into the waiting area. She was breathing heavily from running and had her two boys in tow. Both Mark and Steven were slender in build and had dark hair and brown eyes like their mother. She ordered them to sit quietly and read. They did as they were told, sprawling in two chairs, their long legs stretched out before them. The boys opened their books but continued to look around the room, obviously fascinated by the ongoing action.

As soon as she could turn her attention from her sons to the situation at hand, Judee was brought up to speed on Josie's accident. Then the three women huddled as they waited for information, sipping Coke from a nearby vending machine and worrying in unison.

Within half an hour Gina arrived, clad in her Ritchie's uniform. "I let Sam out for you," she told Valerie and then quickly added to everyone, "I can stay until 4:30 but then I have leave for work."

Coming out of her own concerned reverie, Val looked at Gina with appreciation. "Oh, thanks, Gina." She suddenly realized that she had just given Sam a pat and run out the door. "I didn't even think about letting her out."

By the time the four had shared all the known details about Josie's accident, a young male doctor, tall, slender and blonde, strolled down the main hallway toward the waiting area. "Lanie Olson?" he asked, glancing around.

Lanie quickly stood up and approached him.

"I'm Dr. Arnold, taking care of Josie Turner." The physician was businesslike but warm. "Are you family?" he asked Lanie.

She nodded in the direction of her friends, whose eyes were all focused on her and the physician. "Her birth family won't be involved in this. We're close friends and as much of a family as Josie has," she said.

Dr. Arnold studied her briefly and then gave an understanding nod. "Well, we'll have forms for Miss Turner to fill out that will allow you visitation even though you are not formally family members," he said. "Essentially, so you have some idea what is going on here, Miss Turner's left leg has sustained severe trauma. While the femur in her upper leg has only a hairline fracture, the tibia in her lower leg has two distinct breaks. The downside is that it will require surgery and the use of pins to stabilize the bone. The good side is that the fractures are near the center of the tibia rather than near the knee or the ankle. This will make bracing the leg, therapy, and the recovery much easier, although Miss Turner can expect weeks of real pain followed by months of discomfort and limitation before she is totally healed.

"Now," he added, "the reality of her situation is that she's going to be in a long cast and will have limited movement for several weeks. From what she's been able to tell me about her insurance coverage and her concerns as a student, she wants us to treat her as quickly as possible and send her home."

He paused for a moment to let the information sink in. "It's obviously rather early to be talking about this and normally I wouldn't, but since she's so concerned about the cost I will give you an outline of what is likely to happen. Even if we assume that there are no complications from the surgery or post-op care here in the hospital, she is going to have to have someone available to assist her 24 hours a day for an indefinite period of time. She will also need to be driven to physical therapy when she is ready for that. She will need a caregiver plan, before we can even consider releasing her," he said.

Lanie looked at her friends and they nodded, as if reading her mind. "We'll put a team together, and we'll do it around the clock for as long as it takes," she assured him.

"Okay, that's good to know," the doctor said, giving them all a warm smile. "Now, for the immediate situation, she is sedated but awake. She will go into surgery tomorrow morning. I can't let all of you go in, but you," he nodded to Lanie, "as I recall you came in with her and helped with the registration. I'll take you back with me as a family representative, and I'll get the forms signed by tomorrow that will allow all of you to visit her.

"She'll probably go to sleep soon from the pain medication and the sedatives, so you all should go home and get some rest. And work on coming up with your best plan for her post-hospital care. If all goes well, she'll be in recovery tomorrow afternoon and able to have visitors either tomorrow evening or the next day. If you each give me your name, I'll list you for Miss Turner's signature so we can get you in to see her then."

Judee, Valerie, and Gina gave him their names, and he moved off to the nurses' station to make notations about visits. While the doctor was gone Lanie leaned over to Valerie and asked, "Do you think he's gay?"

Valerie shrugged. "Could be. Gay friendly, anyway. I think he got the picture quite well."

Dr. Arnold returned and addressed Lanie. "Now if you'll follow me," he said and led her down the hall.

Lanie returned to the waiting room shortly and shared with the others what she had seen. She had been very shocked by the severity of Josie's fall, even beyond the mangled leg. Josie had deep scratches on both arms, her face was bruised and swollen, and she had stitches above her left eye. That was going to be very black by the next day. Despite her obvious pain and grogginess, Josie seemed very relieved to see Lanie and to know the others were there as well.

After Lanie finished her report, they quietly discussed their schedules—when each could visit and when each could help out after Josie was released. There never seemed to be any question whether they would all pitch in.

They split soon afterward—Gina to work, Judee to take her sons home to feed them dinner, Lanie for a real estate appointment, and Valerie home to take care of Sam.

Val lay awake, tossing and turning late into the night. Her mind kept going over the events of the day, recalling how everything started off positively and suddenly changed into a crisis. Josie's fall, hospitalization, confinement, and then subsequent recovery would test to the max the depth of the group's friendship.

It was easy to be friends during the good times: poker nights, movies, dinners out. Those were fun and brought them all together to enjoy each other. But Josie's injury would mean pain, fear, and frustration for her and a lot of sacrifice on the part of everyone else. The women would discover new things about each other and they would learn just how willing they were to give up important events—and time they really needed for themselves—in order to care for Josie. And it would be several weeks, if not months, before all of their lives returned to some semblance of normal. Val had had her own experiences with Doreen, as well as friends in San Francisco who had died of AIDS. She knew how draining a situation like this was on everyone. At least, in this case, there should eventually be full recovery. Josie was young, strong, and pretty determined. She'd be scared, but she would do whatever it took to get over this fall.

Valerie also thought about Josie's little apartment and her roommate, Sarah, who hadn't yet been considered at all. Had she even been notified? Val or someone in the group should call and talk with her. Valerie thought that the two shared the apartment mostly out of convenience. She didn't believe there was any romantic attachment between them. At least Josie had never suggested any intimacy with Sarah. If having all these people in and out of that tiny apartment would be uncomfortable for that girl, then it might cause some friction. And maybe, Val considered, that little place, really barely more than a studio, wasn't the best spot for Josie to go when she was released from the hospital.

Almost inevitably, Val's mind shifted to the empty bedroom in her own house. It was on the second floor, but there was a full bath across the hall so the location could work adequately while Josie was confined. When she began to move around, they might have to set up a bed in the living room for her to lessen the number of trips up and down the stairs. And there was a partial bath on the ground floor.

But in this scenario there was also Gina to consider. She had so little time to herself now, with those three jobs, that helping care for Josie would be an added burden—although one that, at least for now, Gina seemed quite willing to undertake. If they brought Josie into this house, it would be a further invasion of Gina's limited privacy. While it was Valerie's final decision to make an offer to care for Josie, she would at least talk to Gina first and give her a chance to express any concerns she might have. Lanie and Judee would probably welcome this offer because they were so accustomed to hanging out at Val's house anyway. And if Josie had to be anywhere but in her own bed, she would probably be happiest at Valerie's.

At the moment, Val felt she was reluctantly bowing to something unavoidable. After going through home nursing care for months with Doreen she really didn't want to do it again, but at least Josie's prognosis was a lot better than Doreen's fatal bout with cancer. Valerie quickly tried to refocus her thoughts on the present. It did her no good to dwell on the past. And at any rate, these ideas would all have to be considered over the next few days as they watched Josie's progress after surgery.

Since she couldn't resolve any of this now, Val tried to let it go. She rearranged her pillows, pulled the covers up tightly around herself, and attempted to get some sleep.

Early the next evening they all—except Gina, who was working her shift at Ritchie's Grill—gathered back in the waiting room at St. Joseph Hospital. Lanie had arrived first and had managed to get an update on Josie's condition, thanks to the intervention of Dr. Arnold. He had obtained the necessary signatures from Josie and had left specific instructions at the nurses' station regarding the "cousins."

Lanie passed the information on to the others as they waited for a nurse to tell them that they could briefly visit Josie.

"She's out of recovery and has been sleeping," Lanie explained to Valerie and Judee. "They woke her at dinner time to see if she was able to eat anything, and she had a little bit of liquid. She's pretty groggy and will be back to sleep shortly, but they promised we could at least say hi and let her know we are here."

Shortly a tall, athletic-looking nurse with close-cropped auburn hair and rimless glasses came briskly down the hallway, pointed to Lanie, and motioned her to follow. Lanie jumped up from her chair to obey.

"That nurse is MOT, I think," whispered Judee to Val, who just smiled and nodded. *Always looking for a lesbian in the woodpile,* she thought to herself.

Trying to make themselves comfortable, Valerie and Judee sat and waited, leafing through magazines and observing people come and go.

Soon Lanie returned to the waiting area, and Judee was escorted down the hall.

"How is she?" Valerie asked.

"Pretty good, all things considered. She's groggy as all get out, but she still hasn't lost her sense of humor. Her leg is all splinted up and suspended from some contraption. I don't know how she'll sleep like that, but I guess the drugs will knock her out."

In a couple of minutes Judee was back, and Valerie followed the nurse down the hall.

"Your friend is lucky," the nurse commented to Val, "to have such a large extended family."

Valerie looked at her askance, wondering how sarcastic she was being. "Yes, it's lucky we all have each other," she said, pointedly. "Some people have no one."

Without further comment, the nurse ushered her into Josie's room and said, "I'll be out here at the nurse's station if you need me. No more than three or four minutes, at the most."

Val nodded.

Josie looked pale and her eyelids drooped. One eye was puffy and blackened. She was clearly ready to drop back into sleep but she managed a vague smile for Valerie, who put a hand on Josie's arm and said quietly, "How are you doin', trooper?"

"I'm okay," Josie assured her, her speech slightly slurred. "They got me so doped, I can hardly stay awake. Do I sound drunk?"

"Well considering what you've been through, you sound pretty good to me. I just want you to know that we're all here for you and not to worry. Gina's working right now but she'll visit when she can."

Josie offered a slight nod. "I don't know how to thank you. I don't know how you guys managed to get in here. I was so scared about everything, but Judee says she can help me with school—as soon as they let up on these meds." Josie struggled to get the words out.

"Don't worry, kiddo," Val assured her. "We'll figure out how to solve all the problems as soon as you're ready to tackle them. Everything is kosher for us to be visiting you. Dr. Arnold got you to sign some forms—you were probably so sedated you don't remember—that name us as members of your family, cousins I think, so we're in for the duration."

"That's good," Josie murmured, her eyelids closing as she began to drift off.

Valerie gave her another gentle pat on the arm and left the room.

That evening Val remained downstairs in the living room, reading a paperback while she waited for Gina to get home from work. She knew Gina would have questions about Josie, and she wanted to be there to answer them. If they talked it out, they both would probably sleep better.

Just before 10 p.m., after she had let Sam out for the last time and just before she had reached the climax of her murder mystery, Val heard the engine whine of Gina's Beetle as it came up the street. A few moments later the front door opened.

Gina looked exhausted and, obviously thinking she would be alone, started to strip off her uniform shirt as soon as she closed the door and headed for the staircase. Then she saw the light in the living room and, flushing with embarrassment, pulled her top back in place. "Hi," she called to Valerie. At the same time she reached down to pet Sam, who had gone to the front hallway to greet her.

"Come in here for a moment," Val called out. When Gina appeared, Valerie pointed to a leather chair next to her recliner. "Have a seat. I bet you are really beat."

Gina nodded and plopped into the chair. "How is Josie?" she asked.

"Doing pretty well, I think. Thanks to Dr. Arnold and a with-it nurse, we all got in to see her for a few minutes this evening. She was pretty dopey, but I think she'll remember tomorrow that we were there and she'll feel our support."

Gina smiled. "That's good. I'm glad. Hopefully I can see her tomorrow. Do you know yet how long she'll be in the hospital?"

Valerie shook her head. "I don't know anything for sure, but I would assume she'll be there for several days." She laughed. "She'll be out as soon as they'll let her go, of that I'm sure!"

"Right," Gina agreed.

"I've been thinking," Valerie added, "but I wanted to ask you first, about suggesting that Josie be brought here when she is released rather than going to the small apartment she shares with Sarah Green."

Gina's brow furrowed as she considered Val's idea for a moment. Then her face brightened. "I think it's a good idea. You have the space, and everyone is used to gathering here. It's centrally located. And as for me, I would get to spend more time with her because I'd be right here. I could help you more."

"You're sure it's not an imposition? If I rented out the other bedroom, you'd have to share with another person. But Josie is different. She is going to need a lot of care and attention around the clock for several weeks. It will be like Grand Central Station around here. And you get very little private time as it is. I want to be fair to you."

Gina smiled. "Thanks for the consideration, but I want to help and I think I can do it better this way. I'm all for bringing her here."

Valerie closed her book. "Well, thank you. I'll mention it tomorrow to Judee and Lanie, and, if we're all agreed, we'll find a way to bring it up with Dr. Arnold before Josie is released."

"Good. But if you don't mind, I'm going to hit the hay," Gina said, suppressing a yawn.

"Me, too."

They climbed the first set of stairs together, with Sam at their heels.

"Goodnight," Val said as she went down the hallway and on up to her attic room. Gina responded in kind.

Once in bed, and before she dropped off to sleep, Valerie thought some more about her offer to bring Josie to the house and she considered Gina's support. Although that gal looked as if you could blow her away with a feather and seemed so terribly introverted, Gina had recently shown some real strength of character. And Val certainly hadn't forgotten her unexpected, and quite surprising, physical response to Gina when they danced the other night at the Purple Priscilla. She sighed. Gina was a fascinating puzzle, but there was no time to focus on her right now. There were other, more urgent things to think about at the moment.

Two days later, between her morning job at the record shop and her late-afternoon shift at Ritchie's, Gina managed to visit Josie in the hospital. Although Gina was feeling a little pressed for time, she was very relieved to see that Josie was alert and obviously feeling much better.

"I'm sorry I didn't have time to get you a stuffed animal or flowers or anything," Gina apologized. "I'm here, and I guess I'm the present."

Josie laughed. "Geez! Given your schedule, I'm really honored that you came to see me."

They were both quiet for a moment. Neither knew the other really well. All their conversations had been in the midst of the poker foursome, or the "fivesome" when Gina attended.

Finally Gina looked at the way Josie's leg was encased in some kind of medical contraption and hanging from a sling. "How is your leg coming along? Any less pain today?"

"Much better," Josie said. "It still hurts like hell, but I know it's improving. The doctor seemed much closer to giving me a date for getting out of here. I hate hospitals."

"Yeah, me too," Gina said, almost without thinking. Then she paled and bit her lip. She didn't want to talk about hospitals, or being in them.

Josie didn't seem to notice. "The nurses are really nice, but I mostly want out because of the money," she said. "I never really thought too much about what hospitals cost, but I'm getting the picture. I can see my college education going down the tube, and I'll have a debt to pay off that will take the rest of my life. It's real scary."

Gina touched Josie's arm and smiled understandingly. "I don't think it will be that bad. Your doctor sounded really cooperative and I'm sure you'll work something out. But I understand about having a big debt hanging over your head. That's why I'm working three jobs, to pay off a large bill I owe."

"Wouldn't you make more money teaching?" Josie asked. "You have tons of education."

Gina uttered a deep sigh and plopped down in a chair near Josie's bed. After briefly considering it, she decided to share part of her own story. It might help Josie. "Well, after graduate school I had some emotional problems," she explained, "and was in a hospital briefly. Then I had to have therapy. It cost a lot of money and now I've got to pay off the debt. I had to kind of start over again, to build up my confidence. Maybe someday I'll be ready to teach, or maybe I'll write. Or both. Right now I'm not sure."

"Did your problems have anything to do with being a lesbian?"

Gina hesitated but then nodded, surprising herself by admitting this to Josie.

"I went to a counselor once, about being gay," Josie said. "My parents pretty much threw me out of the house when they found out. They didn't want a lesbian daughter and they didn't want me tellin' family secrets to a therapist. I was 19 and ready for college, but I would have had to live at home even though I had a scholarship. So when they threw me out I had to find a job and a place to live. The scholarship disappeared, and any dreams of college I had were put on hold. For years. And that's why, finally, I've been workin' and goin' to school part time. It's kinda hard, but tryin' to live any other way is even harder."

"Yeah, I guess it is," Gina said. "You're lucky, though, you've made some real friends."

"I know. I can't believe how supportive everyone is. It's like, incredible!"

"I hope you'll count me as one of your friends," Gina offered.

"Sure. I mean, I was a little overwhelmed when I first met you. I don't do so well in school—I get by, but I'm certainly not an A student. When I think of all the college you've had and how smart you must be, I'm kinda in awe," Josie admitted.

Gina smiled. "Underneath everything, I'm a just farm girl from Illinois. I've milked cows, swept out barns, collected eggs, and changed the oil on a tractor. I'm really a basic person so don't pay much attention to my college degrees. If my mother hadn't been a teacher and pushed me to go to college, I'd be doing some kind of outdoor work like you, most likely."

"Really?" Josie asked. "You don't seem like the outdoor type to me."

"I used to be, when I was a kid. A real tomboy. But several years of school, intense studies, late hours, emotional problems, and now a heavy workload have kind of taken their toll. I was always slender, but I used to be strong as an ox. I think I could get it back if I worked on it. That's just not my priority right now."

"I understand," Josie said. "I'm a chunk, always was a chunk, and will always be a chunk, no matter what. Can't help it. But I do love working in landscaping. I feel like it's my calling, you know what I mean?"

"Yep, and that's great, to know what you want to do. You'll do it, too."

Soon it was time for Gina to take off for Ritchie's, but when she left Josie she felt much better than when she had arrived. Opening up to Josie was a good thing. Josie was smarter and more aware of things than she had realized. Now they were becoming friends and that felt really good. Gina wasn't sorry, when she looked back on the conversation as she drove to the restaurant, that she had talked about some of her difficult past. Josie had also had a hard life, and they shared that in common.

Chapter Eight

Late the following Saturday morning, Josie was released from St. Joseph. She was taken by ambulance to Valerie's home, where the EMTs used a gurney to carry her up to the second floor. The spare bedroom had been readied for her and included a hospital bed and a wheelchair. Valerie had discussed with her friends the possibility of putting the bed in the living room, but since there was only a partial bathroom on the ground floor everyone agreed that the second floor bedroom was the best choice.

A home-health nurse was scheduled to come to the house for the first few days to help Josie and to teach the volunteer crew how to manage her care. There were also several sheets of written instructions about medications, what to do and not to do in terms of moving Josie, and how to keep the area around her cast clean.

Even under these trying circumstances, Josie was an agreeable houseguest. If she was embarrassed at having her friends taking care of her physical needs, instead of being irritable about it, she covered her discomfort with jokes and laughter. Both were a lot easier for everyone to take. At least once a day Josie or someone in the group came up with a new bedpan joke.

Valerie was very nervous at first, even though she was still glad she had volunteered use of the house. It didn't take her long to discover that it was nice to have another person around, especially one who brought smiles and laughter into the space. Samantha was beside herself with yet another soul to watch over, sniff, and lick. Despite being in considerable discomfort, Josie was able to enjoy Sam's antics as well.

During the first week, the nurse came in the mornings while Valerie and Gina were at work. She was a hefty, middle-aged woman with graying hair, dark-rimmed glasses, and plenty of experience in moving unyielding objects in restricted space. Once Val and Gina arrived home just after noon the nurse, Amanda Cardwell, showed them what to do and then left the two in charge. Valerie and Gina spelled each other, so each could get some personal things done. When Gina went to work at Ritchie's Grill, Valerie took over. Judee and Lanie supported her in the evening.

On the weekends everyone helped out. Judee brought textbooks and assignments from Josie's classes, but since Josie would be out for several weeks there were plans afoot to hook her up through the Internet to her classrooms. Otherwise she wouldn't be able to keep up with the work and would lose the whole semester. Josie seemed overwhelmed by the Internet proposal, but Judee told her that the university staff had funds for just such situations, would set it up, and would show her how to use the equipment. Thanks to modern technology, home confinement was a whole lot less "confining"—at least in terms of education.

As the first days turned into two and then three weeks, Valerie was relieved to see how well her friends cooperated and followed through with Josie's care and companionship. She had been a bit worried that she would end up doing most of the work herself and would have to bear the financial burden as well. Even though she owned the house, she didn't really have extra cash to pay for increased utilities or any other added expenses. But Judee and Lanie cornered her the first day and offered some money. They also brought in food when they came. Fresh sandwiches and homemade soup, enough for both Josie and Valerie. This unexpected contribution helped a lot during Josie's recovery.

Val was particularly impressed with how much time Gina continually gave to Josie's care, despite her own heavy workload. She carried her fair share of everything they did for Josie. Valerie began to look forward to the moment when Gina arrived each day because she could trust her to take over and do a good job. Even though she was the newest member of this little group of friends, she was proving very responsible and Val's respect for her grew.

An unexpected side benefit, Valerie considered, was the way in which they were getting to know each other better. When you emptied bed pans and administered sponge baths you got to know a person a lot better than sitting around a poker table. They also saw each other in new ways. Lanie wasn't really a cook, but she knew where the best and healthiest sandwiches could be found and she brought plenty. Judee, who *was* a good cook, prepared big pots of homemade soup and large pans of lasagna that could last several days. When Judee came in the evening, sometimes she had to bring her kids along. Sometimes they spent the evenings at homes of their friends, but when they were at Valerie's house, the two boys did their homework at the dining room table or watched television in the living room. Valerie's appreciation for Judee's parenting skills rose as she saw how they could have fun, like their mother, but also be quiet and respectful in someone else's home. One evening, when there was a scheduling conflict, Lanie took Mark and Steven to an action movie at the multiplex so that Judee was free to come and help Josie with her homework.

Valerie was surprised but pleased when Judee mentioned to her one evening before leaving the house that Josie had less than good study habits. "She's not stupid, you know," Judee explained. "Actually, she's quite bright. But her schooling has been so sporadic that she's never learned real discipline. I've got some questions about her family and the environment where she grew up. But, that aside, I've been helping her study for tests and do papers. I've also been showing her how to organize her studying to achieve the best results. I think she'll be a better student from now on." Val had thanked Judee for her insight and her help. When Judee was gone, Valerie shook her head in wonder. She seemed like such a joker but the inner Judee was very sharp. Had to be, Val mused, to keep up with her two boys. Counseling probably would be a very good career for her once she graduated.

Gina scooted into the room, and Valerie slipped out the door. "I'll be in the studio if you need me," she called as she passed. "Oh, and if you need any laundry done, I can run a load through for you."

"Thanks, but I'm good," Gina called back, winking at Josie as she then spoke quietly to her. "Things are getting really good around here, thanks to you."

They both laughed and Josie whispered, "You mean we're getting your strict landlady to relax a little?" Their laughter turned into giggles, which they tried unsuccessfully to smother.

Gina watched Josie and could see instantly that she was feeling much better. Her eyes were brighter and her smile, always there, was less tense, less pained. The bruising on her face had almost totally disappeared.

"So how's the recovering landscape gardener?" Gina asked.

"Really good. Dr. Arnold called this morning, and he's ordered an ambulance to take me in for an X-ray tomorrow. After they look at the pictures and if everything is okay, they are planning to put a walking brace on me. I'll be able to get out of bed more easily and start moving around. Then I can start physical therapy very soon. I feel like I'm really beginning to mend," Josie said in an unusual flurry of words.

"Hey, that's great!" Gina exclaimed. Then she took a look at the book Josie had been reading. "One of those sexy lesbian romance novels, I see. I thought you were studying your biology."

Josie grinned. "I get biology this evening when Judee comes. Right now I'm having my relaxation period."

"Oh, I see!" Gina grinned at her.

Josie motioned Gina to lean over near her. "Speaking of romance, I think Valerie likes you," she whispered.

Gina blushed. "Really? What makes you think so?"

Josie shrugged. "The way she looks at you. It's subtle, but something changes when you walk into the room. Her eyes soften." Then she whispered, "And she just offered to do your laundry for you." She grinned. "I've watched Valerie long enough to know that is a *big* one for her."

"Well, could be you're right, but maybe you are reading too many lesbian novels."

"Yeah, sure. But what do you think of her?"

Gina shrugged. "I like her a lot. She's a decent landlady. She's admittedly an attractive woman but, geez, she's nearly 20 years older than I am. That's about the age of my mother or that shrink I used to see," she confessed.

"So no attraction, huh?"

Gina reddened even more. "Mmmm, I don't know about that, but she can be a bit intimidating." She felt uncomfortable talking about Valerie this way.

There was a moment of silence as Josie studied her. "So you really had some heavy counseling, huh?"

Gina nodded. "Yeah." She considered Josie, then decided to share some more. "I was very homophobic—I'm sure you know what I mean. I had never considered myself to be anything but straight. After all, what else is there?" They both smothered a laugh.

Settling herself into the blue velour-covered chair near Josie's bed, Gina continued. "I hadn't dated a lot, since I was busy with school, and I just thought that sort of stuff would come later. Then, after I'd finished graduate school, this woman came onto me. Totally unexpected. It really freaked me out. After all the pressures of classes and writing my dissertation, I guess I was kind of fragile. This incident put me over the edge."

"So you had to go in the hospital?"

Gina nodded. "Yeah, for a little while. They piece you together and get you out on the street as fast as they can. Insurance, as you well know. But then I had to have outpatient therapy and that got really intense."

"Did it help you?"

Gina sighed and thought for a moment. "Well, ultimately I came to some peace about being gay, so I guess it helped. But it worked backward because this shrink thought she could make me straight, or at least she said she could. And in the beginning I wanted desperately to be straight so I bought into it."

"What did she do?"

"She was a psychoanalyst, like, you know, Sigmund Freud. The couch and a lot of listening. They get you to talk about all sorts of things and, while you're spilling your guts out, you are unconsciously becoming emotionally attached to the therapist."

"That sounds scary," Josie admitted.

"It is. I mean they have all these technical terms for it, like 'transference,' and for them it's all a head trip. But when you are the patient you *feel* all this stuff, and it's painful, and you sometimes wish you were dead instead of experiencing all this intense emotion. You feel like you're losing it. Then they tell you that all these deep feelings aren't real. That part is *really* agonizing." Gina shuddered. It still upset her so much that she had never spoken with anyone in depth about this part of her past before. As she talked, she looked away or down at the floor most of the time.

When she did risk a glance at Josie, she saw that her friend was studying her with compassion. Gina swallowed and then went on with her story, forcing herself to look directly at Josie. "This woman, Dr. Reitman, was 17 or 18 years older than I am. I felt like I was in love with her, obsessed with her. I was panicked about my feelings. I wanted her sexually and that scared me too, since I was so terrified of being gay. Then, finally, after feeling all this stuff and not being able to act on it with her, I got really frustrated and angry. Gradually I turned toward other women. Women who were more like me and less overpowering. I guess that's the way therapy works, but it's awful to go through it."

"So that's why Valerie makes you uncomfortable, her age, I mean?"

"Kind of. It sounds stupid, and maybe it is, but that's where I'm at right now. I want to be with an equal, someone more my own age. And there are good reasons for that, besides my kooky ones."

"Yeah, I suppose, like having more things in common," Josie admitted. "But Valerie is a real cool lady, don't you think?"

Gina nodded. "Yes, she's quite special. And pretty. 'Zaftig,' I think the German word is, soft and round and voluptuous—things I'll never be. Beanpole, that's what I am." She winked at Josie. "And I admire her painting. I think she's very talented." She suddenly laughed with embarrassment. "But let's talk about something else. What are YOU looking for in a partner? Or do you want a partner?"

Josie grinned. "Well, it would be a little awkward right now, having a partner." She looked down at her leg. "But when I'm on my feet and school is over, I'd like someone to do things with. I guess I want a physical person, someone who loves the outdoors—hiking, kayaking, climbing. And of course, flowers. Got to be a flower lover."

Gina chuckled. "Well, if you're not into Sylvia Plath or Virginia Woolf, I guess we'll never be lovers."

Josie laughed. "Probably not. But you are becoming a friend, and I really do like you. Right now good friends are what I need most. As a friend, you have some great qualities."

"Thanks," Gina said, acknowledging the compliment, as her cheeks again turned pink. "And I think," she added, "for me, right now, good friends are where it's at. That's why I feel so lucky that I saw Val's name on the bulletin board at Humboldt State and that I came to this house, because doing that has led me to some good, very stable friends."

They chatted for a while about less personal stuff. When Gina got ready to leave the room, she turned to Josie and whispered to her, "What I told you about the therapist—that's between us, right?"

"Sure," Josie replied, sounding very sincere. "I'm your friend. You can trust me."

Gina stood at the kitchen counter at Ritchie's, waiting for her next order. It was a slow evening and she was restless. Her mind wouldn't stay focused. She hadn't been this restless for a long time. It must have been the conversation with Josie. She worried that she had said too much. Spilling the beans about therapy, about those horrible months and, yes, years she had been under Dr. Reitman's spell, was something she had planned never to do. She had so much personal shame about that time.

Yet, as she shouldered a tray of food to take to her customers, she admitted to herself that talking about it gave her a new chance to review the reality of the past and to consider whether she had put up unnecessary walls against other people because of it. Was age really an issue? Laura Reitman had been a very controlling person, and being a therapist permitted her to encourage her dependent clients to relinquish their control over their own lives. Although the psychoanalyst intended consciously to help her patients, she also could run their lives and she seemed to enjoy doing it. Yes, Gina thought, a transference, while painful for a patient, could be a power trip for the therapist. All that adoration—who wouldn't, deep down inside, enjoy being the center of someone else's universe?

With a warm smile Gina set the plates before a family of four and moved away from the table to resume her inner thoughts. She had also talked about relationships with Josie—and Valerie. That surprised her. Gina didn't spend time thinking about relationships, partly because she was too busy. But was she avoiding something? And what would she personally look for, in a relationship? She knew that she needed someone who would appreciate her mind, her desire to write, and her sensitivities. Those qualities were certainly more important than how old a partner was. Yes, age had its issues. People of all ages often saw things differently, although not always. But age wasn't the only thing. Maybe she should keep an open mind, allow herself to be open, when the time came. A good woman, whatever her age, could be a good fit in other, more important ways.

Gina finally let all these thoughts slide and got back into the swing of the job. A young couple and a family, including three small children, had just come into the restaurant and she had two new tables to serve.

The next Saturday evening at the theater, Rick sidled up to Gina while they were cleaning an auditorium. "Where have you been? We haven't seen you at the Purple Priscilla in weeks."

"Missed me, huh?"

"Yeah, I had all these beautiful dames lined up for you to check out, and you've been a no show. You're giving me a bad rep."

"Sorry," Gina apologized. "I've been extra busy helping Valerie take care of our friend Josie. I just haven't had the time or energy to get to the club. But things are getting better and I'm thinking of coming tonight. How's that?"

"Great. I'll see you later then." He was off, whistling as he pushed his cleaning cart out of the auditorium.

Gina smiled to herself. Rick could be so over the top, but he was a good person at heart. And she needed some stress relief. It would be good to go to the Purple Priscilla again.

After the multiplex closed for the night, she changed into her street clothes, threw her uniform in the back of her car, and followed Rick over to Arcata. When they arrived at the bar, Eric and Paul were already there. They had with them a couple of young women. Types

Gina would have called "bull dykes," but when she talked with them they both seemed pleasant despite the tough exterior.

One of the two, P.J.—tall, dark, and dressed in leather—asked Gina to dance. Gina went out on the floor and quickly found that she had to assume the feminine role and allow P.J. to lead. Bull dykes, Gina decided, must be the "male" in any pairing. She felt a bit uncomfortable and stumbled over herself at first, but P.J. wasn't all that bad a dance partner. The evening went well and was fun. Gina could not, however, help remembering the last time she was here, when she danced with Valerie. She couldn't forget the electricity that had surged through her body when they touched.

Soon Josie had her walking brace and life at Valerie's house began to normalize. Josie was able to get around more on her own and take care of her personal needs. She leaned on the support team less. Val could sense Lanie and Judee's relief as their time helping was shortened and they could return to their own lives. Valerie knew she would miss Josie when she left, but Val was also well aware that she would be glad to get back to the quieter existence she had had before Josie's accident. And back to her painting on a regular basis.

All things considered, Josie's accident and recovery had turned out pretty well. She was going to be able to finish her semester at college, and her initial debt for medical care, while sizable, was being negotiated into a long-term payment plan. While more bills certainly would follow and she would be saddled with a large debt, she still would be able to go on with her life. Even her gardening customers, who had called during the weeks she was totally disabled, were staying loyal to her and promising work for her when she could return. "I'll have a lot of weeds to tackle," Josie groaned. It was now well into late spring and everything, especially weeds, had been growing in her absence.

When Josie, on crutches and aided by the flexible brace, was ready to go home they held a party at the house and everyone came. Judee brought wine, Lanie chips and dip. They shared stories about how each had coped, stories that Josie couldn't have enjoyed until she was feeling a lot better. They laughed, joked, and hugged. Valerie wanted to show Josie that life had not totally stopped during the past few weeks, so she invited them into the studio to show them a new painting she had managed to finish during Josie's home care. They all "ooh'd" and "aah'd" over it.

The next morning Valerie loaded her Volvo wagon with Josie's things and drove her back to her apartment.

"I don't know how to thank you for all you've done for me," Josie said, when they arrived at her little stucco apartment building.

Val smiled. "I won't say it was nothing, because we both know it was hard work for everyone, but you are very welcome. You were the world's best patient. I'm just glad to see you on your feet and on the mend."

Josie's roommate, slender and bespectacled Sarah Green, greeted them and helped Val bring in a couple of boxes of books and other personal items as well as two small suitcases full of clothes. Although Sarah hadn't been free to spend too much time at Valerie's house during the past few weeks, she did seem to care about Josie and Val thought Josie would be in good hands. Sarah had volunteered to drive Josie around town, until she was able to safely navigate her truck again. When Sarah couldn't help out, the team would pick up the slack. "Thank goodness I didn't break my right leg," Josie had quipped when they made their plans, "and that I had the good sense to buy a truck with an automatic transmission."

Josie stood at the front door of her apartment, leaning on crutches. She waved as Valerie pulled away from the curb, and Val felt a wave of relief that the worst of their trial was over. While Josie would require assistance for some time to come, probably several months, the recovery period at her house had ended. Val was glad of that. At the same time she was happy to have been able to help. Josie's injury had provided a good opportunity for all of them to share and give to a friend. She thought the experience had brought all of them closer together, which was a good thing. She had been afraid they they would all get tired of pushing aside their own needs and doing for Josie. Especially Gina, whose work schedule was demanding and often kept her isolated. Yet she had contributed considerably. Val was learning yet again that Gina was not the lightweight that she had first thought when Gina landed on her doorstep.

Gina also heaved a sigh of relief when she waved goodbye to Josie at Val's house. Her own life would be a bit simpler now. At the same time, she had to admit that she had grown from this experience and had actually enjoyed being a part of it. Four women with a common goal, no bitching or complaining, just pitching in and doing what was needed. It was the best experience she had ever had with lesbians, and she was beginning to find that beneath the bravado and occasional quirky habits and dress styles, these women were just people. Good people. Trustworthy people. Being phobic about women, lesbian women, was beginning to seem unreal to her, and these ideas and fears were gradually slipping away. This therapy out in the real world, and she knew all this *was* therapeutic, was more rewarding and felt a whole lot better than those hours spent with Dr. Reitman.

The inevitable bill in her mailbox the following Saturday also gave Gina new hope. Her therapy balance was now just under $1,000, an amount she had begun to think she would never see. Provided she didn't have any other emergencies or car trouble, in a few months the bill would be paid off completely. Then she could plan her move to San Francisco. It was funny, she thought as she wrote out a check to the psychoanalyst and posted it in the mail slot, as much as she was excited about going to the City she also knew that she would miss Eureka—and all the people she had formed friendships with there.

Chapter Nine

Valerie sold a painting, her first significant sale since moving to the North Coast. The path to this major success began when Paulina Johansen, an attractive 40-something redhead, had posed for photos in the photography studio with her dog—a miniature schnauzer named Max—as a gift for her husband, Jim. When the proofs were ready, Paulina had come to the studio to decide which one to have printed and framed for her husband's birthday.

"I thought I'd sneak in this morning," she said pleasantly, pushing her sunglasses back on her head. "Jim is out on the boat and he won't know I've done this."

"You have a boat?" Valerie's curiosity was aroused.

"Yes, a 50-foot sailboat. We're just getting into the season where we can enjoy it. We've had the sloop in dry dock for the winter down in the Bay Area. Jim just sailed it up the coast and is now out testing the rigging, doing some fine tuning to get ready for the summer."

"I love sailboats," admitted Valerie. "I used to be fascinated just watching them glide by on San Francisco Bay."

"Do you sail?" Paulina asked.

"Well, I'm not an expert. I have been out a couple of times, enough to know that I don't get too seasick and that sailing is a lot quieter and more fun for me than power boating."

"Yes, I agree with you. I'd never make a power boater, or a 'stink potter,' as they kiddingly say," Paulina mused. "I'll always be a 'rag bagger,' as the power boaters tauntingly call us sailors."

They both laughed.

Valerie acknowledged that sailboats made good subjects for painting and that she had done watercolors and oils featuring sailing craft.

"I didn't know you painted." Paulina was surprised. But she expressed an interest and asked if she could see some of Val's work. They made arrangements to get together, and Paulina came to the house the following week. Valerie showed her around her studio and pulled out several of her paintings for her to see. Paulina was clearly impressed.

"And here I thought you were just a photographer's assistant," she exclaimed. "Hiding your light under the proverbial bushel barrel, are you?" She thought for a moment and then added, "You should ask Lyn to display some of your paintings!"

Val's mouth dropped open in surprise. "I never thought of that. I bet she would allow it. Thanks for the suggestion."

Paulina chose one of the sailboat paintings, offered Valerie a very good price for it, and picked it up the next week. As she was loading the carefully wrapped painting into her silver Lexus SUV, she turned and smiled at Val. "My husband would like to meet you. I've raved so much about your work. Of course, at this time of the year, he's totally involved with the boat. How would you like to come out for an afternoon sail one of these days?"

Valerie was taken aback. "That would be wonderful," she said. She had always believed that people who had enough money to own luxury cars and boats were very selective about their guests, so she felt quite honored to be asked. Whether it would ever come to pass was another matter. California was famous for the "let's do lunch" line, but lunch often never happened.

But Paulina seemed serious. As she climbed into the Lexus, she suggested, "The next time we are going out, I'll give you a call. I'll try to give you some warning, though. And please bring a friend."

Despite Paulina's seeming sincerity, Valerie allowed the offer to slip to the back of her mind, as one of those things that would probably never happen. When the phone rang the next Friday afternoon, she was quite surprised to hear Paulina's voice on the other end of the line.

"Jim is planning to go out on the boat tomorrow afternoon," Paulina announced. "The weather forecast is for a truly rare sunny day. It looks like it will be perfect for sailing. Are you free to come with us?"

Valerie thought quickly. She had no fixed plans for the weekend, just household chores that could wait. Her gang had not planned a poker party this week for various reasons.

"Yes, I think so," she decided. "I would love to come along."

Paulina gave her instructions to the marina and then told her what to wear for warmth against the ocean wind. "Don't worry about bringing anything else. There will be plenty of food and beverages on board.

"And, remember, feel free to bring a friend," she reminded.

Valerie hung up the phone and considered the invitation. *Bring a friend.* Paulina probably meant a male friend, and she might be in for a surprise when Val showed up with a woman. Oh well, so be it. Her first choice would be Lanie, who was always a lot of fun. They hadn't done much together, just the two of them, since Josie's accident.

"What's up?" Lanie sounded cheerful when she heard Valerie's voice on the phone.

"I've just had a wonderful invitation to go sailing tomorrow."

"Wow! How did you manage that?"

"Paulina Johansen, this woman I sold a painting to. She and her husband own a sailboat—a pretty big one, I think. She just called and asked me to go out on it tomorrow and said I could bring a friend."

"Is that why you called, to invite me?"

"Yes, of course!"

"Oh, that's wonderful!" Lanie sounded really excited, but then her voice fell. "But wait, I've got a house to show tomorrow afternoon to this couple from San Diego. They seem really interested and will only be in town for the day. It could mean a big sale for me, and I can't put them off. I'm really disappointed, but I can't go with you," Lanie said, sounding really down about it.

"I'm sorry, I would have loved for you to come."

"Can you ask someone else?"

"I'm sure I'll find someone, but I wish it could have been you."

"Maybe next time. Don't fall overboard, but have a good time and tell me all about it later!" Lanie could never stay down for long. "Bye," she said, already bouncing back with her natural enthusiasm.

Valerie sighed and hung up. She called Judee, but she had the boys for the weekend and couldn't get away. They had a softball game and she had promised to watch them play. Josie wasn't steady enough on her feet yet to risk bouncing around on a sailboat. Besides she was just starting back to her gardening work. Saturday would be a very busy day for her, and she needed every penny she could earn.

Just then Gina came in the front door and called out a hello. Sam ran to greet her, tail in rapid motion.

"It's a beautiful afternoon," Gina said, with a big grin. "And the weekend is supposed to be gorgeous."

Valerie thought a minute. "Do you work tomorrow?"

"Yes, tomorrow evening. Why, do you need something?"

"Well, I've been invited to go sailing tomorrow. They told me I could bring a friend, and I wondered if you would like to go. But it's possible we might not get back in time for you to make your shift at work."

Gina bit at her upper lip, looking thoughtful. "I've never been sailing and I might get seasick, but I'd sure like to try it. It sounds wonderful." Making a decision, she nodded to Valerie. "Let me make some calls and see if I can cover my hours at the theater."

She ran up the stairs with Sam at her heels, quickly entered her room, and called the theater manager on her cell. She asked for names of people she could call to cover for her or with whom she could trade shifts. She made some notes, thanked her boss, and started dialing.

A few minutes later Gina came bouncing back downstairs, looking for Valerie who was still sitting at the dining room table, deep in thought.

"I'm covered. So I can go," Gina said, barely masking her excitement.

"Is this a big sacrifice for you?" Valerie asked, knowing how much Gina depended on her work income.

"I traded. I'll work an extra shift next weekend to make it up. It's okay and I really *want* to go. It sounds like a once in a lifetime opportunity."

Valerie smiled. "Good! I'm glad you can come along."

"What do I need to do, or wear, or what?"

"Paulina said to wear sports shoes with white or light soles. Something about not marking up the deck." She shrugged. "And to be comfortable, but wear warm layers and to bring some sunscreen and a hat. She said it will be chilly on the ocean, but the sun could feel warm and by the afternoon we might be stripping down to shirtsleeves."

"What time do we go?"

"Paulina said to be at the marina at 11 a.m. She gave me instructions on how to find the right dock and where to leave the car," Valerie explained.

"Wow, this is really exciting!" Gina exclaimed.

"I know," Val said with a big grin. "I'm taking a camera and my sketch pad," she added.

"Oh, yeah, that reminds me. I've got plenty of sunscreen, if you need any," Gina offered. "Couldn't live without that in Tucson!"

"Thanks." Valerie nodded.

Clapping her hands in excitement, Gina disappeared up the stairs to change for her evening job at Ritchie's Grill.

"What do you want for breakfast tomorrow?" she hollered down the stairs. "I'm cooking."

The two women were on their way out the front door on Saturday morning, their stomachs filled with pancakes, toast, sausages, fresh fruit, and hot tea, when Valerie suddenly exclaimed, "Sam! I didn't think about how long we're going to be gone. Poor Sam. I need to do something about her."

Gina stared at her. Befuddled, she tried to help. "What if—?"

Miraculously, Josie appeared around the corner of the house. "I heard that. And go on. I've got a key to the house, and Sam will be fine. I'll see that she gets out."

Valerie was so happy to see Josie back on her feet, in her overalls with a pair of clippers in one hand. With her cropped hair, a smudge of dirt on her face, and her soon-ready-for-the-washbin clothes, she was obviously happy and back in her element. Her left leg was still in a brace, but she had learned to work around it and was gradually resuming a more normal life. She no longer needed crutches and could drive herself wherever she had to go.

Val was greatly relieved. "Oh, thanks, Josie, that's perfect."

Valerie gave Josie a quick squeeze, and Gina offered her a big smile.

"We'll take lots of pictures and tell you all about it," Val called back as the two women sprinted to the Volvo, dumped their gear and jackets in the back of the wagon, and took off.

They located the Woodley Island Marina, parked the wagon, and worked their way along the docks, gawking at the many sailboats and fishing craft until they saw the right finger, Dock D, with the big sailing vessel *Sweet Dreams* tied at the end of it. They both nearly gasped at the size and splendor of the boat. A gleaming white hull with a tall mast and wood trim everywhere on deck. Mahogany, really beautiful.

Paulina stood in the cockpit. She greeted them both and watched closely as they stepped carefully from the dock onto the slightly rocking boat. Her husband, gray headed and balding with just the hint of a paunch, came forward, and Paulina said, "This is my husband, Jim."

"Jim, this is the artist, Valerie Stephans. I've told you all about her. And this is?"

Before Gina could answer, Val spoke up. "This is my friend, Dr. Gina Fortenham."

Gina almost gasped and gave Valerie a perplexed look, but she kept her mouth shut. There were nods and handshakes all around. Jim took charge and told them where they could put their jackets and other gear and where they should sit in the cockpit. He showed them how to fasten their orange life vests, which he explained were called "PFDs." The boat's engine was already running and Jim said they would be leaving shortly.

"Oh, Jim," called Paulina, "take them down into the cabin and show them where the head is and the galley—before things start really rocking and rolling." She chuckled to herself.

As she climbed down the ladder into the cabin, Valerie surveyed the beauty of the sailboat with amazement. The rich mahogany surfaces everywhere she looked—bookshelves, the sleeping quarters, the deluxe galley, and the captain's table for dining. "Wow," Gina whispered to her, and Val nodded in agreement.

Jim offered them some seasickness medication, since neither had taken any, and they both accepted. "You may not need it, but it's better to be prepared," he said kindly. His weathered blue eyes twinkled. "A small amount of Bonine shouldn't make you drowsy but it will really keep your stomachs settled."

Food on board included fruit, bottled water on ice, cold cuts and bread for sandwiches, salads, cookies, and other snacks. Valerie could see that they wouldn't go hungry.

Shortly Paulina released the mooring lines as Jim backed away from the dock and pointed the bow of *Sweet Dreams* out into Humboldt Bay. Once in the bay, he raised the sails, which he explained were on "roller-furling" and opened almost automatically at the touch of a button. Jim tied down lines while Paulina stood at the big spoked wheel, which she called "the helm."

"I love sailing," Paulina commented with a smile, "as long as it isn't too much work. The helm I can manage."

Soon they had passed the breakwater opening and were out on the Pacific Ocean. The big boat began to gently heel over, but Jim, now back on the helm, cut the engine and kept *Sweet Dreams* steady. Gina and Valerie both held tight to the railing and stared with open mouths up into the large white sails now filling with wind.

"We're lucky today," Paulina explained, "the wind is light but steady and the seas are predicted to have very slight swells. Since you haven't sailed before, Gina, this is about as good an introduction as you could get."

Even the light wind on the ocean was nippy, and Gina and Valerie both pulled their jackets close to keep warm. Gina had thought to bring a watch cap, and she pulled it down around her ears. Valerie had forgotten to bring a hat, but she did have a headband on, and she pulled it over her ears. That helped.

After watching Jim move easily around the boat, Gina became curious about what it would look like up front, at "the bow," as Jim had called it. Holding onto the handrails carefully, she worked her way from the cockpit forward until she reached an open area just behind the bow. Once she was there, Paulina called to her to stay low in case the jib sail shifted suddenly. Wearing a PFD wouldn't prevent her from being knocked overboard into the ocean, Paulina warned.

With the engine no longer running, all that could be heard was the wind and the sound of water as the bow of the boat cut into the waves and swirling water washed up against the hull. From the expression on her face Gina obviously loved the soft slapping sounds of the water and the feel of the boat's rocking motion.

Valerie, still in the cockpit, soon began to wonder what Gina was seeing. She also made her way to the bow. Gina motioned her to be very still, so she could hear the ocean and the wind, and Val nodded. She had not told Gina that she had been sailing before and just kept quiet, enjoying Gina's excitement.

Soon the two of them were lying side by side on the deck, faces up, relaxing in the bright sunshine. Lying flat cut down on the wind and soon they began to feel warm. They slipped out of their jackets and lay on top of them. Within minutes both were drifting off to sleep.

Valerie stood on the foredeck of The Ancient Mariner, *hanging from the lines and grinning upward as the Golden Gate Bridge passed overhead. Doreen was next to her, tall and tanned.*

It was a wondrous San Francisco summer day, and they had come aboard the 30-foot sailboat with their friends, Rob Randall and Steve Wieman—two young couples having the time of their lives.

Steve was at the helm, slender, bearded, wearing dark glasses. Rob, muscular and stocky, handled the lines. "Look at that bridge!" Rob called to them from the cockpit. Valerie and Doreen both turned and nodded and smiled at the same time. The Golden Gate was breathtaking, whether in sun or fog or rain, and sailing under her magnificent red superstructure was even more amazing.

In late morning, they had left the dock from a marina not too far from Fisherman's Wharf, first following a gradually increasing wind across the big bay and back again. They had passed Alcatraz Island and then, since the wind was just right, had headed for the Golden Gate and the ocean beyond.

While San Francisco had many treasures to offer, sailing on a summer day ranked at the top of Valerie's list, both in her dreams and now in the reality of it. She wanted to pinch herself to believe this was actually happening. Doreen's broad grin showed that she, too, was having the time of her life.

Initially clad in jeans and sweats over bathing suits, Valerie and Doreen had stripped to their swimwear by early afternoon and quickly slathered each other with sunscreen.

As the Golden Gate Bridge, its red girders bright in the sunlight, slipped behind them, they gradually turned their attention to the ocean. There were several sailboats on the water, slipping along in this direction and that. And even though it was Sunday afternoon, there were several giant freighters in the shipping lanes, heading into San Francisco Bay.

Steve watched the wheel carefully and periodically checked the radar and compass. Valerie and Doreen had come back to the cockpit from the bow and Steve explained to them some readings he was getting on the radar screen.

"You've got all the latest gear on this boat," Valerie observed.

Steve nodded. "Yeah, it cost a bundle, but it's worth it. You have to stay out of the shipping lanes, unless you want to be run over by a freighter! And sudden fog can catch us out here. Without knowing what is around us, we could really be in trouble."

Rob came up from the galley with trays of food that he passed around. Steve managed to hold the helm with one hand and tackle a sandwich with the other. They all drank bottled water for lunch, but there was wine below deck for later.

Once they had finished their food Rob went below and turned on some music. There were speakers in the cockpit, and the mellow sounds from the CD in the galley washed over them soothingly. Valerie and Doreen relaxed on deck cushions. Doreen's head nestled in Val's lap. Val ran her fingers through Doreen's auburn hair.

"Feels so good," Doreen murmured, closing her brown eyes. Valerie leaned down and placed a light kiss on her lips. "That's even better," Doreen whispered.

Rob moved over to Steve at the helm, slipped his arm around his waist, and offered him a kiss. Steven returned it and the two smiled.

"Okay, you gals," Steve said with amusement. "You look like you need some private time. We've got the perfect place for that, a bed down below in the bow. All nice clean sheets, and you can close the door."

Valerie smiled mischievously at Steve. "And what are you going to do while we're down there?"

"That's easy," Steve replied with a devilish grin. "We're safely out of the shipping lanes, so we're going to drop the sails, throw out a couple of anchors for drag to keep us from drifting, and enjoy each other's company up here in the cockpit."

"Will we all be safe?" Doreen asked.

"That's why we're staying up here. If any danger comes our way, we have plenty of time to react," Steve assured them both.

Taken off guard but curious about this arrangement, Valerie and Doreen stepped through the entryway and down the ladder into the cabin. The boat was swaying and they hung onto the railings, but by the time they got up to the bow and its tiny private space they realized that they were safe as soon as they lay down on the sheets.

In seconds, their excitement over the day's sailing turned into excitement over each other. First a kiss, then a stroke, then a nibble. Soon the swimsuits were abandoned and they hugged, kissed, and explored each other's bodies. Perhaps a decade into their relationship, they discovered that the new surroundings made their sexual encounter fresh and wild. They rolled, and rocked with the boat, and took each other to ecstacy. Then they lay spooned together, sated and deliriously happy.

Paulina stood over the two sleeping women. Both were on their stomachs, and Valerie's right arm was resting on Gina's back. "Wake up, girls," Paulina said, "you don't want to get sunburned out here. And we're having sandwiches. You might enjoy having some food with us."

Totally surprised at where they were and that they had both dozed off, Valerie and Gina abruptly sat up. Val, obviously uncomfortable, quickly pulled her arm away from Gina, and Gina looked at her quizzically. The two struggled to their feet and awkwardly followed Paulina back to the cockpit. Jim gave them a big smile when they were safely seated.

"I can't believe I fell asleep," Valerie said. She also couldn't believe that she had put her arm over Gina and had slept that way. She felt embarrassed at the unplanned intimacy. She vaguely remembered something she had dreamed, something about Doreen and sailing, and now she wondered in confusion if she had reached out to Gina because she was unconsciously back with Doreen.

"Me, too," Gina added, her questioning gaze again going to Val, who looked away. "Could it be the medication we took?"

Jim laughed. "Just ocean air, most likely." He was at the helm, steering by moving the big wheel a spoke to the left or the right. "The most tense people in the world can relax on a sailboat. It's wonderful therapy for whatever ails you."

Sensing some tension between her guests, Paulina passed around a tray filled with sandwiches and fruit. "Eat up," she encouraged them. "I brought Jim's favorite sailing food, and there is plenty for all of us." They each took a ham and cheese sandwich and Valerie quickly realized that out in the open air she was ravenously hungry. Gina seemed to be digging quickly into her sandwich, as well. Paulina encouraged them to drink a lot of water, because the sun would be pulling moisture from their bodies without them being aware of it.

After their meal, Paulina took the helm so Jim could eat more comfortably. Jim focused on Valerie.

"I like your painting, young woman," he said. "Paulina came home and raved about your work. I wasn't sure until I opened the package on my birthday. Then I was impressed. I've seen a lot of landscapes in my time, lots of sailboats and lighthouses, all painted diligently but most lacking some special touch to make them unique. You have done that, taken something very real and moved it beyond realism. I like that very much. We've placed your painting in a prominent position within our collection."

Valerie, already a bit pink from the sun and wind, blushed at the compliment. "Thank you very much. It's always nice to receive praise from someone who can recognize the difference in artists' work and styles. Some people buy just to own, without understanding."

"Paulina says," Jim continued between bites of food, "that you are from San Francisco. We've sailed down there any number of times. Beautiful area. What caused you to move away from there to live up here?"

"Well," Valerie confessed, "I was born there and lived in the City all my life and it is beautiful. At times I really miss it." She paused a moment and then decided to just say it all. "But my life partner died of cancer and I needed to make a change. It was just too hard, being surrounded everywhere by memories." Well, she thought to herself, she had never lied to anyone about her life or lifestyle and she didn't want to start now. For a moment, she wondered how this information would be accepted by her hosts.

Jim didn't miss a beat. "Say, Eureka is a good place for starting over. It's not overcrowded, yet there is culture and a sense of history. The Victorian architecture throughout the town is beautiful. I'm sure you'll do well here," he said supportively.

He turned to Gina. "And you are a doctor. Medical?"

"No," Gina said. "Doctor of philosophy. English literature."

"Oh, interesting. Do you teach?"

"Not right now," Gina said, looking at Valerie.

"And what brings *you*—from somewhere in the Midwest, I take it from your accent—to Eureka?"

"Long story," Gina said, with a hesitant smile. "Let's just say I'm starting over, too."

Paulina turned from the helm. "Are you two a couple?" she asked.

Valerie and Gina both reddened visibly.

"No," Valerie said.

"I—," Gina started.

"Gina and I share a house and a dog, Samantha, but we are not partners." Valerie cut in and finished before Gina could admit to being her roomer.

Paulina studied them for a split second and then shrugged, evidently deciding not to pursue the topic. "Jim and I are New Englanders," she explained. "We're retired, and we wanted to experience the West Coast. Chilly winters and heavy rainfall are not unknown in the Northeast, but the climate here is still a little less extreme. We get our cake and eat it, too, as they say."

Valerie considered them too young to be retired, although Jim might be in his late 50s she now decided. "You must have been very successful, to be retired so young."

Jim grinned. "Pharmaceuticals," he acknowledged. "I sold them for several years. Very good money. I invested in the market and luckily got out before the big downturn in 2000. I didn't have any insider information, but I was close enough to the trends to sense what was coming. Some of my friends didn't move quickly enough and lost their shirts.

"Yes," he continued, "I was very lucky. I bought *Sweet Dreams* and I sleep well at night."

Valerie pursued another thought that had occurred to her. "We have very little real summer here on the North Coast. Quite chilly and still often rainy days. How do you get enough sailing time to make it worth bringing such a beautiful boat up here?"

"Good question," Jim responded with a warm smile. "We get out when we can, when it's decent enough. But in late August and early September there is a little spot where the weather along the Northwest Coast is usually nicer than the rest of the year. When we get to that time, we pack our gear and head north along the Oregon and Washington coast. A real holiday and a real cruise."

"Sometimes," Paulina added, "we are able to get as far as the Puget Sound, the San Juan Islands, and even do some exploring along Vancouver Island in British Columbia. There are so many places to go that it would take a lifetime to see them all."

Valerie noticed that Gina seemed a little uncomfortable with the conversation. High finance, big sailboats, and lengthy cruises certainly didn't match her current life as roomer and worker at three entry-level jobs. Val felt for her. But if Gina's personal problems hadn't gotten in the way and she had taken a good teaching job, she might be talking about the stock market and making money too. Gina was young so maybe financial success would still come to her one day. Val, herself, was on more familiar turf, having had professional parents and having lived in a major urban area all her life. She had known many people like the Johansens and was comfortable around them.

"Does your dog Max like sailing?" Valerie asked, steering conversation to a little easier territory.

Jim laughed. "We've brought Max out a couple of times, but he doesn't really like it. He shivers and shakes the whole time and it's wrong to put him through that. We leave him at home with the housekeeper," he said.

Gina turned to Valerie. "What do you think Sam would do?"

Valerie grinned. "She'd love it but she'd be over the side in a moment, because she's fearless and so used to jumping around and bounding up and down stairs. She's chased birds into the water at the beach. I don't think that she would realize that to jump here she'd be in the deep ocean."

They sailed in a northwesterly direction most of the afternoon, since the wind was from the south-southwest and filled their big white sails when they were on a starboard tack. "Starboard is the right side of the boat," Jim explained to Gina. "Port is the left." Later in the day he steered a bit closer to land. "The coast here is really pretty in the late afternoon, so we'll come along it on our way home. The wind is supposed to shift to the west and that will help us a lot," he said.

Gina seemed fascinated with the mechanics of sailing. Jim showed her the wind vane at the top of the mast, the compass, how he set a heading and then steered by it, and how the lines were tied and loosened when they shifted direction. Jim put her on the helm, and soon Gina was calling "Ready to come about." Paulina looked amused, watching her take over. Val wondered if she was seeing a budding sailor in Gina.

"You call this boat a sloop?" Gina asked Jim.

"Yes," Jim replied with a smile. He was obviously enjoying her interest in his craft. "A sloop has one mast and usually it has two sails—one rigged from the mast and going back toward the stern and one coming from the mast but also attached to the bow, up front, called the jib. This sloop is a cutter-rigged sloop, because it has two sails before, or in front of, the mast."

"Wow," Gina said.

Valerie smiled at her technical interest. The earlier tension over her physical contact with Gina now forgotten, she just enjoyed relaxing. Val soon picked up her sketchpad and, after some adjustments to the motion of the boat, she was able to make sketches of *Sweet Dreams* from a variety of angles. She could see a painting or two coming from this afternoon's sail. She also got out her camera and photographed Paulina and Jim and then Gina at the helm. Gina was obviously ecstatic. Gina in turn took the camera and photographed Valerie holding the wheel for a moment. And Paulina took a picture of the two of them together at the big wheel, smiling broadly. Gina, too, now seemed comfortable with Val again.

Late in the afternoon they came along the coast, and Jim pointed out landmarks on shore that they would recognize, including Mad River Beach where they had gone that one Saturday with Sam.

Before dark, the sails were taken down and they were motoring through Humboldt Bay on the way to the docks. They had been on a marvelous adventure, both Valerie and Gina told each other. Food for the soul, Valerie would muse to herself.

They hugged Jim and Paulina on the dock, offering thanks to their two hosts. As they piled their belongings into the Volvo, they chattered happily about the experience and the fun they had. Gina climbed into the passenger seat and slid down low. "Wow, what a day!" she exclaimed.

"You can say that again," Val agreed, as she put her key in the ignition. "I don't know when I've had so much fun."

On the drive home, neither of them mentioned Val's arm finding its way over Gina's shoulders as they had slept on the deck of *Sweet Dreams*.

Sam barked at the front door when Valerie's wagon turned into the driveway. "Coming," Valerie called out, hoping to appease the retriever. She and Gina unloaded the car and went up to the front door. Val opened it with her key, only to be practically knocked down by Sam in her enthusiasm to see them again.

Val ruffled her fur. "Sorry, girl, I know it's been a long day. I'll take you for a walk in just a minute."

Gina put her duffle bag by the door. "You want me to take her out?"

Val sighed. "Would you? I'm totally bushed."

"Sure." Gina found Sam's leash, clipped it on, and took the dog out to the sidewalk for an around-the-block before sundown stroll.

Sam looked back toward the house to see if Val was coming and then turned her attention to Gina, following her with a wagging tail.

Val watched them from the dining room window for a moment. She smiled to herself and then collapsed into a chair. The sailing was great, but it had certainly taken a lot out of her energy reserves. Whew!

Later that evening, as she cleaned up the kitchen after a dinner snack of soup and crackers shared with Gina, Valerie put down a bowl of kibble for Sam. Gina had disappeared upstairs, and the dog had gone with her. "Sam," Val called out, "your dinner is ready."

The dog didn't appear, and Valerie murmured to herself. "I think Sam really is Gina's dog now." She shrugged. The food was there, the dog would get to it eventually, and it was natural for her to miss Gina as well as Val when both had been gone all day.

She switched off the lights in the kitchen and sat down in the living room for a few moments. The house was quiet, and Valerie started thinking back over the day's adventure. It had been a very good change after the weeks of confinement with Josie. It was as if the universe had rewarded them for their caring.

She considered Paulina and Jim and their successful lives, and she was grateful that they were basically real and unpretentious people who were willing to share their bounty with others. She would have to do something nice for them to say thank you. Maybe a small painting of their boat.

And Gina. She had loved watching Gina come to life. She had seen many sides of her in the past months, but most of them were serious. Gina could and did laugh at times, and she could be enthusiastic. But there was a core to her that, perhaps because of her troubles and the debt she had to pay off, was basically heavy. Today she had been different, a sea sprite. Jim had obviously enjoyed teaching her about sailing, and she had taken to it avidly. It was cute and Gina had been adorable out there on the sloop, her ponytail flopping in the wind. Valerie liked the way the day had gone for all of them. She did still wonder about that dream. The details had already begun to fade from her memory, but why had she dreamed about that, and why had she, in sleep, reached out physically to Gina? She forcefully pushed the question away. *There is no point in going down that path*, she told herself.

Gina's skin was burning and she put on some lotion before climbing into bed. She didn't care if she had gotten sunburned. She was so happy to have gone sailing, and she couldn't wait to tell Rick and her other friends at the theater about it. She hoped to be able to go out on the ocean again someday.

After sending Sam upstairs to be with Val, Gina turned out her light and settled into the bed. She punched her pillows so they were just right and cuddled up surrounded by her comforter.

Gina smiled to herself when she thought about the fact that Valerie had introduced her as a Ph.D. and hidden the fact that she was a roomer. At first she had been shocked but then, as the atmosphere surrounding these wealthy people began to sink in, she realized that Valerie was kind of protecting her. Giving her a chance to be on an equal footing with them, not like some charity case. She did have her doctorate, but it wasn't a very meaningful part of her life these days. So she found being treated as special rather nice.

What a day! And Valerie had been fun, too, in her quiet sort of way. More mature, more settled. But Gina couldn't help it. Her own enthusiasm just burst out. Sailing was really fun! It had been especially neat when they fell asleep on the foredeck, but what had been going on in Valerie's mind when she put her arm over Gina's shoulder? Gina had been so shocked when Paulina awakened them and she felt the weight—and the intimacy—of Val's touch. She tingled now even thinking of it. But what did it mean? Maybe Valerie was just lonely and missing Doreen and in her sleep just reached out to another woman. But what if she was really expressing something toward Gina? *Should she welcome that, or not?* She had to admit that Val's touch had felt good. Well, whatever the meaning of it, it was a puzzle that she couldn't solve. Gina tried to stop analyzing and drifted off to sleep, just warmed by the memory of that arm over her shoulder.

Chapter Ten

Valerie sat in the shade of a coastal redwood, sketching an enormous tree that rose majestically before her. She really loved the ancient trees that grew in northern California. They were so awe inspiring—how they had lived for thousands of years and during the less rainy summer months the way they had fed their hearty thirst for water by absorbing mist in the daily fog that settled along the coast. Every so often Val took the hour-long drive down the 101 to Humboldt Redwoods State Park and walked, sat and thought or sketched. Other than the ocean, these stands of redwoods were her favorite inspiration for painting.

Walking around the massive base of a redwood, she would stare upward along the trunk that appeared to reach all the way to the sky. She drew these trees both in their realistic form and in softer impressions that emerged within her mind. The trees were awesome, that was for sure, and she tried to capture that amazing spirit in her drawings.

As she sat sketching, she was reminded of what Gina had once said about how being out of doors was better than being in church. Whatever God meant to Valerie, and she was not always too sure about that, she had to admit that redwoods were indeed part of some great spiritual reality. She had been capturing the trees on paper for several hours this summer afternoon, with Sam stretched out by her side. Dogs weren't permitted many places in the spacious state park, but she had found a spot where she could draw while the retriever relaxed nearby.

She thought as she worked. Mulling. Going back over the past few months.

Her life had changed a lot in the year—now more like a year and a half—since Doreen's death. She would always miss her partner, but she had to admit that the present was becoming as rewarding as the past. Paulina and Jim had bought two more of her paintings and had referred friends to her. Those friends had also purchased some of her work. She had, with Lanie's help, set up a web page on the Internet, resulting in several other inquiries. No actual sales yet, but some new possibilities. She had to laugh because she was not into the Internet herself and did not even have her own computer or e-mail address like everyone else she knew. She did understand the power of this modern technology but didn't want to fool with it. Lanie, however, was really "into the Web," as everyone was always saying, and she came up with the plan for Val's web page and took the time to print out the inquiries for her.

"You *are* going to have to get on the Web eventually," Lanie had told her more than once.

Val smiled to herself. She was still resisting the Internet because she knew it would consume a lot of her time. And she was becoming more accustomed to the slower pace of life in Eureka. She *liked* not being as rushed as she had been in San Francisco. And culture *did* exist here—it just didn't overwhelm. A concert here, a movie worth seeing there, an event in a local park. Maybe it was because she was getting older, slowing down herself, that this less intense pace felt good. Doreen aside, she didn't think she would want to live in the city anymore. She didn't feel that she needed the traffic, smog, bustle, crime, or 'Frisco's one hundred theater groups and myriad art houses. Or Castro Street and the extreme gay scene, with political tensions between the radical left and the radical right.

There was plenty of art available on the North Coast. Eureka's Old Town was filled with galleries, art walks, and shows, and she knew in time she would become more involved in that scene. She had started to dream about having her own gallery. Rent wasn't too bad, a little over $300 a month for some spaces, and she had recently joined a couple of local artist organizations. "If I could rent both bedrooms on the second floor of the house, I could have a real studio and gallery right now," she mused aloud to herself. She had visited some galleries on the upper floors of Old Town buildings. She noted that the high ceilings and tall windows allowed considerable natural light. It would be so good for her to work there—so much better than the garage.

Yes, she had discovered that Eureka had many charms for a creative person, but she still had been extremely surprised by the fact that she had developed friendships with lesbian women on the North Coast. Maybe it was the openness of today's society, but gay people seemed easier to find. And her Eureka friends had become *real* friends, not just lesbians looking for sexual exploits or conquests.

She grinned at Sam and reached down to ruffle the dog's fur. "This ol' gal ain't quite done yet," she said whimsically. "I think I might want to have a sexual partner again in this lifetime. I don't know when, and I don't know who—and I wouldn't confess it to anyone but you that I'm thinking about it—but I do believe that eventually it's going to happen." She chuckled as she continued to sketch.

Her mind shifted gears to Gina. She smiled to herself, remembering how unimpressed she had been with that tall, stringy girl on the doorstep that day. A real head case, too, in the beginning. But Gina had opened up and Valerie had to admit that she had stopped thinking of her solely as a renter and as a "kid." Gina had gradually emerged as a friend that Val liked and respected.

She paused in her sketching. *Was it possible that she was on the verge of feeling more than liking for Gina?* She tried to push the thought out of her mind. That would be a bad road to go down. Valerie could only get hurt letting herself feel attracted to Gina, she felt sure of that. Gina had clear goals and they didn't include settling in Eureka. She was headed for San Francisco—with all its urban challenges and potential rewards. Colleges and universities in the Bay Area, where Gina might be able to land some kind of teaching position. Once in the system, she was young enough to work her way up, make a real contribution. Valerie knew that Gina was still sorting out her identity, but the big and varied gay community of San Francisco would support her lesbianism. Val felt sure, when she considered it, that before long the Gina she knew would be past history.

"Oh, well," she said to herself. "Life is just too complicated. I'll just have to take it a day at a time." She looked down at Sam. "Right, Sam?"

Gazing upward with her big brown eyes, Samantha studied Val's face and simply thumped her tail against the grass.

That evening Val was curled up with a book in the living room. It was a Friday, but her friends had been busy with one thing and another and had decided not to get together. They had drifted toward Friday evening activities so that Gina could participate. Alone on this evening, Valerie decided it was a good time to catch up on her reading.

She had just gotten to an exciting part of a good murder mystery when Gina burst in the front door.

"Hi!" Gina's voice was charged with energy. "Guess what? I just got my hands on this lesbian film called *Lianna*. Rick mentioned it to me, and I found a copy at Blockbuster Video. I was surprised they would carry this. See?"

She held out the disc to Valerie, who examined the DVD jacket.

"Looks like a good film," Val observed. She didn't mention that it was a classic and that she had seen it some time ago.

"Well, my computer plays DVDs so I can watch it in my room— unless you want to see it, too." Gina bubbled over with enthusiasm. Then she noticed Valerie's book. "Oh, you're reading. Sorry. I didn't mean to disturb you."

Val put the book down. Gina's excitement could be contagious.

"No, this book can wait." A mischievous smile flickered across Valerie's face. "We could have an old-fashioned movie night, with popcorn and everything."

Gina grinned. "Sure, that would be really neat."

Val got up to go to the kitchen. "Coke, wine, tea?"

Gina paused a moment and then replied, "Hot tea, but chamomile or something without caffeine."

"Okay, you set up the DVD and I'll bring the food."

Gina turned on the television and popped the DVD into the player, then ran upstairs to go to the bathroom. She quickly returned, patted Sam, and gave the dog a treat, all in about the same the time it took Valerie to run a bag of popcorn through the microwave, fill a big bowl for them to share, and heat water for tea.

Soon they were seated together on the large leather sofa with *Lianna* playing away on the TV. They laughed and passed the popcorn bowl back and forth, offering a few kernels to Sam who had stretched out on the carpet before them.

Valerie recalled that *Lianna* told the story of a professor's wife and student in a Midwestern college town who became attracted to a female professor. Lianna's husband was distant and was, as the story began, being unfaithful to her with a female student. Recognizing his infidelity, Lianna decided to turn the tables on him. She enticed the professor and the two women had a passionate sexual encounter that evolved into a relationship. When the husband found out, he turned Lianna out of the house and sued for custody of their children. Lianna, overwhelmed and living alone in a tiny apartment, then faced learning how to live life as a lesbian. Not surprisingly the female professor had a partner back in Canada and ultimately returned to that relationship. No happy ending to this story.

Valerie had forgotten much of the film. She recalled the story line as they began watching the DVD and thought privately that it was a good thought-provoking film for Gina to see. Gina seemed very taken with the movie. Her eyes were open wide and she was totally focused on the television set. They had turned the lights down and sipped their tea in silence, continuing to pass the popcorn bowl back and forth.

At one point, while grabbing some popcorn, Val unintentionally touched Gina's thigh and Valerie felt a jolt of electricity. She was very aware of it but just said "Sorry" for the accidental contact and they turned their attention back to the film. She couldn't help but wonder if Gina had felt the same electrical charge and, if she had, what it may have meant to her. *Gina's going to San Francisco*, Valerie reminded herself quickly. She definitely did not want a casual affair. She would not want to ruin her own life or Gina's, or cause either of them emotional pain.

Gina remained entranced until the film was over. Then her shoulders suddenly slumped and she was silent for a moment.

Finally she spoke. "That was kind of sad, wasn't it? No happy ending. Being a lesbian can be really lonely, can't it?"

"Yes," Valerie agreed. "It can be. But if it's who you are, better to live the truth in loneliness—if it happens that way—than to endure a false life in utter misery."

Gina nodded but suddenly she dropped her head into her hands and began to cry. Her shoulders heaved.

Valerie was stunned. She had never seen Gina lose control like this. Touched and not knowing exactly what to do, Val put her arm around Gina's shoulders. "I'm sorry, Gina," she said gently, "I know you are going through a hard time."

Gina leaned into Valerie, who threw both arms around the younger woman and tried to soothe her. It seemed to Val that all the pent up feelings that Gina had pushed aside to do what she needed to do were suddenly exposed, suddenly on the surface. Valerie patted her gently and instinctively kissed her lightly on the cheek.

Suddenly Gina's eyes, tear stained and a bottomless blue, looked up into Valerie's face, searching for something. And then, even more abruptly, she pushed upward and kissed Val on the mouth. Taken by surprise, Val responded to the kiss.

Before either could think, they were wrapped in a passionate embrace. Mouth on mouth, arms around each other, stroking, holding, reaching, exploring.

Valerie put on the brakes first. She stopped and gently but firmly held Gina away from her. She looked directly into her eyes and said, "Gina, I'm sorry, but this isn't right. I can't do this. We can't hurt each other like this."

Gina appeared distraught and terribly pained, but she sat still and stared back. And then she nodded. "You're right. I'm sorry, too."

She stood up and, with new tears streaming down her face, ran from the room and up the stairs.

Summer school was almost finished. Josie had completed two of her spring courses with passing grades, but two laboratory classes had posed difficulties. She hadn't been able to participate in classroom experiments while she was on bedrest and had been forced to accept incompletes in those classes. She had to finish the work in summer school. Josie hadn't been happy about that, because it took time away from her lawn service, but she needed the passing grades so she did what she had to do.

So on this summer afternoon, a lovely weekend afternoon, Josie sat in the Humboldt State library studying for her last final exam. Abruptly her cell phone vibrated. She asked another student nearby to watch over her books while she returned the call. Then she went outside the library building and quickly hit the button to dial the number showing on her screen.

It was Gina.

"Can I talk with you?" Gina asked. Her voice was strained.

Josie paused for a moment, obviously considering all the studying she needed to do. But Gina needed something. "Sure," she said, keeping her tone light. "I'm over at the college in the library, in the main study area. I can leave my books for a little while if you can come over here and meet me."

"I can be there in 30 minutes. Is that okay?"

Josie agreed and the two hung up.

Gina's Beetle hummed its way up Highway 101 to Arcata, where she left the main roadway at the Humboldt State exit. When she got to the center of the campus, she searched for and found a parking place for visitors and then scurried to the library. She knew her way, having been there a couple of times before. She was so glad that Josie had agreed to see her for a few minutes.

When Gina entered the library, Josie waved. She had been concentrating on her studies but still looking up periodically for her friend. The two left the library and walked to the quad in front of the student union. Josie still moved slowly and with a pronounced limp, so Gina carried her books for her. They found an empty bench in the shade, with a breeze to keep them cool. There they could talk privately.

Gina put Josie's pile of books down beside her. "How are finals going?"

"Really good. Better than I could ever have hoped. Judee's tutoring in the spring really helped me get focused."

Gina smiled. "I'm so glad for you. Maybe you'll actually learn to like school."

"Hmmph," Josie mumbled. "But you didn't drive all the way up here to ask about my exams. So what's up? You sounded like it was something urgent." She grimaced and positioned her braced leg as best she could to keep it from aching.

Gina took a deep breath but waited to speak until Josie was settled. "Well, last night Valerie and I were watching a lesbian movie and she touched me, I think by accident, but I felt this big jolt of electricity go through me. I was really startled——." Gina stumbled over her words, not sure if or how to explain what had happened afterward.

Josie grinned. "Sounds like attraction to me. If you felt it, then the chances are that she did too."

"Is it her sending me a signal or something?"

Josie chuckled. "More like you *both* were sending signals."

"I don't know what to do." Gina looked confused and distraught.

Josie looked at her with amusement. "I told you months ago, when I was lying up there in Val's house with my bum leg, that she *likes* you—maybe a *lot*. You two *live* together in the same house. You've had time to build up feelings for each other, even if you haven't been aware of them, and maybe both of you are living in denial. I'm surprised that this didn't happen a long time ago."

Gina thought for a moment and then admitted, "Well, it sort of did once, at the Purple Priscilla when we danced together, but I wrote it off to the evening, the music, the situation. I didn't take it seriously."

"I think you've been blocking this out for a long time," Josie said, gently touching Gina's arm, "but maybe now you'll have to deal with it."

Gina nodded. "But——."

"But what?" Josie asked. "Do I get a sense that there is something more here?"

Gina sighed. "Last night, after the movie, I got upset. I don't know why but I started crying. Valerie held me, and then we kissed. It was a shock, you know, because I didn't mean—well, I didn't want to do something wrong, but I had this urge. I'm upset and I think she's upset too, and now I really don't know what to do."

Josie looked at Gina and firmly grasped her hand. "Well, my friend, you're gonna have to decide what you *really* want. You and Valerie are, well, not in the same place. You came here to hang out while you settle some debts. Then you're off to San Francisco, right?"

Gina nodded reluctantly and stared at the ground.

"Valerie came to Eureka to build a new life," Josie continued, "and she's doing that. It's been long enough since Doreen's death that her feelings could be waking up. Even if she doesn't consciously know it, she might be ready for a new relationship. But when she opens herself up again, she's not likely to settle for a passing affair.

"If you aren't ready to settle down here in Eureka and be loving and loyal to her until she's old and wrinkled and beyond, then you had best stay away from her."

Gina stared at the ground, frowning, at a loss for words.

Josie finally pushed again. "Are you ready to give up San Francisco?"

Gina sighed and shook her head. Then she studied Josie's face, impressed with her mature assessment of the situation. "Geez, Josie, you should be a psychologist!" she said—adding, with a deep sigh, "Actually that's what I was afraid you'd say. I guess I knew it, way down deep inside. I just didn't want to look at it."

Josie grasped Gina's shoulder. "I can understand that. She's nice, you're nice, and you've had a good place to stay in her house. You've gradually become comfortable with each other. Now you're good friends. Under other circumstances, you could become lovers. It's hard now to sort out things. At some level, you don't want to leave. Why would you?"

Gina nodded. "You're right. But it looks like I'll have to go."

"How much more do you owe that therapist?"

"Maybe $200. Another month will put it behind me."

"Well, you had better make sure you don't have any more intimate evenings with Val. You know how to make yourself busy, you with your million and one jobs. Don't invite her to go dancing, don't hang out around her, and keep very busy. Maybe mention that you'll be leaving for San Francisco soon. Give her a clear message that you are following your original plan. There will be less pain that way. She'll miss you when you leave, but she won't have a broken heart."

Gina gave Josie a hug. "Thanks, Josie, you are really a good friend. Thanks for listening to me."

Josie grinned. "You're welcome. It's kind of fun, giving advice to a Ph.D."

Gina cuffed her playfully. "I bet."

"Well, I've got to get back to my books. You gonna be okay?"

Gina sighed. "Sure, and thanks again."

Josie struggled to get to her feet. "We're all gonna miss you, Gina, but you've got to do what you've got to do. You've waited so long and fought so hard for it."

Gina watched as Josie hoisted her books. "You want me to take those back for you?"

"Nope, I'm fine. See you later."

Gina nodded and watched as Josie, with her persistent limp, headed back across the campus toward the library. Although Josie still had a brace on her leg, Gina admired how far she had come in the months since her potentially tragic fall from the ladder.

It seemed that her fate had been sealed so Gina dragged home empty boxes. She looked at her belongings, the many things she had accumulated during her months in Eureka. Deciding what she would take with her and what she would leave behind, she began loading the boxes with things to go and things destined for a local charity. She avoided any personal conversations with Valerie, and Val said little to her.

She saved every penny she could from her jobs, worked extra hours, and pushed to get that last $200 paid off as quickly as she could. After three weeks she had accumulated the money and she mailed the final check. Then she felt free, as if an immense burden had been lifted.

She phoned Rick to tell him the news. They met that evening at the Purple Priscilla, and Gina danced the night away with several young women. She told Rick that she was about ready to leave Eureka.

"We'll miss you," he said to her. "I don't see that San Francisco has anything to offer that we don't have here, but that's my take on it. I mean what could be greater than the Rhododendron Parade in April and the Kinetic Sculpture Race in May and the Blues by the Bay Festival in August? And then there's that Trucker's Parade, too."

Gina giggled at him and shook her head. "I'm sorry," she said. "I suspect it's not the same thrill as seeing the Golden Gate Bridge or Fisherman's Wharf or riding on a cable car."

"I know, but you've never given Eureka a chance. You've wanted to be down there ever since you got here. So I guess you should go and do it." Rick shrugged. "And I guess that means this is goodbye."

During the last days, Valerie was friendly but continued to keep her distance. When they chatted about anything, Gina mentioned San Francisco. She told Valerie that she had paid off the debt and she left the door to her room open, so that Val could easily see the boxes she was packing up.

Valerie had started a new painting and was spending every hour she could spare on it. Now that she was beginning to sell more of her work, maybe she could soon let go of her part-time job and make a living solely from her art. That would be incredible.

After she had watched *Lianna* with Gina, a night she would prefer to forget, she had become quite aware of the recent changes in Gina. For several months they had seemed to be moving closer to each other, but, since that night, they couldn't be further apart. It was obvious that Gina was practically out the door. Soon Val would be looking for another roomer, partly for the money but also because this house suddenly seemed too big for just her and Sam.

Gina's departure would probably be for the best. Feelings were running too deep, and Val was starting to feel very vulnerable.

She remembered the night they danced at the Purple Priscilla and how her body responded to Gina's closeness. Even now she could feel the wetness between her legs. That had surprised and embarrassed her and yet she had felt pleasure. Because her passionate nature, dormant so long, was coming back to life and because she truly cared for Gina—maybe even was a bit in love with her—she knew she would hurt when Gina left. The longer Gina stayed, the more Val would hurt. And eventually Gina would go, no matter what. She saw her life as being out there somewhere else, not in Eureka.

The phone rang. It was Lanie.

"Hi, I'm just down the street. Can I stop by for a moment?"

"Sure." Valerie brightened at the thought of spending time with a good friend. "I'm in the studio. Just come on in. The front door's unlocked."

Lanie soon popped through the doorway, patted Sam, and pulled up a chair for herself. She commented on Valerie's new painting and then said, "You've been pretty non-communicative the past few weeks. I can't help but notice. What's going on?"

Val wanted to say, "Oh, nothing," but she couldn't really avoid the truth. "Well, Gina's getting ready to leave for San Francisco soon. I think I'm reacting to the reality that she's going to be gone."

"Why am I not surprised?" Lanie asked, smiling at Valerie as gently as brusque Lanie could smile.

Val gave her a rueful smile in return. "Yes, I know, you told me from the beginning to watch out for her."

"Well my opinion of Gina has changed a bit over the months. But she does have a plan for her life, and you aren't at the center of it. You deserve to be at the center of someone's life—someone you love and someone who loves you," Lanie told her.

"I know," Valerie agreed with a deep sigh.

"You and me, kid, we've both been around the block. You once, me several times, and we both know what's going on. If I weren't so completely immersed in selling real estate, I'd probably be chasing after you," Lanie confided, putting her hand on Valerie's arm.

Val chuckled. "Yeah, I suspect so. But you know we make better friends than we would lovers."

Lanie nodded soulfully. "So, as a good friend, I'm telling you to let this go. Let Gina go. Don't make a play for her. She's got an agenda, real or fantasy, and she's got to follow it. Otherwise she'd always blame you for holding her back, keeping her from getting what she believes she wants for herself."

Valerie nodded, her shoulders sagging. "You're right. I know it. But I still feel a big emptiness inside."

"That you can't help. She's been a big presence in your life for nearly a year now. Wave goodbye to her. Place an ad for a new roommate, allow yourself to grieve, and then move on."

"You're right."

Lanie gave her a big hug. "Don't shut me out, huh?"

Val nodded, and Lanie headed out the door to meet a client who was looking for a Victorian house.

On her final night of work at the multiplex, Gina turned in her uniform. Afterward she went to the Purple Priscilla to meet Rick and his friends for the last time. She danced until the place closed and then held Rick in a final goodbye hug.

"Don't forget us," he said at the front door of the bar. "Those 'Frisco fairies can't have all of you."

"I'll write," she promised, as she climbed into her Beetle.

Chapter Eleven

Gina's battered green "Bug" stood at the curb, nearly listing from the weight of clothes and boxes tucked into every available space—decidedly more personal belongings than she had owned when she arrived in Eureka at the beginning of the year.

Valerie had fixed an early breakfast for them both. They sat quietly at the table, an uncomfortable silence between them. Sam too was still, as if she sensed the tension in the air.

Gina's stomach was so tightly wound that she could barely eat. *We're like actors playing out a script*, she thought to herself. If only she could re-write the story, but she just didn't know how. They were stuck in some way and had to just keep going along the path that had been set—that she had set. She sighed, without looking at Valerie, and buttered her blueberry muffin.

After managing to finish her tea, Gina climbed the stairs to get her purse and sweater and to take one last look at her room—now her former room—to see that everything was in order. At the same time Val picked up Sam's leash and prepared to take the dog for a long walk.

Gina went out to her car and was closing the trunk of the Beetle when Valerie came outside with Sam. Gina started to wave a quick goodbye and climb into the driver's seat, but she halted midway and waited. When Val and Sam reached the sidewalk, she asked, "If you are going for a walk, do you mind if I join you? I could use the exercise before a long day in the car."

"Sure," Valerie said, without any particular warmth.

Gina patted Sam, and the trio started down the sidewalk in the direction of the harbor.

"I'm anxious to get to San Francisco," Gina said, as they walked along, "but I want you to know how much this past year has meant to me." The words just tumbled out. "I want you to know how much I appreciate your trusting me enough to take me in off the street when I first got here and for becoming a very special friend, way beyond a landlady. You've given me more than you could ever know—a safe place to grow and find myself." Gina stopped herself, before opening up a pandora's box about the evening they had watched *Lianna* together.

Valerie offered a small smile. "I'm glad that living here has been positive for you," she said genuinely.

They continued walking in silence for a moment, amidst the still-cool morning air and emerging sunshine. Something was blooming. There was a sweet fragrance in the slight breeze off the coast.

Gina finally picked up the thread of what she had been rehashing in her mind. Her voice filled with tension as she risked admitting, "Eureka has been so good to me that sometimes I've wondered whether I am making a mistake by leaving all of this behind. Everybody here, especially you, has been so warm and friendly, and I don't know how long it will be before I enjoy such friendships again. It would be easy to stay, you know——." Given that evening when they had kissed, this speech must sound really stilted, Gina admitted to herself.

Stopping abruptly, Valerie interrupted Gina. Grasping Gina's arm for a brief moment and looking her directly in the eyes, she said firmly. "I think you should go, Gina. This is what you've wanted for a long time, and you owe it to yourself to fulfill your dream. You've lost a lot in your life already, and you've given up many important things. I think you need to do this for yourself."

Gina sighed. A pained look crossed her face as she unconsciously shoved her glasses up on her nose. "You're probably right," she agreed reluctantly. "I really have held onto this dream for a long time. It kept me going in Tucson when things were very bad for me. I want to write, and I want to teach, and I want to experience 'Frisco, the Mecca for gay people. I need to embrace that world, for me."

As they started walking again Gina stubbed her toe on a crack in the sidewalk, nearly tripped but quickly righted herself, and continued. "I just want you to know how easy it would be to let it go. I feel like there is something between you and me that could be developed—."

Valerie interrupted again. "You're not ready, Gina." She tried to be gentle, to keep any edge out of her voice. "You need to go to San Francisco and do this thing for yourself. Lives are built around many things—careers, relationships, personal sacrifice, spiritual growth. Most people juggle many of these things, but always there is always one that is the most important. As much as I love my art I have always known that life for me revolves around meaningful relationships and one special committed relationship. I've watched you blossom this last year, but you're still growing and changing and deciding what's really important for you. You need to do that, above all."

Gina swallowed, and tears came to her eyes. She leaned down and patted Sam and then she reached out and gave Valerie a quick but strong hug. "I guess this is goodbye," she said in a husky voice. Then she turned and ran back toward her waiting car.

Valerie stood with Sam and watched her go. Val too had tears in her eyes. "Drive carefully," she called out. Then, wiping away a tear with her hand, she turned and, with the dog at her heels, walked on.

Gina's Beetle sang its way down the highway and, after a few tearful moments, she began to sing along with it, buoyed by the beautiful redwoods along the roadside and her dreams of San Francisco. She stopped here and there to take a look and shoot photographs—of the redwoods, then a picturesque small town. At Santa Rosa she detoured toward the coast to go through Bodega Bay, where Alfred Hitchcock's *The Birds* had been filmed. Nearly a year earlier, traveling north, she had rushed by, desperate for a job and a place to stay. This time, although anxious to be in the City, she felt she owed it to herself to smell the sea air, save some memories for the future, and enjoy the natural beauty of northern California.

It was very late in the day when coastal Highway 1 finally merged with 101 just north of the art colony Sausalito at the northern end of the Golden Gate Bridge. Although her funds were limited, Gina managed to find a modest motel room in which to spend the night. She wanted to enter San Francisco rested and fresh. Tomorrow, she would really *be* there, she told herself. At dinner in a small, quaint cafe, she picked up a newspaper and circled rental properties in the City, comparing addresses with the maps she had brought. Later, back in her room, she read part of a novel to try to wind down to sleep, but she found that her mind kept wandering—backward to Eureka and Valerie and her friends as well as forward to 'Frisco.

The next morning Sausalito was bathed in dense fog. Gina awoke early. She showered, dressed, and took a brief walk. Then she had some hot tea, a croissant, and sliced bananas at a little coffee shop and loaded up her car. By the time she was ready to leave, the sun was breaking through the low-lying clouds. When she started across the Golden Gate, the blue San Francisco Bay was sparkling. Her heart felt like it was in her throat as she took in the renowned City spread out before her.

Having studied tour books and maps beforehand, Gina felt she knew what she wanted to do and see. She followed Highway 1 through Golden Gate Park and continued southward until she came to the coast, then turned north and headed toward the Cliff House, a famous landmark restaurant facing the ocean. From there she took Geary Boulevard back toward the central part of the City. She had bought a morning newspaper and had circled a few additional ads for rooms for rent that could serve her temporarily until she found good employment and could rent an apartment. Gina knew she couldn't be choosy in the beginning, but she had decided that the place had to be clean, in a reasonably safe neighborhood, and close to buses and trolleys. San Francisco was well known for its public transportation and she would use that whenever possible.

Grabbing an unexpected parking space at the curb on Geary, Gina stopped for a few moments. She picked up her cell phone, took a deep breath—*You can do this*—and began to call each of her selected ads. On her first call, she quickly hung up when a gruff-sounding voice answered the phone. The second and third calls led only to answering machines and gave her little information to go on. She put the phone down on the seat beside her and experienced a rising tide of panic. She was already running out of ideas, and she needed somewhere to stay immediately. If she couldn't get a real lead on a room, she would have to start driving up and down streets looking for posted rentals. That seemed rather futile, and the time, money, and gasoline consumed would be daunting. What could she do to make this easier?

Suddenly she remembered that she had seen a sign pointing toward the University of San Francisco when she was driving into the City. If a university had helped her find a room in Eureka, maybe one here could do the same. *Why hadn't she thought of that before?*

Driving anxiously, but carefully, she managed to make a turn back through urban streets to the university campus, which was busy with vehicles both in motion and parked everywhere and great numbers of students on foot and bicycle. She would have to stash the car someplace and look for a housing office. She was becoming frantic when a car pulled abruptly out of a visitor parking spot just as she turned the corner. Gina quickly whipped the Beetle into the space. Whew! That was a good omen, she knew.

For nearly half an hour she wandered on foot around the campus, her heart pounding with both hope and fear. She looked at the educational buildings with fascination and asked questions of students she passed who strolled or sat somewhere studying. Following a couple of suggestions, she finally reached the housing office and entered the front door.

A young woman with shaggy brown hair and wire-rimmed glasses—probably a student, Gina thought—looked up from a book as Gina approached the counter.

"Do you keep lists of rooms off campus that rent to students?" Gina tried not to let her nervousness show.

The unattractive and frankly overweight young woman eyed her suspiciously and stuck out a hand. "Student ID, please," she said gruffly. Perhaps she was annoyed at being pulled away from her reading.

"I'm sorry, I don't have one," Gina admitted.

"Then you're not a student here?" The tone was terse.

"No," Gina said. "But I plan to enroll next semester." This was not the time, she knew, to trot out her Ph.D. She forced a smile.

"Hmmm," the clerk said. She clearly didn't believe that Gina intended to be a student and considered her critically for a moment. Finally, with a heavy sigh, she admitted, "Well, we have some listings, but most of them are pretty restricted to currently enrolled students." After a long pause, during which she looked at Gina out of the corner of her eye, the clerk decided to flip through a Rolodex. "I do have one, though, that might work for you. There's a woman in North Beach who occasionally takes in a student, usually a more mature woman, and she insists that they don't drink, smoke, or have pets." She stared directly at Gina. "If you fit that description, you might give her a call."

"That's me, to a tee." Gina gave her a friendly grin. She felt with great relief that she must have passed some test, since the clerk now seemed willing to help.

"Well, this lady doesn't advertise anywhere—probably lives in a neighborhood where renting rooms is frowned on or a tad illegal—so between you and me, keep this quiet. If you don't take the room, tear up the phone number, okay?"

"Sure," Gina said. "Right. Got it."

The clerk wrote down a number on a slip of paper and started to push it across the counter. Then she hesitated.

"I'm breaking every rule in the book to give you this, so I hope I'm not making a mistake in trusting you." She offered a raised eyebrow.

Gina looked at her very directly. "You're not making a mistake. I'm very trustworthy."

"Okay, and good luck," the clerk said, passing over the paper. The barest of smiles crossed her lips.

Gina looked at the phone number carefully to be sure she could make out the handwriting and then said, "Thank you very much. I really appreciate this."

The clerk nodded and turned her attention back to her book.

With a farewell wave, Gina left the housing office and stood outside for a moment, catching her breath. She had really feared that the clerk was going to turn her away. Once she had calmed down a bit, she moved along the walkway but away from foot traffic, pulled out her cell and quickly dialed the telephone number. When an elderly woman answered, her voice highly accented, Gina introduced herself, explained that she had gotten the number at the university housing office, and asked if a room was available. At first the woman hesitated but then gave Gina an address in North Beach, a neighborhood that Gina recalled from her research was seemingly decent and located somewhere between Union Square and Fisherman's Wharf.

When Gina eventually found her way there, the address in North Beach was on a block that looked clean and very international, but there was absolutely nowhere to park. Gina drove around the neighborhood several times before finally locating a small spot to stash the Beetle. Then she hiked a number of blocks back to the house number written on her piece of paper. Despite the obvious parking issues, she'd decided that she should at least look at the place. Parking could well be an issue wherever she went.

A tiny, stooped lady answered the door when Gina rang the bell. Mrs. Han seemed to be of some Oriental extraction, but spoke English quite clearly—despite the accent and some incorrect grammar. Mrs. Han appeared relieved to see that Gina was nonthreatening and presentable. The row house, which had windows only on the street and a rear alley, seemed cramped and very dark to Gina. The room available for rent was located on the second floor at the top of a narrow stairway. It was small and equally dark but serviceable—for the present, anyway. Gina mentioned her difficulty in finding a place to park, and Mrs. Han smiled. "We fix that. I don't drive car myself, but I have garage and would rent it to you." The total cost seemed steep to Gina, and she stood considering.

Mrs. Han was not about to let her get away. "Do you have computer?" she asked.

"Yes," Gina admitted, not sure what this had to do with anything.

"Well, I too have computer. I also have 'WiFi,' and if you take room you may sign onto my account to use," Mrs. Han offered, with a knowing smile.

That, of course, did it! Gina couldn't let this deal get away. Relieved, she decided to take the room at once. The price *was* high for her, $450 a month plus $50 for parking, but given the neighborhood and what little she had gleaned from the newspaper and the promised Internet connection, she had a feeling that it was a steal. Handing over to Mrs. Han the first month's rent and a deposit just about cleaned out her cash reserve, but she was determined she would find work soon.

When the deal was complete, Gina hiked through the neighborhood to collect the Beetle and drove to the house. She eased the car into the tiny garage, which was lit by a single naked overhead bulb, and hauled her boxes and bags one by one up the narrow stairs to her room. The biggest plus to her new housing was that Mrs. Han had equipped the room with a small refrigerator and tiny microwave. Remembering with a surprising touch of nostalgia her struggles at

Valerie's house in the beginning months, Gina acknowledged that she had really found a gem in this place.

That evening, after eating a light dinner at a little ethnic restaurant nearby, she tried to organize her belongings and her thoughts. Putting her clothing away in the dresser and the closet, she recalled doing this exact same thing in Eureka. She sighed, and a single tear rolled down her cheek. *How far she had come since that first day at Valerie's house when she had moved in with her duffle bag and box of books.* Her admittedly more extensive wardrobe still fit in the closet here, but she smiled with amusement as she attempted to shove her current pile of books, videos, and CDs into the little bookcase that Mrs. Han had put in the room.

The bed proved comfortable but, as she lay awake that night reliving the day's events, she thought of that beautiful, bright room she had had in Eureka. Her reverie was disturbed by the clanging sounds of a cable car nearby as it rounded a corner and headed uphill—a sound she knew she would have to get used to. San Francisco was definitely different from the quiet world she had known on the North Coast.

Valerie struggled with her feelings. The first tear, after Gina's departure, had led to a flood and a pile of tissues before the day was over. Returning home, she had put fresh sheets on the bed in Gina's room, hoping to dispel the last of Gina's scent. She cleaned the already clean bathroom and put out different towels. By the time she had completed these tasks she was physically ready to move on, but it became clear that getting beyond her current thoughts and feelings would not be as easy.

Despite the fact that she had always known Gina would be leaving and despite the fact that she had constantly reminded herself that Gina was a roomer, not a potential lover—well, a friend at times—Gina had made a deep impact on Valerie. She would miss Gina's coming and going, her steps on the stairs, her occasional laughter. For a relatively serious, rather introverted person, Gina did have a engaging laugh. Then there was her affection for Sam—and her warmth toward Val's friends. And her willingness to work hard, very hard, to go after something she wanted.

If Gina ever seemed open to a change in her plans or had ever indicated that Val was truly important to her, Valerie would have been in real trouble. That one night watching *Lianna*—the slip, when they had kissed—was just a mood of the moment. It hadn't changed anything. But if things had been different at that instant, Valerie would probably have abandoned all or most of her reason—Gina was too young, too focused on her immediate goals, too inexperienced to know what she really wanted yet—and would have become deeply involved with her. Yet by the time Gina had mentioned the possibility of staying, just that last morning, her Beetle was already packed to go to the Bay Area. At that point Valerie had been unwilling to do or say anything that would have altered Gina's plans. She did really feel that Gina needed to go. She still believed that. But knowing that she had almost literally pushed Gina out the door did not make it any easier to get beyond her own feelings of attraction, of caring, perhaps the beginning of love and of loss.

Val lay in her bed that night, alternatively crying, tossing pillows, talking to herself, and saying out loud that she must forget Gina and get on with her own life. *Thank goodness they had not gone all the way and made love.*

Her confusion increased when she realized that Sam had not jumped up on her bed. Val called for the dog. When the retriever didn't come, Valerie climbed out of bed and went downstairs to search for her. She found Sam in Gina's room curled up on the floor by the bed, which Sam had quite neatly turned down with her nose and paws as if waiting for Gina to come home.

Val knelt down and put her arms around the dog, tears flowing freely as she cried into the big red shoulder. "Oh, Sam, she's gone, and we have to get used to it. No more Gina."

After a few moments, Val dried her eyes and signaled for the dog to follow her. Sam cast a longing glance at the empty bed and then trotted, tail hanging low, upstairs with Valerie.

The next morning, which fortunately dawned crisp and clear, Gina hiked uphill and downhill through North Beach, trying to get her bearings. She stuffed her digital camera into her purse so she could take pictures as she walked. There were various businesses along one cable car route, and she noticed a couple of restaurants, a bookstore, a newsstand—where she bought the morning paper—a small delicatessen, a beauty salon, and an Oriental tea room. Needing a break, she stopped at the deli for hot tea and a chance to read the paper. Searching through the want ads she discovered, to her great surprise, that there was a job opening listed at the bookstore she had just passed.

Would her good luck hold? Gina wondered about that as she hurried back to the bookstore, inquired about the job, and filled out an employment application on the spot. The stocky, middle-aged manager, Iris Sanchez, assessed her through heavy spectacles and decided to give her an immediate interview. As they talked, Mrs. Sanchez seemed interested that Gina lived nearby, could walk to work, and that she had recent retail experience. "It makes it easier for me to check since you have worked in California," she noted. "That is good. I also see that you have much education—English literature, that is good for working in a bookstore, I think." Mrs. Sanchez looked at the list of degrees Gina had earned and raised an eyebrow, but she did not choose to ask the inevitable question, "If you have all this education, why are you not teaching?"

The manager thanked Gina for coming in and said that she would get back to her in a few days. Her enthusiasm over Gina's application was obvious, and Gina was encouraged that perhaps she had a chance to get the job. Gina left the store and stood for a moment on the sidewalk, trying to calm her breathing. This was too perfect. She just hoped that in some unknown way she had not blown it. And that her money would hold out until Mrs. Sanchez made a decision.

Emotionally wound up after her unexpected, on-the-spot interview, Gina sprinted down the street to the next cable-car stop and battled her way onto a car headed for Fisherman's Wharf. The ride was invigorating despite the cable car's constant jerking—which caused her to hang onto the support strap for dear life—and the persistent clanging at each street corner and stop. Almost immediately she could distinguish the regular riders who silently clung onto the trolley's rails and straps from the tourists who smiled, pointed to significant buildings, and exclaimed excitedly at every shift of the car's gears as they went up and down hills and around corners.

When Gina arrived at the end of the line near the wharf, she took off walking with long strides. She was hungry to absorb everything. Even though she had to admit that most of the shops seemed filled with souvenirs to attract tourists, she loved the fish stalls and the waterfront smells, the big fishing boats at the docks, and the many seafood restaurants. She treated herself to a loaf of San Francisco sour dough bread, a giant shrimp cocktail, and a large Diet Coke at a stand along Jefferson Street. The operator of the stand humored her by taking her picture holding the bread in one hand and the shrimp cocktail in the other. She saw signs for boat rides around the harbor and excursions to Alcatraz Island and told herself that one day she would take the trip to the former prison. She snapped so many photographs that within a couple of hours she had already consumed all the shots on her camera's video card.

Late in the afternoon, as the breeze off the bay began to turn chilly, she waited in a long line of people—mostly gawking tourists, some American, many from foreign countries—to ride the cable car back to her neighborhood. Her only non-food purchases had been some postcards to send to her friends in Eureka and her parents in Illinois.

The next two days were nerve-wracking. Gina devoured all the local want ads from the papers and on the Internet. She filled out a few online applications and boarded both buses and cable cars to get to locations where there were posted openings or possibilities that she wanted to explore.

She had only one outfit that was suitable for job hunting, and she had to be careful to stay clean as she fought her way through crowds of people getting on and off public transportation. Both evenings she came back to Mrs. Han's house exhausted and a little concerned that maybe her luck had run out. Except for the bookstore, no one had responded very positively to her or she got there after the job already had been filled. She tried not to get too discouraged, reminding herself that she was new to San Francisco and that job hunting was exhausting and frustrating under the best of circumstances. Fighting noise, dust and wind, not knowing where she was going, and always encountering strangers were almost overwhelming. She had to be patient. Somehow, she told herself, her money would last and she would find a job.

Late on the third day of her explorations, just as she hopped off the cable car in North Beach, her cell phone buzzed. Nearly freaking out at the unexpected cellular summons, she pulled the phone out of her pocket to answer. It was Mrs. Sanchez.

"I've checked your references," the manager said, "and all your employers gave you high marks. If you'd still like to have the job, you can start training tomorrow morning at 9:30."

"Oh, yes," Gina said, sighing gratefully. "I'll be there, right on time. Thank you!"

She practically ran to the delicatessen where she had stopped earlier and went to the counter to get a sandwich and some fruit salad for dinner, along with a cinnamon-raisin bagel and a banana for breakfast and a big bottle of water. The next morning she'd use the teapot and hotplate that Valerie had allowed her to keep permanently when she left Eureka. Just like old times. Well, almost. For the moment she was living just as she had then, but when she got some money, she would stock the little refrigerator and begin to use the microwave. She felt certain that life was going to become easier.

Once back in her room, Gina put away her things. She was so relieved that the pressure was off. She sat down at her computer and downloaded the digital photos she had taken the first day. She looked at them and laughed with pleasure at all the sites she had seen and photographed—especially the picture of her with a big grin, holding the loaf of bread and the shrimp cocktail.

Now that she had a job, she could open a local bank account and update her credit accounts. As soon as she got the codes from Mrs. Han, her e-mail address would work. She had e-mail addresses for Josie, Lanie, Judee and Rick. Only Valerie did not have e-mail. Gina wrote a message to everyone about her trip down the coast and her arrival in San Francisco, giving her mailing address, and saved the message in a draft file. When she could send it, she would attach the photo of herself at the wharf and a postscript to Josie, asking her to print out a copy and give it to Valerie. She knew Josie would do that for her. For the moment, that was all she could do. Then she sat down to write her postcards. The first was to Valerie. It was bittersweet to be writing to her, but Gina wanted her to know she was okay. She felt sure that Valerie, despite her coolness when Gina left, would think of her and would wonder. Then she sent a card to Rick and another to her parents.

Just as she was finishing her cards, there was a knock at her door.

When Gina opened the door she encountered Mrs. Han, who had a sweet smile on her face. The old woman had perfect teeth, but it wasn't until a few weeks later that Gina realized she kept them in a glass at night. "I just checking on you," Mrs. Han said. "You have good first days here?"

"Oh, yes," Gina said enthusiastically. "I walked the neighborhood and went on the cable car to Fisherman's Wharf. I loved it! And, most important, I've been looking for a job and I've found one at that bookstore about six blocks down the street."

Mrs. Han nodded. "Very good. Is nice bookstore. I go there sometimes."

Gina smiled. "The next time I'll see you there then."

"Is anything you need? You comfortable here?" the stooped, older lady asked.

"I'm fine, great," Gina said. Then she suddenly thought, "Oh, is there a bank near here?"

Mrs. Han nodded affirmatively. "Yes. U.S.Bank. Good bank. Three blocks up and three blocks over. Open 9 to 5. Not sure about Saturday."

"Thank you. I'll go there as soon as I can," Gina said.

Mrs. Han turned away. "You need anything, you ask," she said.

"The code to use the Internet with your WiFi," Gina mentioned, trying not to sound pushy.

"Ah, yes, I forget. I brought it for you." Mrs. Han pulled a card out of her pocket with the account name and password in neat handwriting.

"Oh, thank you." Gina grabbed the card as if her life depended on it.

Mrs. Han smiled, gave a little bow, and repeated "You need anything else, you ask," as she departed, one hand on the wall as she carefully picked her way down the stairs in the dim light.

By the next time the poker club met, Valerie had recovered most of her equilibrium and Sam had stopped unmaking the bed in what had been Gina's room. The dog had been restless for several days, constantly searching the house, but had gradually settled down.

When Lanie, Josie, and Judee gathered in the dining room to play, they all had a pretty clear idea that Valerie had been wounded by Gina's departure and that maybe talking about it was not a good idea. But the gang was subdued anyway. They went through the motions of getting their drinks and treats and shuffling the cards, while looking a bit furtively at one another.

Finally, Valerie couldn't stand it any longer. "Look," she said. "Gina's gone. I'm sad about it, you're all sad about it, but life has to go on. Can't we just play cards? We used to have fun before she was here, so can't we somehow have fun again?"

Lanie rose to the occasion, on behalf of her good friend. "Yes," she said loudly, "let the fun begin."

Judee let out a Bronx cheer, and they all put down their bets.

The job at Pelican New and Used Books proved to be a good fit for Gina. After two weeks of training, during which she worked part-time, she was offered full-time employment. This meant some benefits, eventually, and it was the first full-time job Gina had had since just after graduate school. The customers she met in the bookstore were very diverse—of all ages, ethnicities, and educational backgrounds. Gina enjoyed helping each person find the books wanted or needed, and at times her English literature background came in handy when she was able to help a reader select a special writer or a work of classic literature. During busy hours, her duties could seem intense, especially at the register, but at the end of the day she felt a real sense of satisfaction. She liked making use of information she had acquired during her college years, and she especially felt gratified in guiding customers to treasured books.

Gina also found the patrons interesting, learning something new from each person she helped. Several of her customers were gay or lesbian and most of them gave her more than a passing glance. Some looked questioningly at her. Others seemed to assume that she was one of them. The store had an "alternative lifestyle" section of books, and Gina found herself guiding any number of people to that corner. One woman even tried to make a date with her. Gina put her off. She had too much going on right now to start some kind of relationship—and, truth be told, in some vague way that played at the edge of her consciousness—she didn't feel free to have one.

Mrs. Sanchez was a good manager and trainer. Gina eventually learned that she was of Greek descent but married to a very gentle and dapper gray-haired Spaniard, Felipe Sanchez, whom Gina met one day when he stopped by the store to take his wife out to lunch. Watching the couple leave the shop together, Gina was enthralled by them and how they symbolized the marvelous cultural mixture she encountered every day in San Francisco.

She was assigned to work in the bookstore on weekends, but she had two days off during the week. This schedule was perfect for her. Gina wanted to get to know the City, and she discovered that it was easier to see things when there were fewer tourists. She also wanted to explore the educational community to see if she could find some kind of teaching job. That process definitely had to be accomplished during the week.

Gina located the nearest branch of the public library and spent an afternoon pouring over catalogues for all the local colleges and universities. She checked the offerings in English literature and read the credentials of the professors in each department. She took notes on the campus addresses, the human resources officials in each school, and their appropriate contact numbers.

That same evening in her room, she went over her notes and considered where she would start. Stanford and UC Berkeley seemed a long shot, with her lack of teaching experience and undistinguished resume. Then there were the San Francisco campus of the state university system and the city college. She also made note of Mills College, a relatively small women's college across the Bay in East Oakland. Maybe there she could get her feet wet, trying to sell herself to an administrator. A smaller institution would be less daunting, and maybe, as a woman, she would even get a positive reception.

The next day Gina swallowed her lifelong anxiety about making phone calls and dialed the office of human resources at Mills. She introduced herself to the receptionist as Dr. Fortenham—which Valerie had shown her was important in some situations—and asked for an appointment to see the director. The receptionist asked her to hold for a moment.

When the woman, who sounded young, maybe a student assistant, came back on the line, she said, "Normally Dr. Weiss is booked for weeks in advance, but she happens to have a cancellation at 3 p.m. this afternoon. If you can make it then, it is yours. Otherwise it will be next month before we can work you in."

"I'll be there," Gina replied quickly, taking down instructions from the receptionist about where to park on campus and how to find the appropriate building.

After lunch Gina dressed in her best clothes, a navy three-piece pant outfit, and drove her Beetle across the Bay Bridge onto the I-580 headed east, and then up MacArthur Boulevard to the Mills College campus. She immediately loved the look of the school, with its many eucalyptus trees, open green fields, and Spanish-style stucco buildings. She enjoyed seeing all of the young women—of definitely diverse backgrounds—walking in any direction she looked. What a fun place to be a student, she thought to herself.

At the human resources office, housed in a white Victorian mansion, Gina was shown quickly into the office of Dr. Rochelle Weiss. Weiss was an attractive woman in her early 50s, Gina would guess, with short, curly red hair and clad in a beige pantsuit.

"How may I help you," Dr. Weiss asked, after they shook hands and had seated themselves.

Gina explained her situation: being new to San Francisco, having a Ph.D. but not having taught, wanting to break into college teaching, and not knowing where to even start looking. She made it clear that she was just asking for advice and information, not applying for a job.

Dr. Weiss studied her thoughtfully. "I see your challenge," she said pleasantly. "Getting that first job can be most difficult." She swiveled in her chair and looked for a long moment out the window at the college's campanile tower.

"I wish we had something to offer you here. It sounds like you could make a good contribution to our campus," she said politely. "But as you can probably imagine, a liberal arts college is a sought-after place for English literature instructors. Most of our professors have been here for a long time and will be here until they retire. I can't think of any of them who have given an indication of leaving in the near future. The dean of the faculty would be the final word on that, but this is a small campus and we know each other pretty well.

"If we had a large evening program, I could try to get you some part-time work to help you get launched, as it were. Even a class or two would provide you with some teaching experience and help you move on to a full-time job.

"But, as a small, essentially residential college, Mills is not large enough to offer an extensive evening program," she explained. "Since you are living in the City, I would suggest that you try a college in the center of San Francisco, one with many day and evening students and one that offers a number of introductory English literature classes. That might be the best place to get your foot in that proverbial door."

Before Gina could say anything, Dr. Weiss pulled up a file from her drawer. "I can give you the name of a colleague of mine at Cal State. You may say that I recommended that you contact her." She wrote down a name and phone number on a piece of paper and handed it to Gina.

"I can't thank you enough," Gina said, breathlessly, as she stood and shook hands again with Dr. Weiss. "I so appreciate your time and your helpfulness."

Although disappointed that the odds were against her ever teaching at a prestigious women's college like Mills, Gina appreciated how kindly she was treated there and how Dr. Weiss had given her a lead at San Francisco State University. Wistfully, she drove out of the main gate of Mills and back to the I-580 freeway.

Valerie had always kept her house clean and relatively free of knickknacks. Her own paintings adorned the walls, but she displayed few framed photographs. There had been many photos at the condo in San Francisco—pictures of her and Doreen at the wharf, on the cable car, in Golden Gate Park, and with their friends.

After Doreen died, all of their photos together had made Val feel sad and depressed. With the exception of one that she especially loved and kept framed by her bed, she had taken all of them down and put them in storage. She couldn't bear to burn or discard them, but she didn't want to look at them either.

So, compared to her friends' houses, Val's Eureka home was Spartan. However, under a magnet on the refrigerator there was one other photograph—Valerie and Gina on *Sweet Dreams*. Every time Val opened the refrigerator door she saw that photograph. She loved that picture. It had been such a beautiful day on the ocean and the photo recorded one of the nicest times she had had since moving to Eureka.

Now, however, it was bittersweet. Every time she looked at Gina's face, Valerie knew that she had gone and would probably never return to the North Coast. She should take the picture down, she knew.

One morning, she actually reached for the photograph to put it away—then withdrew her hand because somehow she just couldn't let the image disappear.

Chapter Twelve

While she waited for an interview with the human resources director at California State University at San Francisco, Gina used the next two weeks to learn as much as she could about the City. She left her Beetle in Mrs. Han's garage and rode local buses. She passed through every neighborhood she could, noting the character and architecture of each. She never ceased to be amazed at how different San Francisco was from any other place she had ever been. She realized that, for her, 'Frisco must be the most beautiful city in the world.

Gina explored the Castro District, often mentioned in the media as the historic home, or hangout, for many homosexuals. While San Francisco's large gay and lesbian population was scattered throughout the area's numerous neighborhoods, the Castro had been the site of some of the most famous events involving homosexuals, including massive and colorful Gay Pride parades and demonstrations. When Gina rode in and out of The Castro, she saw all kinds of people on the street, many of whom appeared rather extreme for her own taste. It seemed as if they wanted to be as shocking as they possibly could, sporting spiky dyed hair, Kabuki-style make-up, black leather, or chains. The clientele at the Purple Priscilla paled by comparison. However, she knew enough to understand that not all gays and lesbians were quite that radical. Most were invisible, looking just like everyone else. Perhaps that was less true in San Francisco—which, by reputation, was more "out" than anywhere else in the United States. But her gradually developing "gaydar" was allowing her to recognize several less obvious women she was sure were lesbian, even if they didn't announce that fact loudly to the world.

At the bookstore in North Beach, Mrs. Sanchez allowed Gina to borrow several used books as long as she handled them with care and returned them in saleable condition. On her coffee breaks and at home, she read about San Francisco and its history, politics, architecture, and culture. She devoured Armistad Maupin's *Tales of the City*. She read about gay businessman Harvey Milk and then watched the DVD *Milk*, based on his life. After she watched *Milk*, it occurred to Gina that Valerie had lived here while he was running for public office and when he was assassinated. This gave her some perspective on what Val had experienced in life, compared to what Gina had known—and had not. She wondered, briefly and with a slight pang, if she was going to the same places, doing the same things, and walking the same streets that Valerie had once walked. Her stomach momentarily turned flip-flops at the thought.

The day of her appointment with the human resources director at CSUSF finally arrived. Gina had scoped out the campus earlier and planned to get there by bus. She hoped she wouldn't sweat too much. 'Frisco could be very humid on a fall afternoon, and also at times very warm. By nightfall it would probably be cold and foggy, but afternoons held a particular challenge. Gina found she really had to layer, starting well covered with a jacket in the morning, stripping down to shirtsleeves in the afternoon, and covering up again by early evening.

The HR director, Mrs. Contreras, was very pleasant to Gina when they met, perhaps because Gina had been referred by Dr. Weiss. But she was not particularly hopeful, shaking her head. "I do not see anything that would suit your situation in the near future," she admitted.

"We have many English literature classes at all levels," she explained, "but we also have numerous available instructors out of English departments in the Bay Area. When we have an opening, we can find an English teacher with a master's degree and with several years of experience for less money than we would have to pay you with your Ph.D. and no teaching experience. We have a pay scale and we can't pay you any less than your degree would warrant."

Mrs. Contreras did provide her with an employment application "for our file" and referred her to the HR director at City College. Gina thanked her for her time and courtesy and then went through the hoops once again.

Gina lay in bed, covers pulled up around her, and considered what it meant to her to be in San Francisco. After her initial excitement at just "being" in the City and starting to explore it, she was feeling rather lonely, especially on evenings like this one. This was such a large place and everything she did seemed to be a major struggle. Tucson had seemed large, at least by comparison with her Illinois farm town. But, in retrospect, Tucson had been an easy place to live. Life had been very casual. Gina had rented an apartment in a small neighborhood, and her days had revolved around that part of town—first graduate school and then her therapy. The latter had offered a ready-made support system. She didn't have that support anymore and San Francisco, although fascinating, could also be totally frustrating. She had met people, especially at the bookstore, but she didn't have any real friends or even anyone to chat with yet. City life was intense and hurried—everyone rushing to work and back, or out to dinner, or some other activity. People pushed by each other but never connected. Gina realized she was feeling quite alone.

This evening she had been leafing through piles of local newspapers and other literature on the gay and lesbian scene. Sometimes, when she felt totally overwhelmed, she gave herself pep talks. "It's not going to happen overnight," she said aloud. "Look at what you've accomplished in a few short weeks."

Right now it was too hard, so she pulled out her computer and worked for a while on a short story, a romantic tale set in Eureka.

What she was writing made her laugh at herself for a moment. And then it made her think of "the gang" back there. She moved to her e-mail to see what she had received since she last checked. Her friends in Eureka had been doing a good job of keeping her up to date on their lives and activities. She hadn't heard anything from Valerie yet, but Josie told her that Val was fine and working a lot in her studio. The group still met for their weekend poker games and everyone was doing well. Rick wrote her funny letters about life at the movie theater. A couple of times when Gina read his letters, she would laugh at his graphically descriptive anecdotes and then start to cry.

There were no new messages tonight. Feeling down, Gina realized that she *really* missed her friends—especially Valerie. She so wished Val would write but understood why she didn't. There wasn't any future in staying connected, just an opportunity for hurt.

Three weeks passed before Gina's appointment with the assistant director of human resources at San Francisco City College. The college's main campus was a long way from where she lived, but she figured out a transit routing and managed to keep the appointment. This time she spoke with a young man of Eurasian descent, a Dr. Kheo. At first he shook his head, but then he brightened. "I've got one idea. It would be handy if you had foreign language skills—Spanish, Japanese, Chinese, or Vietnamese—but we teach a lot of ESL classes here, and having a second language yourself isn't an official requirement."

At Gina's perplexed look, he quickly explained, "ESL, English as a second language. I know this isn't what you wanted when you were taking all those beautiful English literature courses, but it is a way to get started. We hire teaching assistants in some of these classes. We admittedly appreciate bilingual or even multi-lingual instructors who can handle some of the languages that come through the door, but the classes themselves are taught totally in English. It's not much, compared to your life dream, but why don't you attend one of our classes, see how you feel about it, and then let me know. I may be able to set you up as an assistant. Do that for a semester and we'll see where we go from there."

Although scared to death, Gina was excited at this prospect. She took the information on the ESL classes—there were many spread out throughout the neighborhood college campuses—and set aside an evening to attend a class.

Valerie went outside to pick up the mail. Among the various advertisements and requests for money from charities she found a postcard from Gina. She stood for a moment studying the card, for it felt familiar but strange at the same time. Val had never really noticed Gina's handwriting, even though the two had shared the house for nearly a year. Absorbing it now for the first time, she realized that she liked Gina's script: open letters, a slight slant, a bit of extra curl that was artistic, yet basically quite legible. Yes, it looked like Gina. Naïve but creative, inexperienced but intelligent. Reading the message on the card, which told of Gina's first adventures in San Francisco, forced Valerie's heart to skip a few beats and then brought a pang of sadness. She missed the City, she missed Gina—*much as she did not want to admit it*—and getting this card brought a flood of past memories into her mind.

She shoved the postcard back in the pile of mail and went into the house. Reminiscing would only bring pain, she sighed. Yes, it was definitely time to find a new roomer. Gina was truly gone. Val promised herself that she would call the women's center that day and place an ad.

Later that morning, her phone rang. It was Lanie, as she might have expected.

"Hi, Val!" Lanie was in an enthusiastic mood. "I'm surprised to catch you at home this morning. I called the photo studio and Lyn said you weren't in today."

"Yes," Valerie replied. "I'm struggling to finish a painting I promised for this week. You know I don't do much commissioned work—it's a real challenge for me. I took the morning off to try to make some progress."

"I got an e-mail message from Gina last night. Have you heard from her?" Lanie asked.

"Uh, huh. Got a postcard from her this morning. She sounds happy and busy." Valerie tried to keep her own feelings at bay.

"She told me that she misses us and Eureka," Lanie noted.

"She'll get over it." There was a touch of bitterness in Val's voice.

"Mmmm," Lanie observed, "you sound like you miss her, too."

"I'll get over it." Valerie now felt annoyed. "Look, Lanie, I've got to get back to work—okay?"

Lanie chuckled. "All right, I'll get off the phone. But it's so unlike you to be grouchy."

"Later." Val wasn't about to discuss her mood.

"Well, bye," Lanie said. "It will get better, believe me."

Now disgusted with Lanie's cheerfulness, Val hung up the phone and went back to her work. But she was not in the mood. Damn, she said to herself. It was definitely time to call the women's center. She needed to get a roomer, and soon. The empty house was getting to her. *That's all that it is,* she told herself, *just the empty house.*

Yet the moment she put that into words she knew it wasn't exactly true. Ever since Gina had driven away in that terrible old Beetle, Valerie had repeatedly played their last conversation in her mind. Gina had tried to open a door, to build something between them, and Val had slammed it shut. She had believed at the time that she had done the right thing, but had she? Maybe she should have offered Gina some hope—that she'd come visit her after she got settled there or that someday she might consider moving back to San Francisco. Yet the very thought of the City caused her breath to catch, and a sharp pain stabbed her in the gut. She didn't want to go back—not to visit, not to move back, not for anything. And financially, even if in the long run she could sell more paintings there, the cost of living in the Bay Area would be a major stumbling block. Having downsized her life to move to Eureka, it would be very difficult for Val to make the journey back the other way.

Well, she admitted, if San Francisco might be right for Gina, it wasn't right for her. So there could never be anything between them. Better to have let Gina go, without any hope, leaving her free to explore her new world on her own. In time Gina would find new friends and hopefully in time a lover, and she would forget. So would Valerie, eventually, forget—at least she thought so.

Gina arrived in the ESL classroom several minutes before the beginning of the session. The classroom was decorated in city grunge— hospital green walls, linoleum floors, barred windows that didn't open, and an outdated window air-conditioning unit that made more racket than it offered anything like cool or breathable air.

She spoke to the instructor, a wild-haired young Asian man whose pockmarked face was nearly consumed by the thickest glasses Gina had ever seen. When she explained why she was there, he smiled indulgently and pointed to a seat in the front row. She assumed he meant that she should sit there to listen to the class, so she seated herself.

The students trickled in, speaking to each other in various languages. They were of all ages and every nationality imaginable. At first glance, the only thing they seemed to have in common was a seriousness of purpose. They quieted down as they took their seats, opened their notebooks, and looked expectantly at the instructor. Without urging, they gave him their full attention when he started to speak.

The session was a challenge for Gina to follow. The instructor spoke in highly accented American English. Each student spoke in his or her own brand of accented English. During the first half hour Gina could hardly understand a word. Gradually she attuned her ears to these unusual sounds and began to pick up a few words here and there. She could see immediately that grammar was definitely fractured. Vocabulary was so limited that confusion reigned. But the textbook was clearly structured. Gina could see that the lesson plan could eventually give the students a sufficient working knowledge of English that they could participate in regular English-speaking classes. But the patience that it would take to get them there! Patience, she thought, on the part of both student and instructor.

She noted that there were heavy homework assignments and that students were graded regularly. This obviously allowed them keep track of their progress and helped maintain structure within the class. Miss too many assignments, score too low on the assignments, and you were out. The teaching assistants, she could see, were there to help answer individual questions, do a little tutoring when possible, and grade papers between classes.

At the end of the session Gina thanked the instructor for allowing her to attend the class and left the building. She pulled her jacket tight against the chilly, damp night air and walked to the bus stop, where she caught a city bus back to North Beach. She did a lot of thinking on the way home. Teaching, or helping to teach this type of class, would be a real challenge for her and very draining. She had not studied English literature to deal with foreign-born students who didn't understand the language or have an appreciation for English or American history and literature. This was another world entirely. She couldn't help but wonder if entering it would take her down a new and different path or be a step toward the original goal she had chosen when she started graduate school.

In the middle of that night, Gina awakened abruptly. She was bathed in sweat and her heart was pounding wildly. She had just been dreaming that she was in Eureka, walking along the beach with Valerie and Sam. They were laughing and enjoying each other's company on a beautiful sunny day when suddenly Gina felt her body tingling. In an impulse too strong to resist, she turned toward Val, reached out and grabbed her, and kissed her intensely and deeply. Valerie relaxed into her embrace and responded to it. At that point Gina woke up instantly.

She lay there for a long time immersed in this dream, which came on the heels of her visit to the ESL class. One explanation for the dream was that her mind was looking for a way out of the difficulties she would face learning to be an effective assistant in one of these classes. If it's too hard here in San Francisco, escape to something more familiar and comforting in Eureka. *Right*, she mumbled to herself.

But there were other possibilities. What if she was connecting with something deep inside her that should not be ignored? Something that dealt with Val and her feelings for her.

As she often did when confused, Gina turned on the light beside her bed and grabbed a notebook that she kept nearby. Her therapist had encouraged her to keep a journal of her thoughts and feelings, since therapy wouldn't always be available to her. And although she had questions about Dr. Reitman's therapeutic approach, she had to admit that writing in her journal was often very useful. Gina opened to a blank page and made a list of her most important goals in life: satisfying career, financial responsibility, meaningful relationships, adventure and travel, and good health. But which one was—or should be—number one? Which one was truly the most important to her?

She spent a few moments mulling over her list and realized that there was no way she could come to a conclusion this night. She honestly didn't know what was most important. But by writing down her ideas, she would not forget them. With a deep sigh, she settled back down in bed and gradually drifted off to sleep.

At the beginning of the spring semester at City College, Gina felt both scared and excited after being hired to work as an assistant for an ESL class that met on Tuesday and Thursday evenings from 6:30 to 9:30 p.m. She had Tuesdays off at the bookstore, but she worked there on Thursdays. It would be difficult to eat and make bus connections in time for the class.

Thankfully, Mrs. Sanchez was sympathetic. She let Gina go an hour early on Thursdays and made it up by tacking an extra hour on another day—a temporary solution until she could shift work schedules. Gina felt that the manager helped her because she had been an enthusiastic, dedicated employee. She had heard the woman turn down a similar request from another worker who had been less diligent.

The next Tuesday, Gina reported to work at CCSF, arriving with the earliest students. At the front of the classroom stood a woman who took Gina's breath away. "Y'all take a seat," she roared to the incoming group. Gina almost sat down but realized she should introduce herself.

She walked up to the stocky, dark-haired woman and held out a hand. "I'm Gina Fortenham, your assistant."

The woman nodded rather curtly. "I'm Linda Sue Gibbons. Thanks, but for right now jis' sit down." She had a strong Southern accent and was obviously used to giving orders.

Gina did as told, blushing in the process, and then tried to figure out who this person was. Linda Sue Gibbins introduced herself to the class and, as Gina watched her and learned that she went by the handle "Rowdy," she realized that Linda Sue was—*surprise*—a lesbian of what Gina would call the "dyke variety."

Linda Sue appeared before her class dressed in black denim and cowboy boots. She had short cropped hair, and wore no makeup. A scar ran the length of her face on the right side just in front of her ear. She paced, sometimes exposing the scar prominently or turning her face to the other side to hide it. She reeked of cigarette smoke, which Gina could smell from her seat in the second row.

Her classroom strength was that Linda Sue could negotiate four or five foreign languages, at least verbally, and at least well enough to help her students understand what she was trying to assist them in saying or writing in English. She came across as very tough and seemed to be able to handle just about anything that could happen in the classroom.

Gina didn't feel comfortable around "Rowdy," mostly because of her tough appearance, but she soon learned to respect her teaching ability. "Rowdy" could take care of herself and got things done.

After the first class was over, Linda Sue motioned Gina to approach. "Let's go git some coffee," she said. It wasn't an invitation or a request. It was a direct order.

Gina started to refuse, to say that she had to catch a bus and get home, but she thought better of it. If she had to work with this woman, she should at least attempt to get along with her. And try to understand her.

Linda Sue led the way on foot to a small 24-hour coffee shop with outdoor seating near the classroom building, picked out a table and motioned Gina to sit while she ordered some coffee. Gina shivered. She felt really uncomfortable in the tow of this very strong woman, but she pulled her down jacket close and sat obediently while Linda Sue ordered two coffees at the counter, along with Danish rolls. The night air was cold. Why did Linda Sue want to sit outside?

Linda Sue brought the coffee and the pastries back to the table and put Gina's in front of her. Not being a coffee drinker, Gina looked apprehensively at the steaming paper cup. The Danish was fine, although she was not terribly hungry. She picked at the pastry, while Linda Sue downed her hot coffee as if she hadn't had a sip of liquid in months.

"What's the matter with the coffee?" Linda Sue barked, when she had finished drinking and put her cup down.

"I'm not a coffee drinker," Gina confessed. "At this time of the day, I would have to go with herbal tea or I'd be up all night."

Linda Sue laughed suggestively. "That wouldn't be a bad thing, would it?" Gina frowned, and Linda Sue tapped her on the arm. "But seriously, why didn't y'all say so?"

Before she could utter a reply, Linda Sue jumped up and ordered a cup of herbal tea for her. Moments later, the hot tea was before her, and Gina began sipping it. "Thanks," she offered. The tea helped keep her warm.

"Y'all's welcome. No biggie." Linda Sue pulled out her cigarettes and offered Gina one. When Gina declined, "Rowdy" lit her own cigarette and inhaled deeply. She was considerate enough to turn away when she exhaled. So that was why they had to sit outside freezing, Gina thought. Infernal cigarettes!

Linda Sue studied Gina. while she ate. "Y'all's a lesbian, right?"

Gina looked around the area. She still wasn't used to such open discussion among strangers, and there *were* other souls braving the evening chill. She finally nodded.

"But y'all's not from here, right?"

Gina shook her head. "Illinois, with grad school in Arizona. I've been in Eureka the last year. I just got to the City a few weeks ago."

"What are y'all doing in this ESL class?"

"I'm looking for a college teaching job in English lit, and this has been the first thing I could come up with that moves me in that direction."

Linda Sue grunted and puffed on her cigarette. "Y'all in a relationship?"

Gina blushed, increasingly uncomfortable with this very pointed conversation. "Well, there's someone I care about but, no, I'm not officially in a relationship," she admitted, surprising herself by the confession. *Where did that come from?*

Linda Sue nodded. "Y'all been to The Castro yet?"

"I've been through the district on a bus, but I haven't been there to go to a bar or a club or anything."

Linda Sue laughed. "Greenhorn, huh?"

Gina wanted to turn the conversation around. She took a deep breath and asked, "Where are you from? You sound a bit Southern."

Linda Sue smiled at Gina, took a puff, kept silent for a moment, and then decided to answer. "Texas, originally. Been lots of places, picked up a little here an' a little there. Been in 'Frisco for four years, tryin' to git through school. I do this ESL stuff to pay for my tuition. ESL don't take a lot of formal education, because y'all dealin' with such basic English, but it takes guts and tons of patience. I got the guts for it. The patience I'm workin' on." She leaned close to Gina and spoke conspiratorially. "Some o' these folks ain't gonna make it in academia, if y'all git my drift."

"What's your major?" Gina asked, knowing fully well that literature would not be Linda Sue's field.

"Women's studies," the Texan said. She grinned. "I was raised pretty much as a boy on the ranch. I'm tryin' to git a handle on what all this women's issues stuff is all about. I never thought much about myself as a woman, but I guess I am one."

Gina studied her for a moment. "So," she observed, "if you were raised like a boy, you got to do whatever you wanted—just like a boy would. And you don't know what it's like to be told you can't have something or do something because you're a woman?"

Linda Sue laughed uproariously. "Yep, li'l one. Y'all got it. Bein' an oppressed female is outside my life experience."

Gina studied her teacup and nodded. Without further comment, she finished her drink and looked at her watch. It was getting really late. She thanked Linda Sue for the tea and Danish and told her that she needed to catch the next bus. Linda Sue offered to walk her to the bus stop and this offer Gina accepted willingly. She had noticed that this wasn't the best of neighborhoods, especially after dark. Linda Sue walked beside her and stood by her at the corner until the bus came along. Then she waved goodbye as Gina climbed on board.

Gina took a seat on the almost empty bus and thought about her encounter with Linda Sue. She found it hard to think of her as "Rowdy." She shivered. What a strange woman—but someone who could teach her a lot about survival here, as long as she could set firm boundaries. Gina was not an expert on sexual harassment in the workplace, but she suspected that whatever the rules were, Linda Sue would push the edge of the envelope at any time it suited her.

As Gina had anticipated, the ESL classes were tough. She had to concentrate really hard to understand individual questions from the students, who spoke in heavily-accented halting English and often reverted to their native tongue when they got confused. Since Gina couldn't understand them at all in their own language, she had to find a way to steer them back to English. It wasn't easy. And grading their papers was a real pain. Interpreting handwriting that had been learned in another country was difficult at best. She began to think the instructors had the best part of it and the assistants the worst. She had to smile because even *she* knew that such a reality was often the norm in the public workplace and in the academic world as well.

Linda Sue continued to impress Gina as a good instructor—colorful, expressive, down-to-earth, humorous, and somehow able to bridge the gap between English and the many other languages represented in the class. Gina doubted she could ever become that effective in the classroom, and watching Linda Sue at work made her question whether teaching was really her destiny. Gina was so much the quiet intellectual, and getting up in front of a group of people would always be hard for her. She tentatively concluded, as she watched Linda Sue artfully handle the class, that she was more the writer/researcher type than someone to take center stage at the front of a classroom.

At night, in her room, she tossed and turned in bed, processing what she was learning and thinking about what she wanted from life. What *were* her real priorities? She had always put a career in education at the top of her list. Personal relationships were always at the bottom, below adventure, travel, and enough money to keep the bills paid. Was this honestly her? Had education been so important because life was hard on the farm and she saw her mother, a teacher, presenting the only ticket out through higher education? Did she put relationships at the bottom because she had been confused about her sexual identity and avoiding relationships had been easier than figuring out who she really was?

What a paradox. Sometimes she felt she was in a maze, looking for the way through or the way out.

The Beetle needed to run, so Gina backed it out of the garage. Thankfully, the car started right away. She gassed it up, got a cheap car wash, and then drove to Golden Gate Park. Although it was officially winter, San Francisco was having a summer-like day. There was a mild breeze off the ocean. She had learned that 'Frisco could have any climate on any given day. Planning ahead was sometimes difficult because it rained when sun was expected and it got hot when it should be cold. And unlike other places where she had lived, 75 degrees in the City could be *very* hot. The only somewhat predictable element was early morning fog, and that gave no clue as to what the rest of the day would be like.

When she reached the park, she found a place to stash the car and walked for miles, stopping at the museums, the Japanese gardens, and Spreckles Lake. As a woman alone, she knew enough to be careful. She watched for anyone who followed too closely or who was loitering or paying unusual attention to her.

The sun broke through tall eucalyptus trees as she passed onto an open grassy area where a young man was playing Frisbee with his dog. Then she noticed a woman running with a yellow Lab. Her breath caught as her imagination turned them into Valerie and Samantha trotting along the Eureka waterfront. Her eyes misted over and for a moment she felt deeply saddened. Had she done the wrong thing—leaving Valerie and Sam and all their friends, and even Eureka, to chase this dream in San Francisco?

Gina needed to shake off this heavy feeling. She allowed her memories to inspire her and her body responded. She took off on a run, pushing herself for a quarter of a mile. She was out of shape and she was soon winded. Every muscle in her body began to vibrate and complain, but she felt so good that she decided she would keep running every day. Her lungs needed the air. Her muscles needed the workout. Her psyche needed the lift.

After her sprint, the sad mood passed. As Gina continued to explore Golden Gate Park that afternoon, she realized again just how much she adored San Francisco. It was as beautiful as she had dreamed it would be, and she was very glad that she was able to experience the City. And her full time job was satisfying. She had decided to stay with Mrs. Han for a while, because keeping her expenses down allowed her to do so much more. She could go to the movies, shop for clothes, and occasionally attend the opera and the ballet—an awesome experience, even if she had to sit in the last row of the balcony.

And for the first time ever, Gina was able to put a few dollars from each paycheck into a savings account for her future. She had money in her pocket to spend any way she wanted. Compared to the tight times during her childhood on the farm, her frugal college years, and the desperate post-graduate period of therapy, she was free and, by comparison, wealthy. At times she felt almost giddy at her freedom.

Yet her time in Eureka had changed something inside her. San Francisco had always seemed an endpoint—she would get there and she'd be home. Now she was questioning that. Was San Francisco really the end for her, or could there be another adventure along the way? Would she always want to be here? Standing in the middle of beautiful Golden Gate Park, she knew she was happy to be in this place today—and yet she didn't know about tomorrow.

Chapter Thirteen

The Nun's Habit—a dark, dirty bar in the Castro District—more than lived up to its name. Mostly a women's hangout, the venue was populated by a loud band, Sapho's Sibs, and wall-to-wall sweaty female bodies gyrating on the dance floor. The women's restroom reeked of marijuana.

Gina had come there with Linda Sue—she still had trouble with the "Rowdy" moniker—because Linda Sue had asked her if she wanted to explore The Castro. Gina once had been to a gay bookstore in the area and to a lesbian writers' support-group meeting that seemed to function more as a pick-up spot, but she hadn't been to the bars. Her natural curiosity led her to accept Linda Sue's offer.

Gina dressed in her best jeans, a silk top, and a sweater for the occasion. Linda Sue wore her usual black denims and cowboy boots, with a leather-trimmed vest topping a Western shirt. The two sat at a small table in a back corner and both ordered a beer. Linda Sue opted for lager, Gina for "lite." Talking to each other was difficult over the band's loud amp, heavy guitar, bass, and percussion. Gina sipped her beer and hoped for an intermission. Shortly, Linda Sue excused herself to step outside for a smoke.

While she was alone at their table, Gina surveyed the dingy room and began wondering what she was doing in this filthy place. She remembered the Purple Priscilla: Rick, his friends, the lesbians she met there, and, of course, dancing with Val. Gina had liked the little Arcata spot a lot better. This one was grimy without even that stupid purple trim to give it some style. She smiled to herself and shook her head. *Why had she ever left Eureka?*

Just as Linda Sue returned, Sapho's Sibs announced a short break. There was polite applause and the dancers headed for their seats. Gina was grateful for the relative quiet.

Linda Sue leaned back in her chair and studied Gina, who continued to watch the activity around her and check out the variously attired women—some in blue denim, some in black leather, one in a red turtleneck and black jeans. They obviously came from very diverse backgrounds, but predominant among them was a look of hardness that Gina had not previously experienced.

Trying to divert her attention, Linda Sue asked, "Now that y'all been in the classroom a few weeks, how are you feelin'? Gettin' the hang of it?"

Gina pulled her focus back to the table and studied her beer a moment. Then she looked up at Linda Sue. "It's better," she admitted, "although it is difficult for me and I'm glad I'm not depending on this to make a living. Two nights a week is about all I can handle."

Linda Sue took a long pull on her lager. "Well," she observed wryly, "this ain't what y'all set out to do anyway, and besides y'all got a full-time job as well."

"True."

"Y'all gonna stick with it?"

"I think so—well, I'm... I'm not sure." Gina stumbled over her words. "I mean, if this leads to a real teaching job, even at night in a regular English class, yeah, I think so, but if I have to do ESL forever, I don't know."

"What about it don't y'all like?"

"Well, you're right. This isn't exactly what I studied to do. I was picturing a college classroom with some bright students analyzing Shakespeare or John Donne or Virginia Woolf, you know?"

Linda Sue smiled. "Yeah, I git it. But urban America jus' ain't about that anymore. It's about survivin' in shiftin' sand. It's so easy to git swallowed up. Illegal immigrants, street drugs, identity theft.

"It's not pretty anymore, if it ever really was," she added.

Gina agreed. "I do see that and I am trying to decide whether my fascination with big city life is enough to build a future here. Underneath it all, I am a Midwestern farm girl and I have personal values that may not fit in this world."

Before Linda Sue could answer, a server appeared at their table to ask if they wanted another beer. Linda Sue nodded but Gina declined. Before the server could say anything about the bar's two-drink minimum, Linda Sue jumped in, "Bring two beers. I'll drink hers, if she don't want it." When the server moved on, Linda Sue smiled at Gina. "These places always got a cover or a minimum. It's just easier to go along with the program than make a fuss."

Gina nodded. A slight smile crossed her lips. "Sorry. Just write it off to 'small-town girl in the big city.'"

Just then the band members returned and began a new set. Softer music this time, with "You're The Wind Beneath My Wings."

Linda Sue stood up. "Would y'all like to dance?" she asked, bowing formally.

Gina wasn't sure she wanted to dance, but she felt compelled by Linda Sue's request. She rose gallantly and allowed Linda Sue to lead her onto the dance floor. Gina was considerably taller than the Texan, who was powerfully built but slightly below medium height. The music encouraged close dancing and Linda Sue pulled Gina tight to her. Gina could feel her muscular body through her Western attire, but what she smelled most was cigarette smoke. Not a turn on for her. She thought again of dancing with Valerie.

The number ended and the band moved into a faster, highly percussive range that encouraged self-expression. This allowed Gina to relax a bit, given that she wasn't attracted to Linda Sue. The two moved in rhythm to the music, but about two feet apart.

They soon returned to their table, and Linda Sue held out a chair for Gina. "Thanks," Gina said, as she flopped down. She had found some new muscles that hadn't recently been stretched.

Linda Sue slid into her chair. "Y'all're pretty, you know," she commented suggestively.

Gina was taken aback. Was this a sexual approach? "Well, thanks. I don't usually think much about that," she replied, "but if you think so, then I'm glad." She tried to keep it light.

Linda Sue put a hand on her arm. "I'd love to take y'all to bed," she said bluntly.

Gina swallowed. This was her work supervisor and she was technically Linda Sue's employee. Gina didn't welcome this intimate suggestion at all. She had agreed to come as a friend—for fun, but not as a real date. Hadn't she made that clear? Had she been naïve? Now she faced the challenge of talking Linda Sue out of whatever she was attempting to engineer.

"Interesting idea, but then what?"

"What do y'all mean, 'then what?'"

"If you're proposing that we build a relationship together, then bed isn't the place to start, at least for me. If you are looking for a one-night stand, I don't do that anymore. I did that in Tucson, when I first came out. I don't now," Gina said.

"Y'all opposed to just havin' fun?"

"I think you can have fun—and a relationship—with the same person."

Linda Sue contemplated that one. "I see," she said finally. "So if I wanna bed y'all, I hafta court y'all first."

"Something like that. And I may have to change jobs or supervisors, first," Gina responded.

Linda Sue studied her silently, her brow furrowed, and took a few sips of her lager. "Okay, y'all sure know how to stand y'all's ground," she admitted. "But no harm in tryin'? Right?" Her face relaxed into a smile as she apparently gave up the quest.

Gina nodded. "No harm."

They danced a few more numbers, but Linda Sue seemed to have lost some of her steam and she was quiet at the table. Soon Gina made it clear that she needed to leave and they walked out of the bar. Linda Sue's pick-up truck was parked down the street and they headed for it. Linda Sue held the passenger door open for Gina.

When Gina got out of the truck back at Mrs. Han's house in North Beach, Linda Sue left the engine running, glanced up and down the street, and then climbed out to walk Gina to the door.

"I had a nice time," Gina said. "I'm sorry if the evening didn't go the way you had imagined."

Linda Sue shrugged. "It's okay. I had a good time, too." She suddenly reached up and kissed Gina on the cheek, then turned to go back to her truck.

Despite herself, Gina smiled after her.

She stayed up late that night writing in her journal. In retrospect, it had been fun to go to a women's bar in The Castro—to see how it compared to the little places she had been to in Tucson and the Purple Priscilla in Arcata. Being with all those women at the Nun's Habit was a turn on to her body, and she was having a hard time getting calmed down. But she was clear that it wasn't Linda Sue who excited her—more like memories of Valerie and of what Gina had felt then. And what, it was now becoming more and more clear, she still felt for Val.

Gina and Linda Sue had nothing in common, beyond being lesbians who lived in San Francisco and who shared an ESL class. Gina had never thought of being attracted to a "type," as some women said they were, but if subconsciously she had a type it wasn't the type Linda Sue was. Maybe it was because they were both "masculine," even though Gina's masculinity was much less pronounced. She had grown up on the farm, she was in touch with her male side, her physical outdoor side, and she liked taking charge, regardless of the psychological problems she had experienced in Arizona. Being with a woman who outdid her in that way, who was almost more male than female, didn't satisfy her. Didn't turn her on. She wanted a woman, not a man. Valerie had numerous strengths, if Gina compared masculine to being strong. But at the same time Val was very feminine, maternal, and soft, with all kinds of personality traits that were attractive to Gina.

She put her journal aside and turned out the light. As she pulled up the covers, she touched herself and felt the wetness between her legs. No sleeping without some release, she knew. So she stroked herself until she came to a climax and then lay sweating in the dark, wondering what in the world she was going to do.

Gina had hoped that Linda Sue would take the hint and leave her alone, but the Texan was one of those people who just didn't give up. During the rest of the school semester she catered to Gina, doing everything she could to make her class experience more positive. She also wore a light perfume that Gina noticed every time they were together, and her clothes no longer reeked of cigarettes. While Gina appreciated Linda Sue's thoughtfulness and persistence, she also knew that there never would be anything more than a mild, essentially professional working relationship between them.

During her few evenings at home, Gina sent e-mails to her friends in Eureka and kept up on all their activities. Rick was her most constant correspondent, asking about San Francisco, the gay scene, and how she was doing. One message gave her pause for thought:

"*Your friends came to the Purple Priscilla the other night. They took a table and mostly talked and had drinks while they were there. I went up to say hello, and your former landlady remembered me. She said something about it being their poker night. I didn't quite get that but you would, I think. She introduced me to the others. I don't remember all their names, but they seemed nice. I got a kick out of the one with the big eyebrows. She kept wiggling them* at me. What a clown. Later on in the evening I saw Valerie right?—and the short one—Lanie, I think she said—out on the dance floor. They were making some good moves out there. I let it go after a while, because it just made me miss you and our fun talks and evenings at the bar."

Rick's message made it clear that he was lonely. It wasn't so much Gina that he missed, she felt sure of that, but someone special to be with, someone to talk to. She wished he could really get over his former lover and open himself up to a new relationship. Well, she admitted with a sigh, she couldn't solve that one.

Messages from Val's gang included news that Josie had made it into the landscape-design program at Humboldt State. Gina felt happy for her. Judee had made the honor roll, despite her home responsibilities and her two active boys. Lanie had been realtor of the month at her firm and was selling more and bigger houses. It appeared that she was now quite successful in real estate.

Judee had told her about Lanie's award and had also sent a detailed message about Lanie's 49th birthday party:

"Lanie walked around for weeks looking like death warmed over, so we decided to push it to the limit. We got a big cake with black icing. Valerie painted a picture of a casket with huge candles standing at each end and a woman in black in the casket, sitting up and screaming. I was surprised that Val had that much humor in her. She's often so serious, especially about her painting. We all met at Val's house, dressed in black from head to toe. When Lanie arrived at the front door, we greeted her with a funeral dirge playing in the background. We gave her our condolences and told her she had at least a year to live. After she saw the cake and the painting, she finally cracked up. Laughed her head off. Got into the spirit, and then we had some drinks and a good time. I think she'll be okay now."

Judee had added a personal aside that now that Lanie was doing so well she probably would make a play for Valerie. And Val, she had just heard from Josie, had sold several paintings and quit her job in the photography studio to devote full time to her art. She also had income from two roomers. Gina was happy to hear that Valerie was doing well, but she had a strange churning sensation in her belly when she thought of Lanie and Val dating. "Well, silly girl," she said to herself out loud, "you walked away from her and she deserves someone to love her. Lanie's a good friend. Val could do worse." Unfortunately, lecturing herself did not make the churning go away.

A message came from Lanie a few days later that highlighted another change among her friends in Eureka.

"Josie has been getting some additional bills left over from her hospitalization and therapy for her leg. She has been overwhelmed and came to poker night a few days ago saying that she was going to have to quit school and get a second job to pay the bills.

"After she made this announcement, Judee contacted her and invited her to move in with her and the boys. Apparently her ex, Wayne, left empty space in the house when he moved out. Judee had been busy with school and hadn't taken the time to redecorate. She suggested that Josie could turn Wayne's former office into another bedroom for herself. The boys would still have their own room, Judee would have the master suite, which was large enough for her own computer desk and supplies. With only one car in the two-car garage, there was plenty of room there and in the driveway for Josie's truck and her landscaping supplies, which included an open trailer. If Josie could pay a little toward utilities and food and help occasionally with the boys, then Judee would not charge any rent. And the two women could carpool some of the time to Humboldt State and save gas money.

"I heard that Josie nearly cried over this offer. At first she worried about leaving Sarah Green holding the bag on their apartment. But it turned out that Sarah was dating and was about to tell Josie that she was moving out. So the change worked perfectly for both of them.

"I am so happy for Josie. Of all of us she seems the most in need of family, and Judee and the boys will provide that for her. She will contribute but she will be able to pursue her life and not have to give up her dreams. I think it's a great thing!"

Gina was very touched by this message. She realized more and more how fortunate she had been to have spent time in Eureka at Val's house and to have met these wonderful women who had made each other into lifelong friends.

When Gina thought that nothing else could happen, another provocative message came from Rick, who dropped a hint that there was going to be a change in management at the movie theater:

"I think the manager is going to get booted and the assistant manager will be promoted. That will leave a hole in the assistant-manager slot. I'd go for it myself, but I don't think I want to be in the movie business full time. But geez, there's benefits and everything. I couldn't entice you to come back, could I? Just kidding."

Gina spent the rest of that evening thinking for the umpteenth time about her priorities.

Chapter Fourteen

Gina was stooped over, shelving several new paperbacks in the philosophy section, when she suddenly sensed someone standing behind her. She quickly turned and found herself looking upward into the face of a lovely young American-Asian woman. Almond-shaped brown eyes, with a slight cast, peered out from under straight, dark bangs and a warm smile greeted Gina's surprised stare.

"Excuse me," a soft voice with a mild Asian accent murmured, "Could you help me find books by Virginia Woolf?"

Rising to her full height, Gina grinned. "Sure." She guided the patron to the literature section of the store, to shelves she knew quite well herself.

Pointing to a row of books just below eye level, Gina observed, "I think we have most of her works in either hardcover or paperback. Are you looking for anything in particular?"

The young woman smiled shyly. "I saw the movie *The Hours* and I was fascinated by the story of Virginia Woolf's life, so I wanted to read something by her. I hadn't heard of her before."

Gina could hardly contain her enthusiasm but, since this reader was new to Virginia Woolf, it would hardly do to start rattling off what she had learned in grad school. She stopped herself and tried to put herself in this person's place. "Well," she began, "*The Hours* was based on Woolf's most famous book, *Mrs. Dalloway*. That might be a good place for you to begin, to experience her writing style and her use of character and language. If you enjoy that one, you might move on to something less familiar to you."

The young woman tilted her head slightly. "Thank you very much. I'll do that."

Gina handed her both the hardcover and paperback editions and the young woman chose the quality paperback, a better buy.

She nodded and smiled sweetly at Gina. "Thank you again for your help."

Gina watched her as she moved gracefully in the direction of the checkout counter. There was something special about this woman. Was it just the Asian influence? She was quite pretty, slender, of medium height, and tastefully dressed in dark brown slacks and a cream-colored sweater. Her English, Gina noted, while accented was impeccable and grammatically correct.

That one could be trouble, Gina thought to herself as she resumed shelving.

Four days later the young woman showed up at the store again. She sought out Gina. "I loved the book," she said enthusiastically. "Could you recommend another?"

Gina located another work by Virginia Woolf. Then the woman asked about the alternative-lifestyle section. Without comment, Gina led her to the gay, lesbian, bisexual, and transgender volumes. The store had several rows of books, but they were tucked away in a back corner.

"Thank you for helping me," the woman said and then stuck out a small, finely boned hand. "I am Kia Thompson. I was remiss the last time in not introducing myself."

Gina offered her hand and a warm smile. "I'm Gina, Gina Fortenham, and if I can be helpful at any time just let me know."

Kia thanked her and, as she turned to look at the lesbian books, Gina quickly returned to other tasks.

This ritual repeated itself for the next two weeks. Then Kia had a new request, having nothing to do with books. "Do you perhaps have time to meet me next door and have a cup of coffee or something?"

Gina was taken aback. "Well, uh, I do have a break coming up in the next half-hour. I guess I could meet you at the coffee shop then." She wasn't sure this was a wise idea. At the same time she was curious about this Kia Thompson, a stunner who was obviously drawn to her in some way.

By the time she checked out for her break, Kia had disappeared. Gina found her at a table next door at the coffee shop with a steaming cup already in front of her. Kia stood. "Would you like coffee, my treat? Or tea maybe?"

"Tea would be great," Gina admitted, remembering her first outing with Linda Sue. How nice to be asked.

Kia went to a counter and returned momentarily with a tray holding a cup of tea and a side bowl of lemons along with a packet of honey. "Thank you," Gina said gratefully. "I'll take the honey. I could use a little sugar fix about now."

There was silence between them for a long moment, as both focused a bit awkwardly on their beverages. Then Kia spoke. "I saw you at City College one evening, you know. I think you were assisting in a class. Then I was surprised to see you in the bookstore." She blushed. "I thought you looked interesting and I wanted a chance to meet you."

Gina felt both flattered and embarrassed. "Thank you for noticing. Sometimes I think I'm part of the wall."

"Oh, no. You are very attractive," Kia said, the pink blush spreading. "Just because you are kind of shy doesn't make you any less beautiful. Maybe more attractive."

Now it was Gina's turn to blush. *Ooh, this was making her a bit uncomfortable.* She tried to get the focus off herself. "You're attending City College?"

Kia nodded. "Yes, I'm studying English literature. I haven't been in this country for very long, so I had to start at City College. I am doing well now and I hope to transfer to Berkeley soon."

"Wow!" Gina raised an eyebrow. "Where are you from?"

"Well, my father is American but my mother is Vietnamese. I grew up in Vietnam with my mother. She wanted me to have more opportunities, so it was arranged for me to come here and live with my father—so I could go to school here."

Gina nodded. "When you graduate, will you go home?"

Kia sighed. "I hope not. I want to stay here. I like it in America. I like San Francisco. I feel free here, free to be who I am."

"Meaning?" Gina was almost afraid to hear the answer. *Then why did I ask?* she wondered to herself.

"I'm a lesbian. That is much easier here than in Vietnam."

Gina nodded noncommittally. *This was getting heavy.* "You know I appreciate the tea, but I need to get back to work. It was good talking with you." She stood and put out her hand.

Kia stared deeply into Gina's eyes. "Would you go out to dinner with me sometime?"

Gina almost gasped. "I—I don't know. I need to think about it. Stop by again in a day or so and I'll have an answer for you." She waved goodbye and turned quickly toward the bookstore.

The rest of the day Gina struggled to keep her mind on her work. She had been right from the beginning. This Kia could be real trouble. She had no real reason *not* to go out to dinner with her. Then why was she reluctant? Was she scared?

At the end of her shift, Gina punched her timecard and walked out the front door only to find Kia waiting for her outside. Gina almost freaked out. *This was too, too much.*

"Please excuse me," Kia entreated immediately. "But I wish to talk with you and I know no other way to do it except to go out to dinner. Will you please indulge me?"

Gina caved. "Okay. Tomorrow night I'm at City College, but Wednesday evening I could go out for a while after work. Can you meet me here or do you want me to meet you at a restaurant?"

"I'll be here on Wednesday. Same time as today?"

Gina nodded. "Yes, same as today."

Kia nodded then disappeared suddenly.

When Gina checked out from her shift two days later, Kia was waiting outside the bookstore. She led Gina to a nearby Asian restaurant with a dark interior and comfortable booths. The menu featured a variety of Asian foods. Gina was drawn to the Chinese dishes, which were more familiar to her, and Kia ordered for herself from the Vietnamese menu.

Once they had ordered Gina looked at Kia and asked, "You are surrounded by students at the college. Out of all the choices available to you for conversation and friendship, why did you pick me?"

Kia's cheeks colored as she stared at her silverware. Haltingly and uneasily she began. "Well, I think you are beautiful. I heard from a friend taking an ESL class that you have an advanced degree in English literature and I just wanted to get to know you."

Gina shrugged. "No, *you* are exotic. A really beautiful young woman. The best of two worlds, East and West. When I look in the mirror I see a Midwestern American hayseed. Nothing special. So it's hard for me to understand—"

Kia interrupted, "That I see beauty in you?"

Gina was rescued from her discomfort and Kia's uncustomary directness by the arrival of their dinner. They ate in silence for a minute or two. *This Kia was really in her face.* Not like Linda Sue, but in her face nevertheless. Kia was what—23 or 24 at the most—and Gina was pushing 35. Apart from both being lesbians and liking and studying English literature, what was their common ground? Yes, she found Kia attractive, she had to admit that, and Kia had hardly masked her own intentions. But pure attraction could only lead to a sexual fling, nothing more, and Gina had had her fill of those back in Arizona. She wasn't looking for another one, not with this attractive Kia any more than she had been with the not-so-attractive Linda Sue.

Gina and Kia were silent again as they sampled their dishes. Kia offered Gina a taste of a couple of the Vietnamese entrees, which she accepted and found enjoyable. They drank their tea while quietly, almost secretly, observing each other.

Gina finally broached the subject that most concerned her. "What is it that you really want?"

Kia gazed into her eyes. "To talk with you. To spend time with you. Maybe to touch you. And maybe to touch your heart."

Gina almost exploded. *This was much too much and way too fast.* "I think it's time I go home," she said, standing up.

"Wait," Kia begged. "Please don't go, not yet."

Gina struggled with herself. She was totally uncomfortable but Kia had done nothing really wrong, so she shouldn't create a scene. She sat back down. "Okay, we'll complete dinner—but then I'm going."

By the time they finished eating, including tapioca pearls in coconut milk for a light and unusual dessert, Gina had regained some sense of balance. Kia insisted on paying the bill and Gina allowed her to do so. After all, she had come at Kia's invitation.

Kia wanted to walk Gina home and, although she thought it a big mistake, Gina allowed it to happen. Inside she kept mumbling to herself, "I'm in way over my head here."

As they stopped at Mrs. Han's front doorstep, Kia surprised Gina by reaching up, holding her cheeks with both hands, and kissing her deeply, probingly. Then with a "See you," she was gone.

Gina did not get much sleep that night. She tossed and turned, thinking about Eureka and Valerie and the gang up there on the North Coast, her memories from Tucson, her encounters with Linda Sue, and what she wanted out of life. This interlude with Kia just didn't fit in anywhere. Yet Gina had come to San Francisco to be among lesbians and that inevitably invited the chance of a lesbian relationship. Now that the opportunity was right in front of her with someone really attractive, why was she fighting it so desperately?

If Kia would just go away that would settle things, wouldn't it?

But, of course, Kia did not go away. She showed up at City College, she showed up at the bookstore, she asked Gina out to a movie and, beaten down, Gina agreed to go. The movie, which Gina hadn't heard of, turned out to be a lesbian romance with lots of steamy sex scenes. Gina squirmed in her seat and thought she might scream at times, but she didn't.

Again they walked back to Mrs. Han's together and again Kia kissed her, just as passionately as before, and left without anything beyond "See you."

Gina went upstairs to face another sleepless night. This kid was getting to her.

After their third evening out together, Kia abruptly invited Gina back to her apartment a few streets away in another section of North Beach. Gina felt like a horse being broken by a persistent cowgirl. Her mind said no, but her body was saying something totally different and "unprintable" that she mumbled silently to herself.

Kia's place was dark and modern, with touches of Western leather furniture and Asian paintings and photographic art. Exotic, like Kia.

Gina was offered a glass of wine, but before more than a sip or two the kissing began. Undressing, touching, and exploring quickly followed, first on the sofa and then in the bedroom, where deep embraces and deeper kisses produced rising passion and a crashing climax.

Gina had never had a partner as intense as Kia and she had never experienced this much physical desire in herself. Her body throbbed, she shivered from chills not brought on by cold, she inhaled the sweet aroma of womanly flesh, and she thrilled at what she could feel—what they could do together, to each other.

When they were sated and lying side by side, their bodies glistening in moonlight from the nearby window, hands and fingers still stroking, Kia asked, "Did you like it?"

"Oh, yes," Gina confessed breathlessly.

"Do you like me?"

"Yes, yes I do." The words tumbled out. No stopping them.

"Good, because I like you—a lot."

Later that night, Gina lay in her own bed at Mrs. Han's and begged for sleep to overtake her. Her thoughts and the feelings and images of her encounter with Kia were all twisting and turning in her mind.

She was not sorry she had surrendered to Kia. Hopefully no harm was done, and perhaps a lot of good was done. If she still had any doubts about being a lesbian, she knew now for sure that she physically and emotionally wanted, loved, and desired women, not men. It couldn't be clearer.

What was not clear to her was how to fit Kia into a picture bigger than that single night. She was enthralled by the exotic in Kia, by her charisma and physical presence, but beyond the passion what could they have together?

Kia was young, very young, a student. While she wasn't Gina's student, she was still a student. She was different, from a different world. A huge gulf to be crossed for any long-term relationship. Five years from now would they be in the same place? Want the same things? Gina admittedly wasn't finished growing into herself either, but her life was certainly a few steps beyond Kia's. The encounter offered Gina a sense of validation, but she still knew that one-night stands were not her thing. She now felt ready to create a more permanent partnership, and she knew that was unlikely with this young partner. Kia had considerable growth and change ahead of her—first at Berkeley, then out in the world. Many experiences, many relationships perhaps, before a committed one.

Still Gina challenged herself. Maybe *she* was putting up walls. Maybe she wasn't allowing something beautiful to happen. Or maybe, on the other hand, her conflict had nothing to do with Kia, her age, or anything like that at all. Maybe Gina had already, unknowingly, given her heart to someone else. Perhaps only her body was available to Kia—not her mind, not her heart, or her soul. Gina lay in bed awake for hours, mulling over this possibility. And what, if anything, to do about it.

The next time Gina saw Kia she told her how she felt. Disappointed, Kia tried to hold back her tears but seemed to understand. She disappeared from Gina's life as suddenly as she had entered it.

Gina was leaving the bookstore after her shift. She said goodbye to Mrs. Sanchez, pulled her jacket close about her against a chilly breeze, and contemplated dinner at the nearby deli. The Jewish-run delicatessen had become her favorite spot to eat, even though she had to run several miles to work off the extra calories contained in those marvelous sandwiches. She was thankful that her job kept her on her feet most of the time.

She arrived at the deli to find Joel, her favorite counter man, on duty. He assembled her habitual sandwich: brisket of beef on Russian rye with lots of provolone cheese and a dill pickle. She grabbed some chips and a Diet Coke and sat by the front window to eat. It was a slow night, and she and Joel chatted about the San Francisco Giants and the current baseball season. Joel had a game playing on the TV mounted above the end of the counter.

When she had finished her meal, Gina waved to Joel and started down the street to Mrs. Han's row house. Just as she turned the next corner, two bodies bumped against her, slamming her against the wall of a building and down onto the pavement and grabbing her purse. The figures, both young men dressed in black, ran off down the street. She got up, feeling her split lip and the scraped skin near her eye. It was already starting to swell, and her eye would be black. She concluded that nothing was broken, although she was beginning to hurt all over. One wrist throbbed. She walked carefully back to the deli, where Joel called 911 for her and gave her some ice for her eye.

Two policemen, with a rather bored "we've-heard-this-all-before" look on their faces, arrived shortly, made some notes, took a description of her assailants, and said they'd try to find the thieves. "There's been several of these incidents in this neighborhood in the past few weeks," one of the officers acknowledged. "We think it's drug related, and we're trying to find these guys. So far, it's the money they're after, not a desire to hurt anyone." After she told them for the third time that she didn't need to go to a hospital, the cops shrugged, returned to their patrol car, and took off from the curb.

Gina sat for a little while with the ice pack against her swollen face. She was miserable but she knew she was lucky. She usually stuck her wallet in a deep pocket of her jacket, so it wasn't in her purse. They had gotten her favorite handbag. Fortunately it contained only a bottle of water, some snacks, her pill case—which held only aspirin and some antacids. But they had also gotten her journal and cell phone. Thank goodness, she thought to herself, she hadn't invested her funds in a "smart" phone that could have provided the thieves with considerable personal information. She'd call the phone company as soon as she got home. After she reported the loss, she'd be off the hook for any calls the thieves might make. But the journal was irreplaceable. Nothing in it identified anyone else, but it contained so many of her thoughts and feelings and ideas that could be the basis for stories someday. In shock, Gina began quietly crying over that loss.

Joel's replacement arrived and, after the two men tallied the register receipts for his shift, Joel offered to walk Gina home. She accepted, and the two made their way down the sidewalk toward Mrs. Han's row house. Gina was still shaking over the theft. She had always been careful, but she could never have known what this personal violation would feel like until it happened.

After she climbed painfully up the stairs to her room, she found the cell phone information and asked Mrs. Han if she could use her phone. Mrs. Han was most sympathetic over the attack on the street and bustled about bringing first-aid cream and bandages for Gina's face.

Later that evening, Gina rested uncomfortably in bed. The worst was over, she had to admit to herself, and the phone company would close her account immediately. She could get a new cell phone the next day, open a new account, and life would go on. Her face would look like hell for a week or so, and then it would heal. The purse could be replaced.

What could not be fixed was the way she was feeling—about the City, about her life here, about what was important to her. The attack could have happened in any city, including Eureka, and, by itself, wasn't the problem. Maybe it was time to face the real issues. Heaving a sigh, she climbed out of bed, opened her laptop, and wrote two letters: one to the movie theater in Eureka and one to the human-resources department at Humboldt State University.

A week later, Joel left a message with Mrs. Han that the police had been by the delicatessen trying to locate her. "They found your purse," he had said.

When Gina came home, she immediately got in touch with Joel and located the officer who had found her handbag. She had to go to a nearby police substation to pick it up. "The thieves were disappointed when there was no money in the purse," the duty officer told her. "They just tossed it a few blocks away. They did take the cell phone, but otherwise I think you'll find everything you reported missing."

She took the somewhat battered purse and held it tightly, thanking the policeman.

When she arrived back home, she thumbed through her journal. It seemed intact, and she was very relieved to have her personal thoughts and writing back again. The thieves had not stolen her words.

The semester was over, and Gina felt some sense of accomplishment at seeing how many of the ESL students were more proficient in English at the end of the class than they were at the beginning. She had really enjoyed watching several of them grow and hoped they would do well in their studies and continue their acculturation into American society. At the last class meeting, Linda Sue threw a little party, with punch and cookies, and they all congratulated each other. Several students came up to Gina and told her in their halting, but improved, English how grateful they were for her help during the semester. She appreciated the acknowledgment and thanked them and wished them all well.

Three weeks before the end of the semester, Linda Sue had allowed—"ordered" would probably be a more accurate word—Gina to teach a session. The class had gone reasonably well, and Gina was proud of herself for standing before the students and for successfully, while struggling at times, following the syllabus. She wouldn't give herself an A+, but she had faced the classroom and survived. So had the students.

After the last class and the party, Linda Sue invited Gina to coffee. She said that she had something important to share. Gina accepted the invitation, hoping this wasn't yet another attempt at a personal relationship.

The two nibbled on some biscotti, and Gina drank herbal tea while Linda Sue downed a large cup of decaf coffee. They joked about the semester and some of the funny language miscues that had happened along the way.

"The reason I asked y'all to come," Linda Sue finally said with some seriousness, "aside from the pleasure of y'all's company, is to let y'all know that I recommended y'all for a teachin' assignment in the ESL program. A class of y'all's own, with more pay and y'all's own assistant to do the scutt work, 'scuse my English."

Gina was taken aback. "I don't know what to say—"

Linda Sue stopped her. "Y'all done a good job supportin' me, and it's the least I can do in return. Y'all're very well educated, and y'all should be doin' more than gradin' papers for someone less well prepared."

"I can't begin to teach the way you do. Are you sure I'm ready for more responsibility?" Gina asked.

"Y'all handled the students well and they ain't that easy. Y'all seen me teach, and y'all handled a session on y'all's own. I'm sure y'all would do a good job as a teacher," Linda Sue explained. "And once y'all become an instructor, we'll be on the same footing professionally and—"

Gina could see where she was headed. "There's only one problem," Gina said. "I'm not sure I'll be here in the fall."

Linda Sue played with her coffee cup. She allowed herself a deep sigh. "I ain't surprised somehow," she murmured. "Goin' back to Eureka?"

Gina shrugged. "I'm not sure. Possibly." She put her hand on Linda Sue's arm. "But you've been really nice and fair with me, and I might need that recommendation here or somewhere else down the road. I'd very much appreciate it."

"Well, since y'all ain't as hard to read as y'all think," Linda Sue said, "I brought a copy of my letter. Another copy is in y'all's file at City College. This may help y'all, wherever y'all end up." She pulled a folder out of her briefcase and handed it to Gina.

Gina glanced at the brief letter the folder contained. Linda Sue had written it intelligently, but she had outlined qualities that Gina hadn't recognized in herself and found difficult to believe. "This is overwhelming," she admitted.

"It's deserved, little one, believe me. I'm a bit disappointed that we ain't gotten to know one another better in the way I might like, but I gotta respect y'all. Y'all're ethical. Y'all know where the limits are. So many people, includin' lots of lesbians I know, ain't got a clue what the word 'boundary' means."

Gina could feel her cheeks burning. "Thanks," she said, "I really appreciate this."

"Y'all're welcome. If y'all have a change of mind, I'm around. I ain't goin' nowhere anytime soon," Linda Sue said, taking Gina's hand as gently as her tough persona would allow.

Gina leaned over and planted a light kiss on Linda Sue's forehead. "I won't forget you," she said.

It was time to go. Gina tucked the letter away in her new purse, which would forever remind her of the robbery a few weeks back, and walked with Linda Sue to the bus stop. There they said a final goodbye.

Chapter Fifteen

Spattered by flecks of green paint, Valerie was poised to lay brush to canvas one summer morning when the front doorbell rang. She wondered who that could be. None of her friends ever rang the doorbell. They just walked in. Her latest roomer, a female college student, was away for the weekend with her boyfriend. Val put down her paintbrush. She wiped her hands on a towel and ran a hand through her hair. Decided to let her smock be. Accompanied by Sam—who suddenly seemed agitated—she walked to the front door.

Opening it, Val was shocked to see Gina standing there, neatly dressed in tan slacks, a white shell top, and a suede leather jacket. Her light-brown hair had been cut in an appealing pageboy, and she wore stunning sunglasses. In her hand was a bouquet of crimson roses.

Flabbergasted, Valerie froze on the spot, but Sam dashed through the doorway and jumped up on Gina, licking her face before she could defend herself. Gina just laughed and petted the dog with her free hand while she kept her eyes focused directly on Val.

"Wow," Val gasped, finally finding her voice. "Gina. What a surprise! Uh, come in."

"Thanks," Gina said, stepping across the threshold into the house where she had once lived. "I brought you these," she added, handing the bouquet to Valerie. "I'd like to say they came from San Francisco but, truth is, they would have wilted in the heat during the long trip up. My Beetle's air conditioning isn't very reliable. So these came from a little shop near the Boardwalk here in Eureka." She slid her sunglasses back on her head.

"I don't know what to say," Valerie sputtered. She accepted the flowers and sniffed their fragrance as she tried to recover her emotional balance. "I have the perfect vase for these. Come into the kitchen while I find it."

She headed through the dining room. Gina followed with Sam on her heels.

"What has happened to you? Are you visiting for the weekend or what?" Valerie asked, still flustered. Her heart had begun pounding the moment her hazel eyes met Gina's deep blue ones.

Gina just smiled. "When you can sit down for a moment, I'll tell you all about it."

Valerie found a vase and put the flowers in the middle of the dining room table. "I've been painting and I'm a mess," she stammered nervously. She slipped out of her smock, under which she wore jeans and a short-sleeve T-shirt. She motioned Gina toward the living room, where the two of them collapsed into the leather recliners.

Gina was quiet for a moment. They stared at each other, both with hesitant smiles.

Valerie finally couldn't stand the silence and demanded, "So tell!"

"Well," Gina began, suppressing a grin. "I'm back. I start Monday as assistant manager at the movie complex where I used to work. That's full time, with benefits. And I've got an interview at Humboldt State for a part-time teaching position for an evening class. I have an apartment here in Eureka."

She paused, as Valerie stared unbelieving. Gina looked so different, so well put together. Her eyes were even deeper blue and even more intense than Val had remembered.

Gina finally spoke again. "And I'm here to ask you out to dinner. Tonight, tomorrow, whenever you are free." She paused for a second and then added, "As a date."

Valerie was totally confused. "What happened to San Francisco?"

Gina shook her head. "That's as much as I'm telling you now. If you decide to risk going out with me, at dinner I'll tell you the rest," she promised.

After a moment of absolute silence, Gina stood up. A grin now crept across her face. "You may need time to think, because I know you've long since written me out of your life. But I've put my address and phone number down on this card. If you decide to, give me a call. Okay?"

Before Valerie could gather her wits, Gina had patted Sam on the head and slipped out the front door. Val sat for a long time in her chair and studied the card—the handwriting on it was familiar, but the person she had just seen seemed so radically different from the Gina she had known a year ago.

Valerie drove north on the 101 with Sam at her side, as she always did in good times and bad and whenever she wanted to sort things out. She had planned to go back to work on her painting but her mind wouldn't focus. All she could think about was Gina's sudden appearance on her doorstep. So she had abandoned the studio and driven up the 101 to Trinidad State Beach. She needed a long, long walk.

Eventually, physically and mentally wiped out, she sat down on a large rock and pulled Sam close to her. "What are we going to do, girl?" she asked.

Val was utterly shocked. She had been so careful not to communicate with Gina. She had literally forced herself to take only a mild interest in the letters and cards she received from San Francisco or news of Gina that her friends had shared with her. At first she felt sad and only harbored a touch of bitterness. Gina had been a very meaningful part of her life. But she had left and gradually Val had let go of even that. Gina had gone to the Bay Area and, as far as Valerie was concerned, she had gone permanently. After a few months passed, Val had opened herself up to Lanie's increasing attention. The two had gone out to dinner and movies and had started to take long walks together. Nothing physical yet—about that Val was very cautious—but in time sexual intimacy might come. She had accepted that possibility.

Now Gina was back. And this new Gina was coming on like gangbusters, with a job lined up, her own place, flowers in her hand, and a dinner invitation.

But did Valerie *want* her back in Eureka? Was her return a good thing, or was Val better off without Gina in her life? Had she been relieved, when all was said and done, that Gina had gone on with her own life and lived and worked down the highway in San Francisco? Was Val relieved that Gina wasn't around to tempt her, consciously or unconsciously, into some kind of more committed attachment? Or a sexual involvement? Maybe it would have been better for her if Gina had stayed in 'Frisco and never returned to Eureka?

And was this sudden appearance just another tug at her heartstrings? Would Gina come for six months and then leave for somewhere else? Val certainly didn't want to play that sort of game.

On the other hand, Valerie asked herself if she was overreacting because of the pain she had felt over Doreen's death? Was she afraid to consider how much Gina had come to mean to her during that year—and might mean again, now or in the future?

A big part of her wanted to pretend that Gina hadn't come back so she could go on with her life as it had been until two hours ago. Was that possible? She sighed to herself, as she realized that she was probably—inevitably, perhaps—going to have to deal with Gina.

"Well, Sam, should I go to dinner with Gina or not?" she asked the dog.

Sam merely panted, licked Valerie's hand, and wagged her tail.

The restaurant overlooked the Pacific Ocean and was decorated in a nautical theme. Paintings and photographs of lighthouses hung on every wall, and small working models of lighthouses were positioned throughout the restaurant. Even the salt and peppershakers were shaped like lighthouses.

Gina had made a reservation at this very special restaurant along the coast south of Eureka. She and Valerie were now seated at a white, linen-covered table in a very private area just inside glass windows that overlooked a bluff and the water beyond. They could see the sailboats returning to Humboldt Bay after an afternoon on the ocean. Waves crashed on the rocks below and the sun was starting to dip toward the horizon.

Valerie had recovered from her initial shock at seeing Gina again and had agreed to join her for dinner. Like the poker player she was, Val had bet on only the next upturned card—in this case, dinner—nothing beyond that. That is, until she could hear what Gina had to say. Val was very nervous, but she *had* accepted the invitation.

Gina looked anxious as if she had a lot at stake in the conversation of this evening and perhaps many other evenings to follow. Valerie noticed that Gina had worn a sharp-looking outfit: white slacks and V-neck tee, with a navy bush jacket. Val wore tan, a color that accented her honey blonde hair and hazel eyes.

The two decided to share a bottle of merlot, which they sipped slowly while stealing glances at each other and then quickly averting their eyes to stare at the ocean. A server appeared and they placed their order, for grilled fish to be shared. Conversation was clearly difficult.

Finally Valerie took a deep breath and demanded, "You promised to tell me more, and I'm here. I can't stand it any longer, so tell me!"

Gina chuckled with surprise at Val's unexpected vehemence. "Okay, I'll talk. But I don't know where to start."

"Tell me about San Francisco! What happened there that caused you to come back here?"

"Well, I loved San Francisco," Gina began, her blue eyes sparkling.

"It was everything I had ever dreamed it would be. But while I was there—working in a bookstore, and assisting in teaching an English class for non-English speaking students two nights a week—I had a lot of time to think. I had time to consider things, put them in perspective." She paused and played with her silverware, as if trying to find the right words.

"I guess," she finally continued, "I did a lot of growing up there. I didn't have parents to tell me what to do, or teachers, or therapists, or even a kind landlady to watch over me." She gave Valerie one of her slightly crooked smiles. "I was living in this row house with an elderly Asian lady who was pleasant and helpful but not involved, so I was totally on my own. I had a full-time job with benefits, for the first time ever, and I learned what that felt like. I didn't have a big debt anymore, so my money was my own. I had a chance to find out what I wanted to do with money when I had it to spend."

She paused a second to look out at the ocean. "Then I finally got into a classroom, and I learned some new things about teaching—like what I enjoyed and didn't enjoy. I saw how hard the competition is to get into college teaching in the Bay Area and how I could spend years opening that first door. I began questioning just how much I wanted to teach, if it was worth the battle to me."

"That's interesting," Valerie interrupted. "Are you saying that you now may not want to teach? After all that education you've had?"

Gina smiled at her indulgently. Val was being maternal again. "Well, I'd hate to go that far," she explained, taking a deep breath. "But I think I've realigned its importance to me. I think I originally wanted to be a teacher because my mother was a teacher. Going to school got me off the farm and gave me opportunities to experience culture and travel that I'd never have had in that rural part of Illinois. That's a plus. It will always be there. But I've questioned whether I really wanted to be a teacher for myself or because I saw my mom doing it. Maybe I wanted to teach because I thought she expected it of me. Apart from everything else, I figured out that I want to write, and I've been doing more of that."

"What kind of writing?" Valerie asked.

Gina frowned and straightened her cloth napkin. "I've done some short stories, but beyond that I don't know exactly. I will allow that to come in time. But that isn't really what I'm trying to share with you," she said.

Valerie nodded, realizing in her nervousness she wasn't letting Gina express herself. *Hold your tongue, woman*, she thought to herself.

"While I was in San Francisco," Gina continued, "I started to ask myself what is truly important to me, what I am running to because it's all I know, or because I think I'm supposed to. And what am I running away from? Am I afraid, or is it because I've been hurt—?" She stopped for a moment. She took a sip of wine and carefully studied a lighthouse painting high on the wall directly in front of her.

The waiter brought steaming bowls of clam chowder, and they both cut through the tension in the air by picking up their spoons and sampling the hot soup.

After a few moments, Gina again took up the thread of her story. "In 'Frisco, I had a chance to think about what I had known here in Eureka and what I could see there. I began to compare what my life could be like in both places. That was something new to me—to have this chance to see down two roads."

Gina downed a spoonful of the chowder and began again. "I thought I wanted to be in a big city because life on the farm hadn't satisfied me. I wanted the bright lights, the culture, and the beautiful things to experience sensually, but by the time I got to San Francisco I had lived in a small community that *was* satisfying, that had a lot to offer. I had wanted to be in San Francisco because of the gay community and because I thought that I would be able to live there openly as a lesbian. But by the time I got to the City, I already had done that. So, I satisfied my dreams by taking all the tours, riding the city buses and the BART, visiting Golden Gate Park, going to art films, the ballet, opera, The Castro, bookstores and bars—and it was all wonderful. I enjoyed everything very much, but now I realize that I don't need it all the time. I can *visit* San Francisco—I don't need to live there."

Gina looked directly into Valerie's eyes.

An efficient young waiter interrupted them by bringing their dinners and, for a time, they ate in silence. They pretty much cleaned their plates, except for a small helping of salmon that Val put in a box for Sam. Suddenly Valerie looked at Gina expectantly. She was beginning to see a thread in the conversation, but she knew that the younger woman had still not come to the point.

"I started thinking about home—about what was good in Illinois," Gina explained. "It was the people—how we were there for each other. Looking back, now I can see that my parents had a solid marriage and they both made compromises to make it work. Their relationship was their rock, and it made everything else in their lives possible, including the sacrifices they made to get me through school.

"Because I was sexually ambivalent, I avoided relationships or any kind of deep or personal commitment. And now I realize it was only my sexual confusion, not my personal beliefs. I believe in commitment to friends and to one special person for life. In San Francisco I started to realize that I was putting career at the top of my list of important things, when relationships are really the most important to me." Gina took a deep breath. "It was something I wasn't ready to hear when you talked about relationships being important to you before I left Eureka.

"When I got clear about myself, I started thinking about coming back to Eureka. The best things I've ever known have been here, and the best person I've ever known is here—you. And so I'm here to say those words and see where they take me, or us, to be exact." Gina stopped abruptly, looking as if she was not sure she should continue.

Valerie stared at her, shocked by Gina's revelations. "Wow!" was all she could say.

There was silence for a moment. Gina shifted uncomfortably in her chair and then started to speak again. "Coming back was scary because you never wrote to me. I didn't know if you would even see me, even speak to me."

Valerie sighed. "I shied away from you on purpose. You were headed to San Francisco. I knew I was never going back there. It seemed pointless to pursue anything that could only lead to pain."

Gina nodded and stared out at the ocean.

"Well," she said finally, "My coming back now is a lot to absorb, I'm sure, and you've not been there in the middle of my head while this was going on. I don't expect you to understand all of it, or to respond right now. You've given me a big gift by coming out to dinner with me and just listening."

Valerie stared at her. "I really don't know what to say," she said.

"I know." Gina smiled. "It's a lot for you. You don't have to say anything."

They settled on crème brulee for desert, one dish with two spoons, to share. They had shared food in the past, including the salmon at dinner this evening, so this little intimacy was not uncomfortable. For the moment, it was as far as they could go toward each other.

When they arrived back at Valerie's house, Gina got out quickly, opened the passenger door of the Beetle, and walked Val up to the front door. She said goodnight. Then, "I'd like to do this again, but I want to give you a few days to think about it. I'll call you."

Valerie nodded. Gina gave her a quick hug and then departed just as quickly.

Val took Sam up the 101, this time to Little River State Beach. She walked a long distance with the dog before she settled on a large mound of sand and sat for awhile to soak up some afternoon sun. The retriever sat by her, sniffing the ocean breeze. Val was so thankful for these secluded places where she could come to think and get right with herself.

Her head had been spinning since Gina's abrupt return from San Francisco. The dinner discussion had made it clear to her that Gina had done a lot of deep thinking and was serious about pursuing a relationship. Given that she had set goals before—like getting a Ph.D., paying off her debt, and going to San Francisco—and had met all of them, Gina's determination wasn't to be taken lightly.

But what, Val asked herself, did *she* want? Was Doreen far enough in her past not to interfere with another relationship? Did Valerie even want another relationship, or did she want to stay focused on her art now that it was beginning to sell? If she permitted a relationship to enter her life, did she want one with Gina, who was so much younger, or with Lanie, who had more in common age-wise and who had a full life of her own—who wouldn't be so intense?

Gina had seemed so young when she first came to the house that it had been easy then to write her off. She had grown up now and had become much more a force to be reckoned with. But Gina was still a work in progress, and her intense needs showed clearly in her eyes—or could that have been desire? A relationship with Gina could prove all-consuming. It would undoubtedly be exciting at times and challenging at times, but less stable in certain subtle ways than a relationship with someone who was at the stage that Val was in her life. *Could Valerie handle that inequity? Did she even want to invest in such a relationship?*

Okay, she admitted to herself, she hadn't forgotten how much she had enjoyed having Gina living in her home and how much Sam had taken to her. And Val hadn't forgotten the moments of sexual attraction between them. If she let her body decide, she'd be in bed with Gina before the week was out.

An amused smile was followed by a frown. This was no time to make such a casual, impulsive decision. She had the rest of her life to consider. She wouldn't even explore the possibility of a life with Gina unless the commitment was a shared one between them. And she had to be sure that Gina was the kind of person who would be there down the road. Valerie had already proved herself loyal, faithful, and willing to take hard knocks—to be at a dying lover's side. She knew what she had to offer and didn't want any less in return. Given her age, should they become a couple, the odds were that Gina would someday be where Val had already been with Doreen, facing loss and loneliness.

Her mind rattled on. *What about sex, if they did go to bed?* Valerie had been with Doreen for 20 years and with no one since her death. Gina had been, so she implied, with several partners briefly, although nothing lasting. What kind of sexual partner would Gina make? Or Val herself?

"Oh, phooey," she said to Sam. "I feel like I'm on a roller coaster way up at the top of the lift hill, ready to hang on for dear life. I think I want to get off." She looked at the dog. "Or do I?"

Valerie's phone rang. It was Lanie. "I hear rumors that Gina is back in town," she began before Val could even say hello.

"Yep, the rumors are true," Val affirmed.

"Just visiting?"

"She says she's here to stay. Got a job at the movie theater, assistant manager I think she said, found an apartment, and she's applying for teaching work at Humboldt State."

"Wow! How do you feel about that?"

"I honestly don't know," Val admitted. "She looks good, and she's so much more confident. It's like San Francisco made her into a new person."

"Hmmm," Lanie said and was quiet for a moment.

"I know she wrote to you," Valerie said. "She didn't mention that she was thinking of coming back?"

"No, not a word."

"Well, it sure was a surprise to me," Val acknowledged. "The doorbell rang, and there she was on the front porch. I was shocked."

"Hmmn," Lanie said again. "I somehow suspect she'll be courting you, if she hasn't already." She laughed sardonically. "I guess I should have made my move sooner."

Valerie could feel her pain. "Oh, my dear, I'm so sorry. The timing is terrible, isn't it? I treasure you so much. You've been such a loyal friend. But I don't at this point know what I am going to do, beyond listening and thinking and trying to decide what is right for me. I'm sorry if Gina's coming back is hurtful to you."

"Yeah, well a girl can dream," Lanie commented wryly. "I thought Gina was gone for good. Then when I started selling real estate and making good money, that you'd change your mind about us being a duo." She sighed. "Oh, well. I'm still your friend. Just keep me informed, so I know whether to wish you the best or come by and hold your hand."

Gina was behind the snack bar running a register tape when Rick came on duty for his shift. It was the first time she had seen him since she had returned to Eureka. Rick's eyes lit up, and he instinctively started to approach her to give her a big hug. Then he saw her blue manager's suit and stopped.

"You did it!" he gasped. "You're a manager!"

"Assistant in training," Gina replied with a grin.

"Well look at you in those duds!" Rick danced around in front of her. Then he realized he was making a display. "Sorry," he said, bringing himself under control. "You're a manager now. I'll have to show more respect."

"Probably," Gina said, but she smiled. "Save the other stuff for after hours. You're still my friend when we're not on duty."

Rick started down the hallway to clean an auditorium and then turned back. "It's so good to see you again," he said. A big grin spread across his face as he pushed his cart through a doorway.

Gina locked the register, grabbed her paper tapes, and headed for the box office. She was struggling with her job, as she had known she would. The paperwork and computer operations for a manager were so much more complicated than the tasks she had been responsible for as a staff member. But she liked it and she knew that in a few weeks she would be more at ease in the job. And the position required such weird hours, including night and weekend shifts, that she could do some writing and also handle a part-time teaching job. One full-time job made it easier to juggle her other interests and obligations.

She had located a reasonably comfortable furnished apartment. Using other people's things didn't bother her. She had made do with recycled furniture many times. But she had plans to fix up the apartment, add her own personal touches, and it would feel like her own very soon. It was great to have a small kitchen with her own full-sized refrigerator—a *whole* refrigerator in which to put whatever she wanted. She didn't have all the shelves filled yet but she would.

And soon, she had promised herself, she would trade the battered Beetle for a better car. It had served her faithfully through graduate school and in the years afterwards, but it was time for a more suitable, more *adult* car, maybe even an SUV.

"Right," she said aloud to no one in particular. "You want to make an impression on Valerie, don't you?"

When Val returned from her morning walk with Sam, she found an envelope tucked under her front doormat. Inside were four movie passes and a note. "Bring the gang, on me. Gina."

Valerie chuckled to herself and was soon on the phone to Lanie, Josie, and Judee. They all checked their schedules and decided they could go to the movies on the following Saturday evening. The three met at Val's house and rode to the theater in her Volvo. Despite a chilly evening with heavy fog rolling in from the ocean, they were all excited to be seeing Gina again.

The new assistant manager was tearing tickets at the front door, something the management staff did on busy nights. Valerie thought Gina was impressive in her navy blue uniform. Gina smiled warmly when she saw her old friends standing in line but maintained her professional composure and quickly tore their tickets. "That's theater three to your right," she said, directing them to their auditorium and quickly turning to the next customer.

Judee, Josie, and Lanie bantered with each other as they walked down the hallway. "Doesn't she look great?" Judee exclaimed.

"I love her new hairdo," Josie whispered, then looked at Valerie, who seemed preoccupied. "I thought we'd lost her to San Francisco forever," she said. "But I'm glad she's back, aren't you?"

Val came out of her funk and nodded. "Yes," she replied, "I am."

Josie left the group a few minutes later to pick up a large popcorn to share with her friends. She was surprised to see Gina behind the concession counter helping out the staff.

Josie got in line and, when her turn came, gave Gina a welcoming smile.

Gina looked a bit flustered but her blue eyes sparkled as she greeted her old friend. "Hi, Josie." Her head turned to the sound of business around her, and then she looked back at Josie. "Is there something I can get for you?"

"Large size popcorn for the gang. Please."

Gina nodded and went back to the popper, picking up a big corn barrel on the way. "You want butter?" she asked, looking over her shoulder at Josie.

"Little bit, thanks."

Gina buttered the corn, then reached under the counter and pulled out a brown rectangular box. She brought both items back to the place where Josie stood watching her. "That'll be $5.75," Gina said. "And take this extra box, so it will be easier to share. Just pour some out of the barrel into the box."

"Oh, thanks." Josie handed her a bill.

Gina counted out the change from the register and came back to Josie. She put the change in Josie's hand and started to turn toward another customer.

Josie stopped her by putting her other hand on Gina's arm. She looked deeply into Gina's eyes. "You came back for Valerie, didn't you?"

Gina's eyes widened, but a small smile played about her lips. "We'll see," she said and quickly faced the next person in line.

Valerie's phone hadn't been this busy for months. Whenever she picked up the receiver, Lanie, Josie, or Judee was on the other end of the line, asking if she had heard anything more from Gina or had seen Gina around town. Val could honestly say that she had not, and she was beginning to feel a little concerned. She tried not to let her discomfort show. Gina's new job must be taking up a lot of her time. Surely she'd call when she could.

The following week the phone rang, and this time it *was* Gina. Val was surprised, never having heard the sound of Gina's voice on a telephone before. She held her tongue, tempted to comment on the fact that Gina was now using what she had once thought of as a dreaded instrument.

"Hi," Gina said brightly. "I'm sorry it took so long for me to get back to you, but I was getting organized as a manager. I've still got a lot to learn but it's getting better. I have Thursday evening off, and I was wondering if you would be free to go to dinner and maybe dancing afterward."

Valerie paused a second, wanting to sound casual and to hide her deep-seated nervousness. "Yes, I'd like that," she finally managed.

"Good. How about I pick you up at 6?"

When Valerie put down the phone, she took several deep breaths. She could sense that, whether she was ready or not, the roller-coaster ride was about to begin.

Chapter Sixteen

Despite her fears and reservations, Valerie found it hard not to be totally awed by Gina. The new Gina, that is, who seemed so independent and capable. The ongoing courtship was very apparent—flowers, nice restaurants, arrival at Valerie's door well-groomed and smiling. And Valerie's defenses were crumbling, as if a young girl still existed inside her just waiting to be enticed out of hiding and flattered by attention. Even her adult, often cynical self was melting in the heat of Gina's constant attention.

On Thursday Gina arrived with a bouquet of red carnations. She had gotten her hair styled. It was a bit shorter and framed her face nicely. "Goes with the uniform," she had joked, when Valerie complimented her on her "new do." But Gina was impressive, no doubt about it. She had put on a few pounds during the past year. Instead of the fragile, scrawny lass she had been when she first arrived in Eureka, she now—while still trim—seemed strong, her clothes fitting instead of hanging on her. And she had healthy color in her cheeks.

Gina opened doors and treated Valerie like a special lady. That was impressive too. In the long run Val knew she would prefer a more casual equality—after all she could open her own door quite well—but she knew that Gina was trying to demonstrate that she was no longer a child-tenant, that Valerie was no longer a landlady-mother, that she could initiate things and could set her own boundaries and rules. So Valerie allowed herself, for a time anyway, to just bask in the attention.

One evening the two drove north around Humboldt Bay to a popular steakhouse in Arcata, where they shared wine, a shrimp cocktail, a large porterhouse steak, and a chocolate monstrosity for dessert. And they talked.

"You seem reserved tonight," Gina noted after their order had been taken.

Valerie smiled. "I'm still absorbing all the changes in you. That excited but scared young woman who left for San Francisco has come back a totally different person."

"Like, how different?" Gina asked, with interest and amusement.

"Well, in charge, in command. It's like, wow, I don't know what to say."

Gina buttered her warm roll, trying to decide what to share. Her enthusiasm sometimes boiled over. "You know," she began "in San Francisco, when I started working in the classroom as a teaching assistant, I had to deal with all these people who didn't speak English, or very little English. Geez, I was terrified. But I wanted to survive so badly that I began to practice bluffing. I've never really been good at bluffing. If I'm scared to death, I look scared to death. You know what I mean? But I started watching the teacher, Linda Sue Gibbins, who was very strong—or else the best bluffer I've ever seen—and I kind of imitated her."

She smiled, remembering. "After a few weeks it got easier to pretend to know what I didn't, until I had a moment to catch up and find the answer to the question. I pretended to be at ease and after a while I gradually felt more at ease. It was like some light bulb had gone off in my head and I knew that I could do things I've never done before. I'd be 'as if' until I really was."

She looked down at the table and toyed with the saltshaker for a moment. "But I'll risk telling you the truth. I'm doing a little bit of bluffing right now. Inside, I'm really scared that you'll tell me to get lost," Gina confessed.

Valerie put her hand gently on Gina's arm. "After knowing you for two years and after seeing your growth, I'd be stupid to tell you to get lost—unless you give me some good reason that I should." She chuckled to herself. "I don't know what I'm going to do with you, but I'm not going to tell you to get lost, believe me."

Gina heaved a sigh of relief, smiled tentatively, and looked down at Valerie's hand touching her. She was getting the old vibrations, like a jolt of electricity running through her body. "Thanks," she said, wanting to keep their conversation light for now. "I appreciate the vote of confidence."

Valerie sipped her wine and she withdrew her hand slowly. Then she asked, "Did you like this Linda Sue Gibbins person?"

Gina giggled. "Who? Rowdy? That's what she called herself. Oh, she was okay."

Gina studied Val for a moment before going on. "She was a lesbian and she took me to a bar one night in The Castro. She had designs on me but she wasn't the one for me. She was a rough dyke, with this big scar running down the side of her face and a cigarette constantly either in her hand or in her mouth. I respected her abilities as an instructor, but I was really turned off to the idea of anything personal with her." She blushed. "All she did was remind me of how special you were."

Val smiled wryly. "So maybe I should be glad that she didn't do it for you, right?"

At that moment a portly, graying waiter brought their humungous porterhouse steak, with two plates, a huge baked potato, and a large order of asparagus. "This is enough for four people," they agreed, as they divided the steak and the trimmings.

For several moments they ate in silence, except for an occasional "Mmmm, so good!"

Valerie, who looked very much to Gina like someone trying to keep emotions in check, finally picked up their conversation. "Gina, you've done all this work on yourself, and you've put so many things together to get yourself to this place. How much have you thought down the road—to the future?"

Gina raised an eyebrow. "Like what?"

"Well," Valerie began, then paused for a moment before continuing, "I'm nearly 20 years older than you are. Somewhere in the next few years I'll be going through menopause. I could turn into some terrible bitch, which is very hard on a relationship." She smiled at Gina before continuing. "Then my hair is going to go gray, and I'm going to dry up like a prune and get all wrinkly. And that's the good part. Who knows what else might happen to me as I age. Is that what you want for yourself? Maybe pushing an old lady around in a wheelchair?"

Gina grinned. "My grandmother was 'all wrinkly,' and she was my favorite person. I loved my grandma more than anyone. What do wrinkles have to do with what's inside?"

"Touché." Val laughed. "But, sweetie," she said, using this word for the first time. "Wouldn't it be a whole lot easier to find someone your own age? You could look forward to 40 or 50 years together. With me, I could die on you and leave you to grow old alone. I've been alone and I've watched someone I loved die. Believe me, it's no picnic. I wouldn't wish it on anyone."

Gina shrugged. "Doreen was your age, wasn't she? That didn't protect you from losing her?"

Valerie looked at her sternly. "That was cruel, my friend."

Gina looked pained. "I'm sorry. But I don't think our age is a real issue. It's a made-up issue, to keep psychologists rich. It only matters if we build our lives around liking the exact same music, which we probably don't, or any other cultural event that will be different because we grew up in different decades. But don't you think it's more important that we are both creative, that we enjoy irregular schedules rather than working 9 to 5, that we both love long ocean walks, that we both adore Sam and she loves us back, that the people you call your friends seem to like me and I care about them as well? Aren't those things more central to our appreciation of life?"

Valerie studied Gina for a long time. "You are *really* strong-willed, aren't you? I knew it, but I don't think I quite saw just how determined you are until this moment."

Gina chuckled. "If I hadn't been, I'd still be in Illinois milking cows and harvesting corn."

Their dessert came, and they kidded each other over the chocolate. Without saying a word, Gina realized that, among other things, they were both chocoholics.

While they waited for the check, Gina studied Val's face.

"What about Lanie?" she suddenly asked.

Valerie's eyes widened. Then she smiled. "Lanie's a friend, a good friend," she said gently, putting her hand on Gina's arm again. "Although I must admit that if you had stayed away or waited longer to come back, she might have become more than that."

Gina heaved a sigh of relief. She had been agonizing over that concern for a long time.

After dinner they walked along the harbor and then went to the Purple Priscilla. They had just found a booth in the back and were settling in when Rick, followed by his ever-present sidekicks Eric and Paul, strolled into the bar.

Spotting them, Gina asked Valerie if she minded if they shared their booth, and Val agreed. Gina called out, and the young men slid in beside them. Their humorous antics kept the evening a bit lighter than it might have become if Gina and Val had remained alone at the table.

Rick kidded Valerie from the start. "Gina really liked you when she lived here before," he whispered to her conspiratorially. "But she had this idea that she HAD to go to San Francisco and she's pretty stubborn." He glanced at Gina with a grin. "So she went. Thank God, she finally saw the light and came back to us."

Val found Rick's expressiveness cute. And she enjoyed his comments. What he said made it clear that Gina's attraction to her had not been a total secret.

The band warmed up and talk became difficult. "Want to dance?" Gina asked.

Valerie shrugged. "Sure," she said with apparent lightness.

Gina took her hand and led her to the dance floor. The first number was fast. They faced each other and shook and moved to the beat, their faces both flushing pink from the exertion.

The next number was slow and close, and Gina encircled Valerie with her arms. Val could smell Gina's subtle perfume and she could feel the warmth of her body. Almost as soon as they touched, the electricity between them started to spark.

Valerie looked into Gina's eyes and for a moment she saw the old Gina there, a young woman both excited and scared. Then the look passed and Gina smiled at her. They held each other tightly through the rest of the number, their bodies doing all of the talking.

Later, when Gina dropped Valerie off at her house, she kissed her goodnight on the doorstep. A deep, passionate, longing kiss that Val returned.

When they separated, Gina put her hands on Valerie's face and looked at her deeply. "If we decide to go all the way, the first time has to be at my place," she said. "We have to break all the old patterns from my days as your roomer."

Valerie nodded. "I'll have to bring Sam," was all she said.

Gina grinned. "Sure."

And Val knew in her heart that the deed was as good as done.

Valerie closed the front door and stood in the hallway, shaking nervously. An emotional bomb was exploding inside her. The roller coaster was now in free fall and she wanted to scream for dear life. She trembled and broke into a sweat.

Thinking about Gina, allowing her back into her life, all that was fine. But the core of her being had not yet spoken. Her gut suddenly filled with a pain so intense that it almost pulled her to the floor—a pain that she was sure was entirely emotional. An agony both old and new told her that she was crossing an abyss so wide that she could never return. She was about to change, finally and forever.

Doreen. No matter what she had done with her life to this day, Doreen had always been somewhere in the background, in her memory, in her feelings, in her heart. If she let Gina into her bed, if she opened her mind, her soul, and her body to Gina, then Doreen's hold on her would be gone. At last she could see herself moving on with her life, and the pain of letting go became suddenly and terribly intense.

As she struggled with her searing emotions, Valerie sensed what she needed to do.

After a tormented, restless night, Val showered just before dawn, dressed neatly in slacks and a sweater, and prepared her Volvo for a trip. She packed food and a warm jacket and cap, grabbed Sam's leash, and with the dog in the passenger's seat, headed south on Highway 101 to San Francisco. She had not been back to the City since Doreen's death and the sale of their Marina home.

Valerie sped down the highway like a madwoman. It was 277 miles, about five and one-half hours on paper—but more in reality—which would put her there in mid-afternoon, if she didn't get stuck behind too many semis or RVs and campers. The 101 was sometimes a real freeway for a few miles and sometimes a winding two-lane road deep in the midst of coastal redwoods. The clouds to the southwest looked threatening. Thankfully for her, the rain held off and the road remained dry and reasonably safe.

She sailed through the small communities on the 101, barely slowing for Willits and Ukiah, then Cloverdale. Her mind was a blur, lost in a past that she had been pushing below consciousness. Doreen's parents, who lived in the San Fernando Valley north of Los Angeles, had never been supportive of their relationship. Distant, sometimes hostile, they had never welcomed the two into their home. The awkwardness of communicating led to fewer and fewer contacts over the years. Doreen had expressed sadness about it, but she was so happy with Valerie and their life together that she refused to allow her traditional family to destroy what she and Val had together. Finally all contact ceased.

When Doreen became ill, Val now recalled with renewed pain as she clung to the roadway, white knuckles on the wheel, she had tried to reach out to that family with no success. They didn't answer or return calls. Val stayed by Doreen's side and had done what she could for her, as she quickly slipped into the grip of the disease. Doreen had faded away without ever seeing her mother and father again.

While it was still possible, they had talked to each other about what each of them wanted if something ever happened to the other. Doreen wanted to be cremated and have her ashes spread in the Pacific Ocean. Earlier in their relationship, Doreen and Valerie had made plans to be buried together but cancer had denied that option. "If you wait to be buried beside me, you'll never allow yourself to have a life," Doreen had wisely said before her death. "This way I can release you."

Valerie had agreed to take care of the cremation. They owned everything jointly, with right of survivorship, and even though California didn't allow lesbians to marry at the time, they thought they were well-covered. But Doreen's illness had spread so rapidly that Val, who was by Doreen's side most of their remaining time, didn't have time to update a will or put in writing what Doreen had decided for herself.

After Doreen passed one gray morning, Valerie stayed with her for a few moments and then realized she had not had food or anything to drink for so long that she was about to pass out. She left the room to go down to the cafeteria to get some coffee and a sweet roll, something to give her a little energy to deal with the arrangements she and Doreen had made.

When she returned to the room, Val was shocked to see the empty bed. She went to the nurse's station and asked what had happened. One of the regular nurses, Joanne, came around the counter and asked Val to join her in a nearby conference room. Perplexed, Valerie followed her.

"While you were gone," Joanne said, putting a hand gently on Val's arm, "Doreen's brother was here. He had a lawyer with him and a representative from a funeral home. They said they came to claim her body and that they had a right to take it. They waved some papers around, and two men from the funeral home entered her room. They put her body on a gurney, covered it, and left down the hallway. There was no chance for any of us to find you or to do anything."

Gritting her teeth and pounding the steering wheel with one fist, Valerie found her mind reeling with the memory of that moment as if it were yesterday. She had felt so vulnerable, so helpless, so unprepared to deal with what had happened. She had collapsed into tears, and the staff had gotten permission to give her a sedative and find a place for her to rest for a little while.

The intrusion of Doreen's family had led in part to the long depression that Val had endured after Doreen's passing. It had had a lot to do with her eventual selling of the condo and moving away from San Francisco. She had needed the closure of seeing that Doreen had been cremated as she had wished and that her ashes had been spread where she wished. Valerie had been denied that and that fact still stuck inside her like a raw wound.

Only when she left the Bay Area did she begin to forget, to see things more positively, and to begin to build a world for herself. She knew she wasn't finished with the past but she didn't know what to do about it. It had been stored mostly below the surface of her subconscious, until Gina had showed up on her doorstep a few weeks earlier.

Val pushed the edge of the envelope, but thankfully traffic was light and nothing got in her way. Just after 3 p.m., she arrived at her destination, a large cemetery outside the city of San Francisco proper. No one had been buried inside San Francisco for many years. Except for two cemeteries, the Presidio and Mission, all other burial grounds—some 16 of them—were in neighboring Colma.

Doreen had been cremated, but the family decided her ashes would be placed in the family crypt. Doreen's grandparents had been from San Francisco and they had purchased several spaces for their family in a Colma mausoleum.

Valerie left Sam in the car once she reached the cemetery. She put on her warm cap and pulled her heavy coat closely about her. The wind was sharp on this cold, gray day. The cemetery seemed deserted except for flowers here and there that left a footprint from earlier visitors.

Val entered the mausoleum and stood misty-eyed before the vault. She too had brought flowers—tulips, Doreen's favorite. She placed them on the small ledge. How ironic, Valerie thought, that the gorgeous pink blossoms—so delicate like the woman who adored them—would have a brief but brilliant life.

"I'm here, Doreen," Val said. Tears began to stream down her cheeks as she reached out to touch the gray marble crypt. "I'm back. You've been in my thoughts and dreams and memories every day, but this is the first time I've come here. The pain was too great, but now I'm finally here." She stopped, using the back of her hand to wipe away the tears.

"I've been angry for a long time," she admitted, almost choking on the words, "at you, for dying, for leaving me. I know that's irrational, because you didn't want to go. But I've also been angry at your family for invading our private world and taking you from me, keeping me from having closure, preventing me from doing what you had asked me to do. I felt so helpless not being able to do anything to stop them. So I ran, and I avoided, and I tried to go on as if nothing had happened."

She heaved a sigh. "But of course everything had happened. Our life together was gone, you were gone, and I was left to deal. I haven't always done too good a job of it, but something in me is finally beginning to change."

Valerie sat in silence for several moments. "I'm sorry" she sighed, "if you've known that I've not been here, if you are out there somewhere in space, some sort of spirit, watching. I'm sorry if I've let you down. I didn't mean to. It just hurt too bad." She cried again for a moment and suddenly began to shiver.

"I love you, I'll always love you, and I will always miss you." She stopped, choking on her words, but quickly began to speak again. "But you told me that you wanted me to have a life after your death, and I think it's beginning to happen. I didn't look for it, I didn't expect it, but someone found me. Her name is Gina. She can't replace you. No one ever could. But I think she is a good person. She wants to build something with me if I can allow it."

She touched the tulips tenderly and her body heaved with deep sobs for several moments.

"It's time, Doreen, to let go of the pain, of the anger," she finally said. "Not the love, not the respect, not the memories, but the bad things. I want to remember the good now."

Valerie stood and let go a deep sigh. She wiped her tears and put her palms against the marble crypt one last time. "Now I've come. I've done it and I'm still standing here—alive, sad but alive. It's time for me to seek the life you wanted for me. But I'll visit more often, I promise. And I'll never forget you."

Then she sighed, squared her shoulders, and turned back toward the Volvo and Sam, who was waiting faithfully for her.

Valerie made sure that Gina was blissfully unaware of her emotional trial, which was how Val wanted it to be. Her devotion to Doreen was baggage from the past. If she was going to be with Gina, to give that relationship a chance, she had to go into it totally dedicated. When she got home late that night, she found Gina had left a message on her home phone. When Val returned Gina's call the next day she was careful not to sound awkward. She did not mention the real reason she had been unavailable that day. She wasn't sure she would ever tell Gina, but aside from that discomfort, she began to feel better. She had gone through what some people would call a "dark night of the soul"—a private moment—and she believed that she had come out stronger on the other end. Stronger and for the most part, free. She knew it would take days, weeks, months even, before she was truly beyond all of this. But she had made a start, the most difficult part. She was ready to face her own demons.

A week later, Gina had an evening and the following day off from work. She knew she would need every minute of that free time. Ever since she had decided to return to Eureka, she had dreamed and fantasized and planned for this day.

Even the weather cooperated. She picked up Valerie and Sam and they went down to the waterfront for a long walk, talking about this and that—friendly talk that went in no particular direction. The sun was just setting in the West when they returned to the Beetle.

Gina drove them to her one-bedroom apartment, which Val

seemed to like. It wasn't fancy, but it was clean, spacious, decently furnished, and in a modern complex near the mall. Gina had prepared a salad and lasagna in advance and had Italian rolls and a bottle of red wine ready. Big bowls of water and kibble were waiting on the kitchen floor for Sam.

They ate quietly. Soft music played in the background.

Finally Valerie admitted, "I really like your apartment."

Gina smiled. "That's good. When I was planning to return to Eureka, I thought about moving back to your house and I knew I couldn't do that. If I was ever to have a chance, if we were ever to have a chance with each other, I had to find a way to even the playing field. I decided to get my own place and promised myself that I wouldn't even think of moving in with you until I could pay my own way. Half of the expenses."

Valerie looked at her for a long time. "That's daring of you. What if I had a huge mortgage?"

"Then we'd have to work it out."

"Thankfully, you lucked out on that one," Valerie kidded. "I don't have a large mortgage and I don't have really high expenses. I think you might have half a chance."

Gina laughed. "This sounds like the lesbian moving company—two dates and we're moving in together. But that's not really true. We've known each other for a long time. And we've seen each other with our hair down so to speak. We know a lot about each other that many partners starting a relationship don't. Right?"

"Right," Valerie agreed with a nod.

Gina thought for a moment. "You know you really impressed me when you took Josie into the house after her fall. I saw how nurturing you were, how you went out of your way to make sure that she was cared for and had a chance to recover fully. It was very selfless of you to do that."

Val smiled. "So it's the mother in me that you like?" She seemed to be teasing, at least partly.

Gina blushed. "That's part of it, the nurturing part. But that was a special thing you did. I've never thought of you like a mother, or my mother, or whatever the psychological mumbo-jumbo would be. You're older, yes, but you're very attractive. And smart. And you don't judge people. I really like that."

"I think I can be just as judgmental as the next person," Valerie countered with a laugh.

"Well," Gina replied, a bit flustered, "you hide it well. You may think it, but you don't say it."

Valerie was silent for a moment, then shrugged. "So you find this 50-plus body attractive?"

Gina really blushed this time, nervously pushing her glasses up as she had the first day she appeared on Valerie's doorstep. "Yes. You have a pretty face and beautiful hair. And gorgeous eyes. And soft curves, and well, you smell good."

Val laughed. "They say it's all about smell, anyway, so I guess that's a good sign."

Valerie looked at Gina for a moment, studying her closely. "I wasn't sure what to make of you when you first came to Eureka. But when I saw you juggling those three jobs, I really started to notice. With the background you had, it would have been so easy for you to give up. But you handled everything without complaining, and I watched you do it. I was awed by your determination. You say you get scared, and I know you do, but you are so strong-willed. Like a bull. I suppose you'll tell me you're a Taurus."

Gina grinned. "Is it all right if I am?"

Valerie just smiled and shook her head. She was silent for a while. Then, "You're good looking, too. I'm so pleased that you've started to take pride in your appearance. I especially like seeing you in your new manager's uniform." She giggled. "Even with the glasses."

Gina smiled. "I'm going to get rid of those one of these days."

"I didn't mean to offend you," Val said, putting a hand on Gina's arm.

"You didn't," Gina replied with a wink.

They finished dinner and sat for a few moments, sipping their wine. Sam was curled up on the floor beside them.

Finally Gina touched Valerie's shoulder. "Would you like to dance?"

Val offered a tentative smile, and Gina knew she was not the only one who was nervous. "Sure," Valerie managed to say.

Gina picked out a CD and put some soft music on the boom box, turned the living room lamp down low, threw her eyeglasses on the table, and led Valerie to the center of the room. They held each other for a long time, dancing almost in place, allowing their heat and desire to build.

Gina was trembling, and she wondered if perhaps Val would have to make a first move. *Nope, if she had to she could bluff her way through it.* She knew where she was going and kissed Valerie gently on the cheek. Then she turned her face toward Val. Their eyes met, then their lips, which soon parted in passionate probing. Their sustained kiss was crushing, and Gina could feel just how much pent-up desire she had pushed down inside her until now.

In what seemed like seconds they moved toward the bedroom, then onto Gina's bed. They hugged and kissed each other, fighting out of their restraining clothing, touching and stroking and touching again. Gina began to explore Valerie's mature body, with its rounded breasts, soft curves, and sweet smell. Val touched Gina's slender, firm, muscled form, with an obvious desire she had not previously allowed herself to recognize or express. She could feel her nipples rise and harden with the intensity of their lovemaking.

Their passion was unrestrained. They inhaled each other, exploring and experiencing a mounting excitement. Licking and kissing each others' breasts, nibbling necks, stroking between legs, and finally going down on each other—Gina first, Valerie next, until each had reached an explosive climax. They fell backward, collapsing together, their bodies intertwined. Exhausted, but not sated.

They lay for a time, hugging and stroking, too overwhelmed for words.

"I don't care how wrinkled you get," Gina finally whispered. "I'll always want you."

Valerie chuckled. "My mother and dad were still going at it in their 80s, so I probably—if genes mean anything at all—have a few years to give you yet."

Gina giggled and held Val close. She tucked her head in under Valerie's arm and lay her head across her breast.

All of a sudden tears touched Valerie's skin. She reached up and felt Gina's face. Gina was crying.

"What's wrong, darling?" Valerie asked.

"Oh, nothing," Gina said. Her tears flowed more openly. "I mean, it's hard to talk about."

"Did I do something wrong?"

"Oh, no. It's just that I used to be so intimidated by you. I thought you were beautiful when I first met you, but I was so overwhelmed. I wasn't sure I could ever overcome it." She was quiet for a moment, trying to find the words that needed to come.

Valerie stroked her arm quietly and waited.

Finally, Gina spoke. "It has to do with being in therapy. This woman that I saw, she was some kind of psychoanalyst—the kind that believes in rebuilding personalities. It's like they strip you down to nothing and then put you back together again. It's very painful to go through. You really get lost in it. And this therapist was an older woman. She dominated me so much that I honestly believed I could never be comfortable in my own skin again.

"When I met you, you seemed so strong to me, so sure of yourself. You had all these rules to keep everyone at a distance. I didn't think I could ever be your equal. It's taken all this time and the experience in San Francisco to make it possible for me to even try," Gina admitted.

Valerie was silent for a moment but she continued stroking Gina's arm. "Even though my mother was a psychologist, I don't know a lot about the intricacies of psychotherapy," she finally said. "But somehow this doesn't sound real positive to me—to be left so naked and defenseless in the presence of someone who is supposed to be helping you."

Gina felt a chill. She pulled the sheets up closer and snuggled up to Val.

"Well," she finally said, "I learned that therapists are human too. They can be controlling just like other people. I came out knowing that I was a lesbian, so that was a benefit because I wasn't living a lie anymore. But I sure got left with a lot of other garbage to sort out."

Valerie seemed to freeze for a moment. "I hope your attraction to me wasn't part of working out your problem, because once you work it out you'll be gone," she risked saying.

Gina hugged her reassuringly. "I thought about that a lot. It could have been. But the more I knew you, the more I realized you had so many qualities that I had always admired. The more the therapy slips into my past, the clearer things become. You are not the problem or the solution. You are simply Valerie, the person I have grown to love and desire and want to be with," Gina said.

"You love me?"

"Yes, I do!"

"That's good, because I love you, too."

"When did you know?"

"Well, I denied it to myself at the time, but it was on *Sweet Dreams* when I saw you at the helm. You were so cute and so excited and thrilled, and I loved watching you be so happy. When did you know?"

"I blew off the whole thing, but it was from the minute we danced together at the Purple Priscilla, when this electric charge went through me."

"You, too?"

They both laughed and then were silent for a moment, exploring each other playfully with their fingers.

"So what was this therapist like?" Valerie asked, her mind not totally settled about Gina's past history.

"You mean Dr. Reitman?"

Val nodded.

"Well, she was classically Jewish. You know, dark hair, dark brown eyes, prominent nose, dark-rimmed glasses, attractive, kind of tall." Gina giggled. "Busty, curvy—middle-aged curvy, you know."

"Except for the pleasingly plump part," Valerie noted, allowing herself a little smile, "I guess I'm not her spitting image."

"No way," Gina agreed.

Val seemed thoughtful for a moment. "I'm glad you shared that with me. It could have become a wall between us otherwise. It helps build trust to talk about it," she said.

Gina held her close.

"When Josie was staying at your house, she and I had some good conversations. I told her a little about the therapist and what had happened to me. It helped me a lot to talk about it to someone, to get it outside of me, but at that time I couldn't have shared it with you. I'm grateful that I'm feeling better about me now and that I can tell you. I feel even better now that I have."

Valerie patted Gina's arm and lay quietly. "I'm glad," she finally said, "that you feel you can be open with me. I like you strong and feisty and able to speak your mind."

"I'm glad, too. It feels good to be open with you. I hope you'll always be open with me."

There was a heavy silence in the room. Gina sensed that Val also had something to say but wasn't sure how to put her thoughts into words.

Finally Valerie spoke. "I've had my own demons, too. Last week, you started to become so real in my life that I panicked. I guess I hadn't really faced letting go of Doreen. There wasn't anything in my life here that challenged the past—until you showed up on my doorstep. Suddenly my feelings just started to tear me up. Finally I drove to Colma to visit Doreen's crypt. I had never gone there before." She sighed. "I said goodbye to her. If I hadn't done that, I don't think I could be here with you tonight."

Gina was touched. She reached up and put her hand gently on Valerie's face. "Thank you for fighting for me."

"You're welcome, sweetheart," Val replied softly.

Gina had more questions and she needed to get them behind her. "Doreen was so important to you and I have no idea what she was like."

Valerie sighed. "Oh, you wouldn't know, would you? I have a picture of her in my bedroom, but I think you've only been up there once when you first came. Doreen had brown eyes, auburn hair, and she was tall and willowy, with a really pretty face."

"Hmmm," Gina observed, "I can't compete with that."

Val hugged her and then continued. "The downside of her being so pretty is that it got her into a lot of trouble when she was young. Everyone wanted to be around her, and she was influenced by some of her friends in the City. She took up smoking and drank too much. I'm sure she experimented with drugs as well. Thankfully, by the time she met me she was becoming aware of her reckless behavior. The drugs were gone, she had limited her drinking to a glass of wine at dinner, and because I objected so much, she cut back her smoking to almost nothing. She never smelled of cigarettes around me, which was good, and she never smoked in my presence. But I'm sure she did it now and then."

"And what kind of cancer did she die of?" Gina asked.

"Lung cancer. The smoking did come back to get her." Valerie's voice was husky.

"That's sad," Gina said softly.

"Yes, it is. I only wish I had met her when she was 16 instead of 26. Maybe I could have saved her from all of that. But then 10 years earlier, I might not have been smart enough to realize what we could have together. So I have to accept that the years we had with each other were what was meant to be."

They were both quiet. They held each other close for several moments in the dark. "Does Sam need to go out?" Gina suddenly asked.

"Wow, I'd forgotten all about her," Val giggled. She called Sam, who was curled up on a rug at the foot of the bed. The retriever had been still, but there, the entire evening. Gina and Valerie both laughed.

"Wonder what she thinks?" they asked each other, as they both stroked the dog's head and fondled her ears. Sam looked at them with one raised eyebrow. The women quickly pulled on their clothes.

"You know, the moon is full tonight," Gina said. "Let's take her for a walk."

Arm in arm, they went out the door of the apartment and took Sam for a leisurely stroll through the neighborhood. "Do you think it's safe?" Valerie asked at one point, looking up and down the rather dark street.

Gina grinned. "With two of us Amazon women and Sam, no one would dare."

As they walked they sniffed the sea air. It was laced with wisps of fog. For a long time they were both silent. Then Val thought of something she wanted to share.

"Did you know that Josie is living with Judee and the boys?"

Gina smiled. "Yes, I got an e-mail to that effect."

"I thought it would be good for Josie when the two of them first mentioned it at poker night. But from the little glances between them in the past few weeks, I'm beginning to think that this roommate arrangement is fast becoming a close friendship and maybe even a romance. It surprised me at first, but the more I thought about it the more it made sense to me," Valerie admitted.

"Josie will be good for the boys," Gina observed. "She's strong and outdoorsy and can do things with them. She's nurturing too."

"Of course, so is Judee. She needs someone to respect all the hard work she puts in as a mother and homemaker and serious student at the same time. Josie sees herself as some kind of hayseed, but she's got smarts and I think she brings a lot to the table."

"What about the age difference?"

"And *you're* talking about age difference? Give me a break!" Valerie gave Gina a light punch on the arm.

They both laughed.

The two women returned to the apartment an hour later. They dropped their clothing on the floor, went back to bed, and started to make love again with much teasing and laughter.

Val and Gina awoke the next morning to find the bedclothes scattered all over the floor. They looked at each other and saw that they both had strands of hair sticking out like pieces of straw. They grinned at each other. Sam broke all the rules by jumping up on the bed and licking them both.

"We'll be doing a three-way before long," Gina giggled.

"Not in my house, we won't," Valerie countered.

Now they both laughed.

"Are you sure you want to do this?" Val asked. "Eureka is an awfully small town. Aren't you going to get bored?"

"We can travel," Gina countered, "on my days off."

"Your single day a week?"

"Once I get a teaching job I'll have summers off, right?"

"Unless you teach summer school."

"When I write the great American novel, I won't have to go to work at all. I can write anywhere I can take my computer."

"And I can paint anywhere, I suppose."

"Sure"

"What about your parents? Are you going to tell them about us?"

"Eventually. You'll have to come back to Illinois with me. They may throw us out, but by then we won't care."

"Mine are no problem, since they've both passed on. We can go to the cemetery, and I'll introduce you."

"You mean you might go to San Francisco with me sometime?"

"Maybe. How are we going to handle my owning a house and you not owning it?"

"You can will it to me and I'll inherit it 30 years from now, according to your calculations."

"Well we could register for a California domestic partnership, and that would cover leaving the house to you. Like marriage, half of mine is yours."

"We could go to Vermont and get married."

"You'd do that?"

"Of course."

"We'd have to have a reception back here, so we could invite all our friends."

"Yes, all three of them—oh, and Rick, too."

"I'm hungry. Let's go straight to the reception so we can eat."

"I'm hungry, too."

Valerie and Gina jumped out of bed, totally naked, and raided the refrigerator. They polished off a bowl of chocolate fudge ice cream together.

"We wasted so much time getting to this place," Gina quipped, spoon poised for another bite of ice cream.

"No we didn't. We were getting rid of our own personal garbage and preparing ourselves to do it right," Val responded.

"It feels right," Gina acknowledged.

"You aren't disappointed?"

"No way!"

Then they continued their processing—raising objections to their relationship and then batting them down—until they were totally exhausted. Then they went back to bed and made love again.

Sam heaved a big sigh and curled up on the rug.

Epilogue

Just like old times, the gang had assembled at Valerie's house for a poker night. So much had happened during the last few months that their gatherings had been few and far between—a reality that made this evening all that more special.

Josie and Judee arrived together, both looking very happy. Val immediately noticed that they were wearing matching gold rings on the third finger of their left hands. "Did you get married?" she gasped.

"Not exactly," Judee quipped. "But we did go up to Trinidad Beach and exchange some verbal vows. And we got these rings to mark the occasion."

Josie stood behind her, silent but blushing and with a big grin on her face.

"You'll have to tell me all about it," Valerie said as Lanie came through the front door.

"Hi, guys," Lanie greeted, holding up a six-pack of beer. "Time to party."

"Where's Gina?" asked Judee.

"Out at Humboldt State. Some staff meeting, but it was to be over by 6 p.m. She should be here in a few minutes."

Josie studied Valerie. "You must be really happy that she's starting a real teaching position this fall."

Val grinned. "Yes, I am. I'm really happy to see her doing what she was trained for, after all these years of financial problems and jobs that didn't really use her talents."

Judee turned to Lanie. She was standing aside rather quietly but at the same time looked a little like a Cheshire cat, hiding something.

"Okay, what's up, Lanie?" Judee asked.

Lanie tried to look serious. "Well, everybody around here has such good news and things are going well for all of you. I was afraid that I was getting left behind, but not so. I'm the sales person of the month again, and I just sold a house to a sexy-looking Oregon gal who turned out to be one bitchin' babe. We're going out on a date tomorrow night."

"Wow!" Josie couldn't hide her enthusiasm. "You'll have to update us on that!"

The front door opened and Gina rushed in. Sam followed her, barking at her heels the minute she entered the hallway.

Gina looked radiant, the familiar eyeglasses now replaced by contacts, her hair cut very short and nicely trimmed. She was wearing a soft blue blouse, black denim slacks, and a beige sport jacket. They all stared at her for a moment. Finally Lanie spoke. "Well, the ugly duckling turns into the beautiful swan!"

"She was never ugly," Valerie exclaimed.

"No," Lanie admitted with a grin. "But certainly not all she could be—all those months, or years, ago when we first met her. Skinny as a rail, with that stringy hair and those terrible, excuse me, glasses."

Gina smiled. "Well, life has gotten just a little better than it was." She wrinkled her nose at Valerie.

"So, professor," Josie interrupted, "how does it feel to be on the faculty full time at Humboldt State?"

Gina stepped over to Val and gave her a hug. "Very good, very satisfying."

Valerie glanced around at the gang. "You all don't know it yet, but Gina has a two-week break before she officially joins the faculty for the fall semester. We've decided to take a trip. Kind of a honeymoon since we never had a chance before now."

"Where are you goin'?" Judee asked.

"Oregon and Washington—up the coast. Then east through the mountains, as far as we can get with the time we have."

Lanie laughed. "I bet you only get as far as the first motel on the beach."

Gina smiled. "Seriously, I want to put some road miles on the RAV-4."

They all nodded dubiously.

Valerie studied them for a moment. "We're trying to decide what to do with Sam. She'd love the trip, but she's slowing down a little. Some parks allow dogs, but otherwise, she'd be left in the car whenever we stop during the day to sightsee."

Lanie took the hint. "If you don't mind my new girlfriend visiting, I'll stay in your guest room and watch out for Sam for you. Her meals might be a little irregular, but I'll see that she gets out and gets fed."

"Oh, thank you, Lanie. That's such a relief," Valerie admitted gratefully. "I was hoping that one of you would be available."

The five women loaded up on beer, wine, chips, and dip and settled into their familiar routine at the poker table. The teasing banter continued.

At one point, Josie looked at Gina. "You know in the last year since you came back to Eureka we've all made changes. But I swear I'd never have thought you would be where you are now from the way things were for you when I first met you here at Val's."

Gina blushed. "Yeah, I never saw me sleeping up in the master suite with Valerie in my arms, my old bedroom turned into my office, a full-time position teaching English literature, a dog I love, and friends I adore. I would have said it wasn't possible."

Josie gave Gina a serious look. "What, professor, was the most important highlight of your big year?"

Gina thought for a split second. "Being with Valerie, of course. But there are two other big, big things for me. One was having two short stories accepted, with payment. And then getting the job at

Humboldt. I was excited enough to land an evening class in the fall semester. Then I picked up another class in the spring. But when Dr. Stark died of a heart attack so unexpectedly and a full-time position became available, I was thrilled just to be able to apply for it. I knew I was in the hunt. But there were tons of applications from everywhere, so I was pretty sure I wasn't at the top of the committee's list. A friend told me that a professor was leaving the College of the Redwoods for a better job somewhere else so I applied for that position, too. When State heard through the rumor mill that I was being considered for the Redwood post, they suddenly noticed me. They looked at my records and at student evaluations from my first class, evoked the old "promote from within" credo, and suddenly I was offered the job. Professionally speaking, in my short and so far inglorious career, that was a stellar event!"

Lanie held up her beer. "Toast, everyone, to Gina." They all toasted. Then they toasted Valerie and her friendship and her love for Gina and Sam.

Judee gave Val an amused glance, eyebrows raised. "Okay, Val, we all know you love your gal and your dog, but what was *your* personal biggest moment of the last year?"

Val smiled. "Having a show in San Francisco at a very prominent gallery near Union Square. Having all my lighthouses, coastal scenes, and sailing paintings all up at one time on the walls of that gallery, and having people respond to them—and buy them! It was heaven for me, as an artist! And the exhibit helped me face the City again, but with Gina at my side, showing me *her* San Francisco. Now I know I can go there occasionally without getting drowned in the past. That was truly important for me."

Josie lifted her glass of wine and toasted Valerie for her success. Then the group raised another toast to Josie and Judee as the new couple. Finally they toasted Lanie for her ongoing success in real estate and in finding a potential new girlfriend.

Finally Lanie proposed a last toast. "And here's to the Beetle. May she rest in peace." They all laughed.

The next morning, everyone showed up to reassemble on the sidewalk, as Valerie and Gina climbed into the new white SUV, loaded down with suitcases and supplies, to begin their journey.

There were hugs all around and best wishes as Val and Gina, in the driver's seat of her new RAV-4, leaned out the open windows to reach this hand or that.

Sam paced, wagged her tail hesitantly, and whimpering once. Lanie gave her a loving pat, and the retriever settled down at her feet. The SUV pulled away from the curb as everyone waved one last time. Gina and Val set off on their first big road-trip together, Google maps at the ready.

"The first of many," Gina said, with an adoring look at Valerie, as they headed for the 101 and turned north to follow the coast.

Acknowledgments

North Coast is a work of pure fiction—although inspired by the true, longtime loving partnership of two lesbian women who were several years apart in age. I have chosen to anchor the story in reality by using, respectfully, the real names of cities, educational institutions, and a few businesses. Beyond that the details are the product of my imagination. I wrote *North Coast* because I believe in love, specifically lesbian love. Love that grows and deepens over time. There are many books about instant lesbian intimacy and fewer about women who want and need more than an inviting or intriguing look and a quick hop into bed.

This novel would never have reached publication without the help and support of many of my friends who read the first, second and third drafts and made comments and offered editing assistance. I am very grateful to Karen Merry, an artist whose move from San Diego to Eureka inspired the setting for *North Coast*, and who also read a later draft; Myrna Oliver, retired from *The Los Angeles Times*, who did some extensive editing for me; Glenna Byork and Lucy Martin, both of whom read the manuscript and offered useful suggestions; Connie Jenkins, who supported me in completing the work and found typos in various drafts that needed to be fixed; and Mary George, retired editor from Harcourt Brace Javanovich, who read different drafts, provided invaluable comments, and did painstaking, detailed editing. Without her, you could not be reading this book.

And finally, the late Vera Foster, whose love for me gave birth to *North Coast*.

CPSIA information can be obtained
at www.ICGtesting.com
Printed in the USA
FSOW01n1602250815
10278FS